if you
live
like me

If You Live Like Me
Text © 2009 Lori Weber

Published by Lobster Press™
1620 Sherbrooke Street West, Suites C & D
Montréal, Québec H3H 1C9
Tel. (514) 904-1100 • Fax (514) 904-1101 • www.lobsterpress.com

Publisher: Alison Fripp
Editor: Meghan Nolan
Editorial Assistants: Brynn Smith-Raska & Susanna Rothschild
Graphic Design & Production: Tammy Desnoyers
Consultant on Font & Cover Design: Christian Fuenfhausen

We acknowledge the financial support of the Government of Canada through the Book
Publishing Industry Development Program (BPIDP) for our publishing activities.

The Canada Council Le Conseil des Arts
for the Arts du Canada

We acknowledge the support of the Canada
Council for the Arts for our publishing program.

Société
de développement
des entreprises
culturelles
Québec

We acknowledge the support of the government of Québec
tax credit for book publishing, administered by SODEC.

Library and Archives Canada Cataloguing in Publication

Weber, Lori, 1959-
   If you live like me / Lori Weber.

ISBN 978-1-897550-12-0

   I. Title.
PS8645.E24I3 2009   jC813'.6   C2008-904589-0

Printed and bound in Canada.

Text is printed on Rolland Enviro 100 Book,
100% recycled post-consumer fibre.

For Lori, the kindest person on The Rock, with whom I shared so much.

Acknowledgments:
Thanks to everyone who lent their words of literary wisdom to this book:
Kevin Bushell, Pierre Paré, Jane Barclay, Lynn Bennett, Cassandra Curtis, and,
as always, Ron Curtis. Thanks also to my astute editor, Meghan Nolan. For their
insight into the great province of Newfoundland, thanks to Lori Fritz, Sam and
Isaac Fritz-Tate, Janet Kergoat — especially for walks on Signal Hill and the
whales — Bart and Rosanna Pierson, and Libby Creelman. Thanks also to Noreen,
Phil, Catherine, and Gabrielle for the use of their home in St. John's, where the
book was finished. Finally, I wish to acknowledge the generous support of
the Canada Council for the Arts.

— Lori Weber

if you
live
like me

LORI WEBER

Lobster Press ™

CHAPTER 1
the rock

The Rock. It's down there somewhere and this plane we're on is sending us speeding toward it, descending in bumpy stages, as if we're going down stairs. My father's voice is blabbing in my ear. *Wow, Cher, look. It's an iceberg. An authentic iceberg. Look! Look!* He's pointing out the window, so excited he's practically drooling, but I absolutely refuse to look. I promised myself I'd stay detached for the entire trip, and so far so good. It's pretty easy to ignore what my father's saying anyway, since my ears have completely plugged up, the way they always do on planes. His voice is small, as though he's speaking to me from far away, at the end of a long tunnel, like one they might build one day under the Atlantic Ocean, to connect North America and Europe.

I shrug and point to my ears, to let him know I'm tuned out.

The plane is vibrating like a washing machine on spin

cycle. The hinges on the wings are creaking, making a metallic sound that manages to seep into my blocked ear canals. I've never been on such a rough ride, even though I've taken lots of planes. Maybe I should have paid attention to the safety video they show before takeoff. With these conditions, there's a good possibility we're in for a crash landing. Maybe we'll all have to slide down the inflatable exit ramp they show in the emergency folder. Except, if we did that here, we'd land squat in the ice-cold water of the north Atlantic where hypothermia would kill us anyway.

Now my mother, who's sitting on the other side of me (my parents insisted I sit between them — as if I'm still five years old), is leaning over me, poking her elbow in my ribs. She's trying to see the iceberg too, following my father's finger into oblivion. I swear, if we had a mild crash and landed in the water, my parents would just make the best of it, swimming around the iceberg like two playful seals. *Wow, it's amazing. So beautiful,* I hear my mom say in an even smaller voice than my father's.

Maybe I should stop chewing gum — I've stuffed a whole package into my mouth — and simply let myself go deaf. That way, I'll be spared entering my fourth school since finishing grade six in Montreal three years ago. My parents think attending so many new schools should make the whole experience easier, but it doesn't. It just gets harder each time. With each school, there's a new batch of faces staring at me, a new set of rules, new teachers, new food in the cafeteria, and a new social scene to try to fit into – or watch from the sidelines, which I've learned to do pretty well. I'd like to see my parents bounce back two decades in time and cope with it all. Both of them went to the same high school all the way through, but they say that was boring and that my experience is much more challenging. As if I care.

The plane is now shaking so hard my cheeks are vibrating. *It's the Arctic air currents* my father calls over my head to my mother, as if she needs reassuring. I peek sideways. She does look kind of green. Ahead of us, the flight attendants are strapped into their backward seats, their hands clutching the armrests fiercely, trying their best to look comforting by plastering Stepford smiles to their faces.

My father tugs my sleeve, pointing out the window again. *You'll regret it if you don't look, Cher.* Oh, whatever! I might as well look and get it over with or he'll never leave me alone. I lean over him and glance outside. It takes me a while to see the iceberg because it's really just a small white spot in the vast grey ocean that's rippling and rolling, like a tossed sheet of metal. When I do find it, it reminds me of the last blob of bubbles that floats in a bath, before swirling down the drain. Now there's a thought. If the Atlantic had a drain, I could pull the plug and we'd lose our purpose for being here. No water, no fishing. No fishing, no fishing culture to study. No fishing culture to study, no reason for my anthropologist father to be taking up another temporary position to study another dying way of life, this time in Newfoundland. Maybe he'd even get a real job, like a dentist or a butcher, something that involves staying put. Something that wouldn't be so hard to explain. Whenever people ask why we moved somewhere, I tell them it's for my dad's job. Then they want to know what he does. If I tell them the truth, that he's here to study people to see how all their bad luck is screwing up their lives, it makes everyone really uncomfortable, including me. So, usually I just say he's here to teach at the university and leave it at that. I can't help it if they discover they're being spied on, but I sure hope they never do.

The closer we get to the iceberg, the more interesting its shape becomes. It's a large circle at the base, with two peaks that spiral upward, twisting as they reach for the sky, like soft ice cream. Even from this height, I can see that it's shining, as though the whole interior is lit by a high-powered lightbulb. It *is* amazing, but there's no way I'm going to admit it. *What do you think?* my father shouts. I shrug, then stick my head back in my Archie comic. I only read these to annoy my parents, who have always surrounded me with good books that might broaden my mind. Right now, Archie is broadening my mind. It's reminding me that, somewhere in North America, everyday teenagers are worrying about what clothes to wear to the mall, or ordering burgers and fries at the local McDonald's, which is exactly what I'd be doing if I still lived in Montreal. And it's probably what my old friends are doing right now. It's been three years since I've seen them. Three of the "crucial years," as my parents like to call adolescence, years when my ideas about life are supposedly forming. This cross-country tour will make me some kind of Canadian teen culture expert, according to my father, who obviously sees me as a mini-him, taking notes and using them when I too become an anthropologist one day. That's what I used to tell him I wanted to be, when I was ten, before this marathon began. And before I caught on that fieldwork involves hiding the truth from people.

The plane is now so low to the water, it looks like we'll be floating in it any second. A minute later, the water vanishes and we touch down, skidding and hopping along the runway. The entire plane full of people starts clapping, but I just let out a sigh. We're here, we're really here. There's nothing to do but follow my parents to their new house. I have no choice. My body has to go where they tell it to. But that doesn't mean the rest of me has to follow.

***

The taxi ride to the new house takes us past a few strip malls that look like any other strip mall I've ever seen, with the same big chain stores. At least there's more here than the last place we lived, in the middle of nowhere on the prairies of Saskatchewan, bread basket of the country. The whole place was like a flat slice of white bread, although my parents wouldn't agree. A dying way of life is always fascinating to them. Besides, they manage to find something positive in every situation. In Saskatchewan, where my dad was studying the loss of farming traditions, it was the night skies, where the orange and purple stripes would go on for miles, like a large overhead canvas. And every night was just as amazing as the last for them. Their enthusiasm was as endless as the prairies themselves, but mine wore thin after the first couple of sunsets, especially since sundown meant bedtime, which led to another school morning. Kids from that area were bussed to a school forty kilometres away. They had been sharing a bus since kindergarten and were a pretty close-knit group. Walking onto that bus for the first time was one of the hardest things I've ever done. Now I completely understand the expression "could've heard a pin drop," only in my case, you could have heard a skin cell drop. Mine – shedding all the way down the aisle.

The taxi driver is talking nonstop. He wants to know where we're from, how long we're staying, if we've ever been to Newfoundland before. He's got a thick accent and he keeps punctuating the ends of his sentences with "la" as though he's asking a question, even when he's just telling us something. Like, *If you gets the weather, she's some lovely, la?* I decide to stop listening, which isn't hard since my ears are still blocked and sore. Instead, I concentrate on memorizing the route from the airport to the new house. I take a mental snapshot of the street we're on – Portugal Cove. Whenever we come to a big intersection – well, one with lights – I take another shot: Elizabeth, Empire, Bonaventure. I'll need to know them for when I find a way to get out of here and back to Montreal. There is absolutely no way I'm going to do grade ten in St. John's, Newfoundland, even if I have to become an official high school dropout, my parents' worst fear, to avoid it. It'll be their fault, not mine. The high school I would've attended, if we'd stayed in Montreal, was practically behind our house. My friends and I would go to plays and concerts in its auditorium every year in elementary school, and we'd memorize the layout and even play a game where we'd choose what group of lockers we were going to monopolize one day.

Now, all my old friends are there without me. I've lost touch with everyone, except Janna, my best friend and neighbour since kindergarten. My parents want me to invite her out to Newfoundland for a visit. I tried that when we were in British Columbia, but it didn't work out, and I didn't dare invite her to Saskatchewan. What would we have done? Watch the wheat grow?

Apparently we can now see Cabot Tower in the distance, off to the left somewhere. *Remember we told you about Cabot Tower, Cherie? The place where Marconi received the first radio signal?* my father asks. I don't respond. Actually, I remember everything. It happened in 1902. I have a really good memory, which is too bad for me, since there are lots of things that have happened to me in the last three years that I'd rather forget.

I should remind my dad not to call me Cherie. Cher is bad enough. I really hate my name, in all its forms. It's too cheery and sweet, like maraschino cherries. *I can swing you's up there for no extra cost, if you likes, la,* the taxi driver says. My mother and father look at each other and smile. *That's awfully kind, but I think we just want to get where we're going,* my mother replies. *Suit yourselves,* he answers. Then he starts whistling. God, I hope everyone here isn't this cheerful. I thought that was just a stereotype, the kind you see on TV whenever they show Newfoundland – the happy fisherman, grinning while he mends his nets, the ocean crashing against the shore behind him, his face wrinkled by a thousand lines.

This is so charming, my mom says when we hit an older part of town. *Look at all these colours.* I can tell that she is already mapping out a new quilt in her mind. My mom designs landscape quilts. Everywhere we've ever lived has been immortalized in cotton. This year, we're renting a house from a family that has gone away on sabbatical for the year. They told us it was in the old part of town, which is just what my parents wanted. No suburbs for them. They wanted the authentic St. John's experience. Saltbox houses, that's what the family said the houses in this area are called. They *are* kind of rectangular, but it's as though the saltbox is turned sideways so that it's the narrow side that faces the street. Some of the houses look so thin you could open your arms and hug the whole front.

Oh my goodness, look, Cher, my mother gasps, as we turn onto Gower, the new street. *This street is amazing. Pink and yellow, blue and green. It really is just like in the pictures. Don't you love all that colour?* She stares straight into my eyes when she says the last bit. I know this is a jab at me because I'm dressed all in black, with bits of metal showing, like on my belt and around my neck. I started doing this last year, just before we moved to Saskatchewan. At that point we were living in British Columbia, in Canada's only desert – Osoyoos. It's not that much was dying there, except the vegetation, but it was an excuse to spend a year in a dry climate for my mother's rheumatism. She made a dozen Rocky Mountain quilts that year, capturing their white peaks and colourful wild-flower slopes. My father taught at the Okanagan College and researched the local Native people, the Nk'Mip, on the side. That was a pretty hard year. I tried to fit in, at first, maybe more than I had tried the previous year in Murdochville, a tiny copper town in the Gaspé area of Quebec. I even joined the school band, on flute, but it didn't help much. And once I knew I'd be leaving soon there didn't seem to be any point. It's hard in a small town anyway. At first kids are all really excited to get to know you because you're new and different. But after a while they get over it and you just kind of become a nobody. I mean, why would someone swap a best friend that they've had for years for someone who just stepped off a plane?

I remember what my mom said to me when I stopped wearing anything that wasn't black. *You're not going to mix in if you go around all in black, especially with your dark hair. People in these small places will think you're a witch.* I just smiled. *Cool. That's just the effect I'm going for. Thanks, Mom.*

The taxi pulls up outside the new house. It's tall, narrow, and yellow, with red geraniums so bright they look like they're about to explode sitting in window boxes. *Good day, now*, the taxi driver says as he plunks the last of our suitcases on the narrow sidewalk. My parents have that excited aura they always have just before we enter a new place, like kids about to be unleashed in a toy store. My father is fishing the key out of his wallet and my mother is practically bouncing up and down behind him. I cross my arms and stand a few feet back, staring at my black nails. I peek at the house next door and see the upstairs curtain move. A tall, dark figure steps back from the window. Big surprise – I'm being gawked at already.

***

My parents have gone to pick up the car we'll be leasing and buy some groceries. I'm upstairs, hanging out in my new room. I can tell it was a boy's room because there are still some basketball and hockey pictures tacked up in the cupboard. Whoever he was, he had the good sense to pull down whatever was up on his actual walls, probably posters of Michael Jordan and Wayne Gretsky. Or worse, the rock band Kiss, or eye candy, like Jessica Alba.

It only takes me twenty minutes to unpack. That's because my entire wardrobe fits into two drawers and two inches of cupboard space. I left most of my clothes behind in Montreal, hanging in the cupboard, along with the rest of my life. I'd have outgrown most stuff by now, and I don't buy many new clothes 'cause I know I'll be packing up at the end of a year.

Luckily, the new room has a CD player, even though it's a crappy one, the kind a twelve-year-old would own, with a powder blue cover and two puny speakers. I put on my favourite Marilyn Manson CD and sing along. This song is perfect for the moment because Marilyn is singing about heavy winds blowing and snowing and people wondering which way they're going – like me.

My parents can't stand his music, or him. They keep telling me that he named himself after a brutal killer, Charles Manson, a monster who killed a woman who was seven months pregnant. But I always remind them that he also named himself after one of their favourites, Marilyn Monroe. My mom says that Marilyn was chewed up and spit out by the Hollywood machine, just because she had a great body but lacked confidence in her intelligence and couldn't fight back. So, it's symbolic, I've tried to tell them. The soft and vulnerable along with the hard and menacing, the two sides of human nature, yin and yang and all that. But they don't buy it.

I haven't had the nerve to sit on the bed yet. It's a boy bed – captain style, with three drawers underneath, which I don't dare open. They're probably full of underwear and old socks. How would that help me forget that I have to sleep in the bed of some strange guy who's probably a pimply geek? Even the desk beside the bed is one of those tacky boy ones, with a map of the world printed into the wood. I can tell it's old because Yugoslavia is still one long green country and the Soviet Union

stretches across the top in a big yellow blob. I find
Newfoundland, in the upper right-hand corner of North
America and trace the route I'll be taking home with my finger.
It seems so close on the map, just a short hop over the ocean to
Nova Scotia and then two inches to the left, down the Saint
Lawrence River to Montreal. Now, if only I really had to travel
five inches instead of thousands of kilometers. Wouldn't that
save me a lot of trouble? Here I am, stuck in a totally foreign
place, which is bad enough. But it *would* have to be somewhere
that is completely cut off from the rest of the world by an ocean.
No land bridge or close spot to row a boat across, except up
near Labrador, and how the hell would I get there?

I place my thumb over the pink dot of this island and
press hard, twisting, the way you would to crush a mosquito.

The sound of barking cuts into the music, drawing me to
the window. I look down to see a guy setting out from the
house next door with a huge black dog on a leash. The dog is
pulling so hard the guy's arm is stretched out in front of him,
completely horizontal. They walk down a ways and then
suddenly vanish, as though they've been sucked into a black
hole. I keep watching to see if they'll reappear, but they don't.
Pretty strange.

Next, I spend some time trying to make the room my

own. You have to do that if you live like me, even if you're only going to be staying a short while. It's too creepy being surrounded by someone else's things, like being permanently stuck in a bed-and-breakfast.

I open up my bag of room stuff. It's a pretty cool assortment of weird things. First, there's my scarf collection, purchased at secondhand stores, like the Salvation Army and Goodwill. They've got crazy things on them, like poodles and skeletons. I tape them up on the walls and drape them over lamp shades, adding a bit of ambiance. Then there's my costume jewelry collection – necklaces with gaudy pink and orange beads the size of fruit, and brooches with bursting flowers – that I hang from whatever nails are sticking out of the walls. My Hollywood postcards are all stuck together, but I manage to separate them and stick them up around my bed. I have old movie stars like Greta Garbo, Charlie Chaplin, Marlon Brando, and Bette Davis. Last but not least are my Japanese fans. These I spread out and tack up to the wall above my dresser. The kimonoed women look pretty content, with their delicate white faces and serene smiles, but that's because they don't know they're on some middle-of-nowhere island in the North Atlantic.

The last thing I hang up is the quilt my mother made me

for my tenth birthday. It's of the Montreal skyline, with Mount Royal rising up from the middle of a ring of skyscrapers. On top of Mount Royal is the famous cross, which in reality is made of hundreds of light bulbs, but on my quilt is made of tiny pom-poms. At the bottom lies the Saint Lawrence River, with its four bridges that hook up with the South Shore. If you followed that river west, you'd end up at Lac St. Louis, which is the lake at the foot of my old street. I look at this quilt whenever I'm afraid that the image of Montreal is fading from my memory. I love to think that one day I'll be back there, cruising between the tall buildings – one day soon, if my plan of finding work, saving money, and getting the hell out of here before school starts works out.

When I'm done I stand back and take it all in. Not bad. At least the room has something of me in it now, something that reflects my personality – well my mobile personality anyway. It's not like I could bring my blow-up chairs or lava lamps along, or any of the movie posters I had up in my old place.

My parents still aren't back. Knowing them, they're driving around sightseeing, getting to know the place. They'll come back bubbling over with observations that they'll want to share. Maybe I'll take a walk, just so I'm not here when they get back.

I follow the exact route that guy and his dog took earlier. It's freezing out here, even though it's July. The heat of whatever little sun there is doesn't last into evening, I guess. I'm in a black tank top and black jeans. My arms are all goose-pimpled. Even the stud in my nose feels like a chip of ice. I'll probably get caught in a freak snowstorm!

On the street, lots of people are sitting out on their stoops – one or two-step concrete squares. Behind them, open front doors let out the sounds of talking, music, or television. Stray cats sniff the little bit of grass and weed clinging to the base of the stoops, and dogs look out the front windows, their paws perched on the sills. In one house, two dogs are looking out, a lace curtain draped like a veil over the small dog, making them look like a bride and groom. A couple of people say hello to me as I pass, and an older man says goodnight. I nod back, thinking how strange it is that he thinks I'm off to bed. Then I wonder if what he meant was more along the lines of what a good night it is. I try my best to smile.

Ahead of me there's a break in the row houses that I couldn't see from my window, just about where the guy and his dog vanished. The street sign says Nunnery Hill. What a weird name. I turn down a narrow lane, not much longer than a driveway. At the bottom is a barrier, the kind that runs beside highways on dangerous turns, separating the lane from a steep drop into a parking lot below. A couple of abandoned shopping carts are pushed against the barrier, as though people brought their groceries to the edge then dumped them over.

I lean on the railing and look up into the distance, into the semi-dark. Spread out before me is the St. John's harbour, an oval pool of water bordered on the other side by a low mountain. Oval-shaped oil drums dot the mountain, looking like a colony of gleaming white spaceships. The open end of the harbour is a thin strip of water that the big ships below must have had to squeeze through. Some of those ships are now lit. One looks enormous, like a cruise ship. I usually picture them on the Caribbean, or the French Riviera, not here, where it's freezing in the middle of summer. I've suddenly got an idea. Cruise ships hire lots of people. I could go down tomorrow and check it out. I wouldn't even mind working in the kitchen, scrubbing pots and pans in exchange for a little cubbyhole to sleep in. As long as it took me away.

"It's some pretty spot, isn't it?" a voice behind me says, making me jump. I turn to face the guy I saw earlier, from my window. Up close he's tall, with longish brown hair and big brown eyes. A faint mustache covers his upper lip.

"What?"

"The view. It's pretty. This here is one of my favourite spots in all of St. John's. Hers too." He points to the dog that's sitting at his feet, looking up at him longingly, her tongue hanging out. "We just came up the hill, from Water Street. We do it every night." He looks behind him and that's when I notice that the lane curves off to the left and continues on. I thought I was on a dead end, but I guess not.

I don't know what to say, so I just smile.

"You're new. I saw you move in," he continues. "I'm Jim. I live next door." He puts his hands in his pockets and looks down. "Robbie told us about you guys coming and moving into his house. He said your father's teaching at the university, like his mother, but I don't remember what subject."

"Anthropology," I say, hoping he won't ask me any more about it.

"Oh. Well that's good. I thought maybe he was one of them people the government keeps bringing in, to teach us how to do something other than fish," Jim says, looking back up.

"No, don't worry. My father doesn't know the first thing about fish."

"Good, I'm glad. I can't stand fishing experts." Jim's expression hardens. "I saw one on TV the other day – it got me so mad I wanted to throw something through the screen. He kept talking about how there was no problem with the cod in Iceland and people were still out making a decent living on the water. Made it sound like we're just dumb and lazy."

I don't know what to say. I can't exactly confess that my dad is here to study Newfoundlanders to see if that might be true. Suddenly, Jim's face breaks into a wide smile, like he's just thought of something funny. "Sorry," he says. "I didn't mean to snap. It's just we've got so many mainlanders coming here these days, most of them to cash in on the offshore oil. We got more millionaires than anywhere else in Canada, I bet."

"Yeah, well, we're not millionaires and we're not here for oil," I say. "Sorry to disappoint you." We both stare out at the water, as if we can't figure out what to say next. I'm not that used to talking to guys, especially ones I just met. The guys at my new schools were always pretty curious about me. I mean, I'm not exactly ugly, but none of them seemed to want to go out of their way to get to know me. They just kind of brushed up against me a lot in the hallway, or sat and stared at me in class, like I was fascinating but untouchable. Especially last year, when I was all in black. I'd put on black lipstick, just to complete the picture.

"There might be whales out there any day now," Jim says, pointing toward the water.

"Really?" I say.

"I can show you tomorrow, if you like. We'll bring Boss — she loves water. One day she's gonna slip and go over, tumble right into the Atlantic. Probably wouldn't hurt her though. Her fur's that thick. And she's got special webbed feet that make her good at swimming. Even her tail's built like a rudder."

"Is she a Newfoundland?" I ask, trying to avoid his comment about tomorrow.

"Only part. She's a mix. She'd be bigger if she was purebred. She's part Lab or something, I think. Makes her a bit smaller. But she's one hundred percent Newfoundland inside. She'd be your best friend if you ever fell in the water. Did you bring any pets?"

I chuckle. "God no. People like us can't have pets."

"Cause you'd scare 'em off," he says, laughing. "Sorry — I mean, I see you go for that dark look, kind of vampire-like." I can't tell if he's joking.

"No, because we move around a lot." I hope he won't pry about our moves because I'm in no mood to explain them so soon after getting here. Part of me is still up in the air, suspended. It always takes me time to settle and accept that I am where I am. Well, not *accept* exactly, more like *believe*.

"Cruise ship's in port," he says, pointing in the direction of the water. "We get lots of those in summer. I sometimes wonder how they fit through the Narrows."

"The what?"

"The Narrows. That's what we call that opening between Signal Hill and the South Side Hills. I guess cause it's so narrow, right?"

I can't tell if he's asking me or telling me, so I just nod.

Suddenly, Boss springs up and starts jumping at Jim's feet.

"She's letting me know it's time to move on," Jim says. "You going in? You can walk back with us if you want."

"Okay."

As we head back up to Gower, I try to think of something to say, but can't. I'm not used to easy, casual conversations, especially with guys I don't know. No one's ever just started talking to me the way Jim just did, not in any town we ever lived in. Each conversation I ever had with a new person was hard to start, like one of those old cars with the crank, but this one just sparked. I'm sure I didn't do anything to spark it though. I barely opened my mouth.

At the door to his house, Jim stops and looks straight at

me. "Well, see you tomorrow maybe," he says.

"Yeah, sure," I respond, waving.

After he's gone, I think that maybe I didn't hear him right. I think he asked me out tomorrow. And I think I said yes. Which is weird, because there was only one thing I wanted to do tomorrow – plan my escape.

***

I was right. My parents are back and they're so excited. They love this city already, even though all they did was buy groceries. I beeline up to my room before they can flood me with details.

I finally sit on the new bed, lowering my back onto the mattress slowly, as if I'm not sure it will hold me. Then I ease my whole body onto it, wiggling around, trying to find my centre. The bed is soft, way softer than I like. And it sags in the middle, as though the kid who usually sleeps here has dug a hole in the middle, a hole that I have to try to fit into.

Tomorrow, I'm going to flip the mattress.

***

I wake up at midnight, sweating. I was dreaming of running through tall fields of wheat, the kind that bordered our farmhouse in Saskatchewan. The wheat was much taller than me and I was completely hidden by it. At first it was fun and I squealed as I ran, darting through the stalks that I separated with my hands. But when there was no end I felt myself panic. With every part I hoped to see blue sky, but part after part just led to more wheat.

I feel like I've just run a marathon.

CHAPTER 2
under eons of history

All three of us just about jump out of our skin when the front door opens around noon the next day and a male voice calls out, "Hello. Anyone home?" My parents, who are buried inside the kitchen cupboards, rearranging the dishes so that my mother can reach things more easily, both smash their heads on the top shelf at the same time. I swear they could have been a hit vaudeville act. My mother calls "Hello?" in a sing-songy voice and a minute later the guy from next door walks into the kitchen.

"Hi. I'm Jim," he says, holding his hand out to my mother. "I'm taking your daughter out. I guess she didn't tell you?"

"No, she didn't, but isn't that nice." My mom turns to look at me, a strange smile on her face. I keep staring at my plate. I'm afraid my cheeks may be crimson. She has no idea how I met this guy.

"Hi, I'm Kevin, Kevin Bander," my dad says, holding out his hand to Jim. "You didn't tell us you met the neighbours already," he adds, glancing at me. He looks like he wants to add something, but doesn't dare.

Of course I didn't tell them anything about Jim. I didn't think he would actually show up, but I can't exactly say that. I can feel my parents looking at me and then at each other, bewildered. They've never seen me go out with a guy before, unless you count the son of the family whose back rooms we rented at the farm house last year. His parents had named him Ewan, because it's the last part of the name of his home province – Saskatchewan. He seemed kind of embarrassed by that and who wouldn't be? If my parents had done that to me I'd be Bec, the French word for kiss. That would've made me a big hit in all my new schools. *Here comes Kiss, pucker up!*

But Ewan was only ten. Going out with him meant riding some old bikes around the farm, or swatting a badminton bird around in the field.

"Yeah, well ..." I say, shrugging and smiling at the same time, hoping that'll be enough to stop them from prying.

"Better bring a jacket," Jim says to me, over my parents' heads. "There's wind where we're going. When the queen was here a few years ago, for Cabot's 500th, her hat almost flew right off. She must've had it Velcroed on."

My parents just smile. For once, they seem speechless, like Jim has caught them off guard and they don't know what to say. *Hey come on*, I feel like telling them. *This is what you wanted. Local culture. Dying cultures. Ask him if he knows anyone affected by the cod moratorium, Dad. He could be your first subject. Exhibit number one — tagged and ready. Except, if you say anything, I'll die.*

I drop my sandwich on the plate, squeeze between my parents, walk past Jim, and grab my black jacket off the hook by the door.

"Let's go," I say, stepping outside. My parents call out "Have a good time" as I shut the door.

"Your parents seem shy," Jim says. "I guess I should've knocked. I'm just not used to it. Where I'm from no one does."

"Where you're from," I repeat. "Aren't you from Newfoundland?" I just assumed he was. He has that accent, not as strong as the taxi driver's, but it's still there.

"Oh, sure, but not St. John's. I came here from a small outport on the South Shore, near Burgeo, to go to school when my old school closed down. Not enough kids. Too many families moved away when the fishery closed up. I'm living with my aunt, to finish up. I have one year to go." That means he's going into grade twelve, two grades higher than me.

I stop suddenly and look around. "Where's your dog?"

"Oh, yeah. I thought I'd leave Boss at home for today. She might get jealous, seeing me with another girl. She's used to having me all to herself," Jim says, smiling.

"Great, I've only been here a day and I'm already competing with a dog. That's a first." I can't exactly tell him that this is all a first, for me. It would make me seem pathetic.

"By the way, if we're spending the day together, I guess I should know your name. Besides, you know mine."

"Cheryl," I reply softly, almost eating the word as it comes out. I never did like my name. It's like a name you'd hear in some sucky 1950s rock-and-roll song about a cheer-leader or something.

"Cheryl," he repeats slowly, rolling the name off his tongue. "No, it doesn't suit you. Sorry, but it doesn't."

"Really? How can you tell? You only met me five minutes ago." Is this guy psychic or something?

"I don't know, but it just doesn't. I mean, I like the name. It's a pretty name. Not that you're not pretty, cause you are, but ..."

I stare down at my feet, too embarrassed to look up.

"Look, forget it. It's a nice name. Besides, remember

what Shakespeare said. 'What's in a name?' Take my name, for example. Jim. It sounds simple, right?"

"Right."

"Straightforward-like."

"You mean you're not?" I'm thinking how, so far, he seems to be. He said he'd take me out and now he's doing it, all without much fuss.

"No way. Don't you know anything about irony? Wait till you really get to know me. You'll see the name's all wrong. It's too plain, too plain by far." Then he smiles as though I'm in for a big treat when he makes his grand revelation.

"Okay, if you say so." Maybe now would be the right time to tell him that I'll be out of here in a few weeks, even if I have to cling to a drifting iceberg to do it. But Jim's already pointing out various landmarks that we either pass or see in the distance, as if he's helping me get my bearings.

"That's the Basilica, the biggest church in St. John's. It was built on top of that hill as a beacon for incoming ships, to help them navigate into the harbour," he says, pointing to a church that's sticking out a few streets above us, its two tall steeples reaching the sky.

The building I'm more curious about is the one to the left of the steeples. It looks like it's made of giant cardboard boxes.

Jim catches me looking and laughs. "Funny looking, isn't it? They're called The Rooms. It's our new museum and art gallery, to pull the tourists in. They think all we got in Newfoundland is fish, so even our art centre's supposed to look like the fishing rooms where they used to make the cod. Next thing you know they'll be casting a giant fishing net over the whole city, just to add to the am-bi-ance." Jim drags out the last word, in an exaggerated French accent.

I laugh a little, wondering at the same time what he meant by making cod.

At the end of Gower Street, we turn right and come to a pretty busy intersection where three different roads meet. On the left is a big white brick hotel, with round windows that look like the ones on ships running up the middle. A doorman is standing outside, wearing a blue suit with red stripes, looking pretty swanky. Jim is pointing the other way.

"This here's Duckworth, one of our main downtown streets," he says. "Here's where you go if you want to sit in a trendy café and sip lattes and read poetry. You know ... be super cool."

"Just your kind of place, I bet?"

"Oh yeah, for sure. You look like you'd fit in all right, but not a bay boy like me."

"Not a what boy?"

"A bay boy. From around the bay, like I am. If I wants to, I can lay the local accent on though, make 'em all laugh," Jim says, sounding more like the taxi driver all of a sudden. I can't help but chuckle again, in spite of not wanting to, which seems to make him happy.

We turn left and keep walking, leaving downtown behind.

"The harbour's down there," Jim says, pointing down the bottom of the hill. We can't see much of it from here, just one ship, a fishing vessel, I think, judging by all the nets hanging off of it. No sign of the cruise ship, which is what I'd really like to see. And possibly get inside, to stow away in.

"What's that?" I ask, pointing to a heap of something piled up at the far end of the harbour.

"That's salt chips. This street's called 'Hill 'O Chips.' We take things literal around here. But wait to see how icy these streets get in winter," Jim says.

"I might not be here then," I respond. "I mean, I might be leaving soon."

"Oh really? That's not what Robbie told us. He said you were here for a year – same length of time he'll be away."

"Well, Robbie kind of got it right. Except, it's my parents

who are staying, not me."

"And where are you going?"

"I'm going back to Montreal."

"Oh, is that where you're from? Robbie didn't know for sure. And what're you going to do? Go back on your own?"

"If I can, yeah. At least, I'm going to try. Somehow."

"Ouch, you haven't even been here a full day and you already want to leave? Newfoundland doesn't usually have that effect on people. So, what, are you thinking of jumping aboard a container ship?"

"Could I really do that?"

Jim starts to laugh. "You could try it, I guess, but it would be pretty dangerous. If it was easy, more people'd be doing it, don't you think, to save on airfare?"

"Very funny." I guess it was pretty dumb of me to take him seriously. He obviously doesn't think I'm serious about going back home alone. Neither do my parents.

We start to climb a steep street, past more colourful row houses. I'm really regretting wearing my heavy black boots. They're not the easiest things to walk in.

"What about the cruise ships?" I ask.

"Stow away on a cruise ship? Are you cracked? They're even harder to get near."

"Not stow away. Work on one. They must need hundreds of employees, those things."

"Sure they do, but not from here. They got everything they need by the time they get here. And they're all American anyway. The tourists come here for two things: whales and icebergs. They come in, see a few of each, drink some screech, maybe kiss a rubber cod or two in one of the pubs, listen to some fiddle music, then they're gone. That ship we saw last night's probably left already, heading across to Bermuda or something."

I feel myself deflating. It's not going to be easy getting out of here. Not unless I can get the money together for a plane ticket, and that could take forever. My parents' idea of allowance is ten dollars a week, for pocket money, which isn't even enough for a movie and popcorn, if I were going to do such a thing.

Further along, past where the houses have ended, we come to a little lake. Jim stops. "So, how do you like it?" he asks.

"Like what?"

"Our lake." A sign by the road says Deadman's Pond.

"Is this what you brought me to see?"

"Sure, don't you like it?

"Oh, yeah. It's fantastic. Almost as good as Niagara Falls,"

I say. Deadman's Pond is just an oval of blackish water. I wonder if it got its name from someone who was forced to do something against his will, like climb a mountain, or kiss a fish, and decided to jump in and drown instead. "I thought you said we might see whales. I doubt there's even a fish in this pond."

"No, but there are lots of skeletons, on account of all the people who got hung up on top. They'd roll the bodies down the hill afterwards."

"Are you kidding me?"

"Of course not. Dead serious. Anyway, Deadman's Pond is just the appetizer. The real treat is at the top of the hill."

We continue to trudge upwards, passing something called "The Geo Centre" on our left, its parking lot full of cars and tour busses. Jim tells me his science class got to help out with setting up some of the displays a few years ago, when it opened. "It's pretty amazing," he says. "If you like rocks, which I do."

Right now, I don't know what I like. I'm in too much pain. I can feel my heels scraping against the leather, building up a couple of good blisters. I'm not used to walking this far, especially in these boots. And this hill is so steep. I wish he'd warned me. Jim's up ahead, coaching me along.

"Come on, girl, you can do it," he says. "We're almost at

the top. Keep working those calves." He pumps his legs in an exaggerated way, like some maniac aerobics instructor, trying to make me laugh. But I don't. I just plunk myself down on a boulder by the side of the road.

"What's so great up there anyway? Can't I just look from here? There's a bit of a view." The horseshoe of downtown St. John's is partly visible behind me, the colourful houses dotting the hill that climbs away from the water, like blocks of Lego.

Jim comes down and joins me. "Okay, we'll take a break. I guess I forgot that not everyone climbs this hill every day."

"You actually do this everyday?" I ask. "Are you seriously deranged?"

"Okay, not every day, but when I can. It's hard in winter though – sheet of ice sometimes."

"Well, I don't need to worry about that," I say. "I'll be gone, remember?"

"Oh sure, so you said. Is it my deodorant or something?" Jims says. Then he actually lifts his arm, sticks his nose in his armpit and inhales. "Nope, not me ... Wait a minute. Maybe it's the other one." Then he lifts his other arm and does the same thing again, only this time he chokes and gasps and actually rolls off the rock onto the grass. He holds his stomach and continues writhing, as though he's been struck with acute appendicitis.

I can't help it. It is pretty funny. Before I know it, I'm laughing out loud. I don't even try to hold it in.

"Ah-hah! I caught you. Committing a cardinal sin. That'll be ten, no twenty, Hail Mary's – by the way, are you Catholic? – for giving in to the temptation of humour. Don't you know where humour can lead you? Before you know it, you might actually start to feel good. And then worse – you could actually find yourself ... happy." Jim is standing now, delivering his insane speech in a dramatic voice, his arms flying out around him like a TV evangelist. People in cars driving up to the summit are looking at him. They don't know whether to be concerned or amused.

"Oh my god, is something wrong with you?" I hiss, tugging on his shirt to get him to sit. He makes himself go all floppy and raggedy, like the scarecrow in the Wizard of Oz. I can almost hear his bones hit the boulder as he crashes.

"Is something wrong with *me*? *You're* walking around in black jeans and black jacket and high black boots in summer, and you're worried about what people are going to think about me? Aren't you urban gothy types supposed to be immune to public opinion?" This time Jim puts on a pretty authentic British accent.

"For your information, I am not goth. That's something completely different."

"I know. That's why I said 'gothy,' remember? You're more witchy, I guess. Hey, if you had a broomstick, you could fly us up."

"Sorry. I left it at Robbie's." It's not the first time I've been compared to a witch. Ewan's friends would sometimes creep around to the back of the house and peek in the windows to see me. Ewan told me they wanted to see if I was brewing potions.

"Well, we either sit here all day or get up to the good stuff. What do you say?" Jim stands up and stretches out his hand toward me. I reach out and grab it, letting him pull me up.

"Okay," I shrug. "If we're going to climb this hill, let's get it over with. The sooner we get up, the sooner we get down. Right?" Then I take off at breakneck speed, pumping up the side of the road so fast in my clumpy boots, Jim actually has to run to keep up.

Around a few more bends, a stone tower becomes visible, looking like the chopped-off turret of a castle. It sits past the end of a long parking lot that is packed with cars. People are standing around, pointing off in all directions as they take in the view, the wind whipping their hair, cameras, and windbreakers. Jim guides me to the left side and points down.

"Well, this is it," he says. His voice is full of pride, as though he's somehow personally responsible for what I'm about to see.

"This is what? Where are we?"

"Signal Hill. The most famous spot in St. John's. Didn't you guess?"

"I suppose I should have, but I'm not very good with directions and landmarks and that kind of thing." In fact, I completely suck at them, probably because I deliberately try to block out where I am most of the time.

"Well, that's Cabot Tower, over there." Jim points to the stone structure behind us. "And that's the Atlantic Ocean," he says, pointing right.

As I look out, I feel the breath, or whatever breath I have left after that climb, gush out of my lungs, leaving me dizzy. Stretching below me are rocky hills that undulate toward the water, the reddish rock topped in parts with grass and moss. Beyond the rock lies the ocean, stretching forever, with no end in sight. The water is actually blue, the way postcard oceans always are. It's not that I've never seen ocean before. When we lived in the Okanagan Valley we made several trips to the Pacific Coast, and that was impressive. But this is different, somehow. It's an odd mixture of rough and pretty all at once. Soft and hard. Yin and yang and all that.

"So, what do you think, city girl?" Jim asks.

"It's ... awesome," I say.

"I knew you'd think so," Jim responds. "That's where we're headed now." He points to a narrow path that winds down over the hills. From here, the path seems to go on forever, over boulders, through patches of vegetation, and, at times, turning into wooden stairs that must be bolted into the rock. People hiking at the bottom, near the water, look an inch tall.

I know I should protest. I should roll my eyes and stamp my boots and absolutely refuse. But the strange thing is this: I want to do it. I want to climb down closer to this amazing shore. I want to do it more than I've wanted to do anything since I was yanked away from Montreal three years ago. Much more than I wanted to taste caribou, or ride a gondola up the Rockies, or witness the explosion of grain elevators. But I can't let Jim know that. I can just see that grin blossoming into a full-fledged gloat. An I-told-you-so gloat. The kind my parents might give me, along with a mini lecture about never counting something out before trying it, 'cause you never know, yadda yadda ...

"Whatever. Might as well get it over with," I say, swinging my legs over the parking lot barrier and planting my boots on the other side. As I stand there, looking down, I realize that my blisters have stopped hurting.

***

We descend for what seems like miles, down the path that is, at times, vertical and at others meanders over rock or through the spongy vegetation. The air is crisp and breezy and smells of salty ocean. Seabirds caw and screech as they soar and dip through the air around us. At one point, we look across a cove of black water to a peninsula, the tip of which is the exact same shape as a dinosaur's head. The pitted rock in the middle of the head, surrounded by wrinkles, looks just like its eye. Jim tells me we're looking down into Cuckolds Cove. Farther along, Jim asks if I want to stop for a while, so we sit on a bed of grass and ferns and just stare out at the ocean. I feel like I'm perched at the tip of the world, like I could just lean forward and plunk myself off the edge, into the Atlantic.

"Do you realize that we're actually closer to Ireland than to British Columbia right now?" Jim says.

"Wow. Are you serious? I used to live in B.C."

"No kidding," Jim says, turning back to stare out at the water. "Lucky."

I think about that word for a minute. I could argue with him, but it would be too hard to get into, so I just focus on the view. I think about how all of Canada, its thousands of miles, lies behind me. I picture the provinces I've lived in floating away like ice floes, leaving me blissfully disconnected. I almost feel light and free for the first time in ages, kind of like the birds soaring high above the water.

We sit there for a long time, just staring out. Even Jim is quiet, for a change. I can almost feel the intensity of his stare beside me. His dark eyes are glassy, like marbles. I suddenly have an urge to ask him some questions, about where he comes from and everything, but I don't want to intrude. He seems so into his thoughts.

"Guess how old the rock that we're sitting on is?" Jim asks suddenly.

"I don't know? Fifty thousand years?"

Jim smiles. "Fifty thousand? That's like newborn to these rocks. Try five hundred million." Jim taps the ground below him as he says this, as if to test for strength. "There's rocks near here that date back to the Precambrian period."

"The what period?"

"Precambrian. Haven't you ever heard of it?"

I shake my head.

"The word is familiar, but I have no idea what it means."

"Yeah, well, not many people do. But I'm really into rocks, especially fossils. I've got a big collection from right here, around St. John's, thanks to Mr. Wells, our science teacher. He's also a rock geek. His first name is Pierre, the French word for stone, 'cause his mother's Acadian. I always wonder if that's what gave him the idea to go into geology. He's taken us on field trips all over the Avalon and this summer he might take a group of us over to Horton Bluffs in Nova Scotia. We fund-raised for the trip all year, but I'm still waiting to hear. It'll be completely awesome if we do go. I've been wanting to go there for ages now. It's world famous, well, in geology circles anyway."

Jim sounds so excited. I wonder what it would be like to have such a strong interest in something. So far, I haven't developed a passion for anything, except getting home again.

"Sounds good," I say.

"Yeah, well, we'll see. It's just a first step for me. I want to be a geologist when I grow up. I want to go to all the hot rock spots in the world and search for fossils."

"Why fossils?"

"There's something so amazing about finding a message from the past etched in stone. You can piece together the evolution of our species from those messages or figure out when the first skeletal creatures appeared in Newfoundland. There's so much neat stuff. Like, many people don't know that the Avalon Peninsula, where St. John's is, was once part of a chain of volcanic islands that were strung along the coast of a huge supercontinent, back in the Late Proterozoic period. Then three hundred million years later it used to be part of a large continental plate called Pangaea. It shared the plate with parts of Europe and Africa. Isn't that cool? I mean, who would think we were once connected to somewhere as different as Africa?"

"Wow. You sure know a lot about it."

"Not as much as I want to. I want to go to Africa one day, to study their rocks too. But I'm not sure if I'll make it. I've only been off the island of Newfoundland once in my life, when I was really young, two years old. My parents took me and my older brothers to visit my mom's cousin in Toronto. But I don't remember a single thing."

I suppose now wouldn't be the best time to tell him that I've been to every province in Canada. Not only that, but I've been to Europe too – twice.

Jim points out some little grey slivers in the distance that he says are boats. We sit there long enough to watch them grow in size and actually sail off to our right, into the harbour. One is a tall sailboat, built out of wood, like in the olden days. Jim tells me it's a tour boat.

"This place is like being home, on top of Mary's Hill," Jim says, softly. "My brothers used to take me up there all the time to throw rocks and watch the whales."

"Are your brothers here too?" I ask.

"No. I haven't seen them for three years. They're in Alberta with my father. They're probably muscular oil men now, with twenty-inch biceps from wrapping those thick chains around drill bits. When I spoke to them last Christmas they said I should come out and join them. They said it would put hair on my chest. Then they both cracked up. I know they didn't mean nothing by it though. They've been teasing me all my life, 'cause I always have my head in a book about rocks or the earth or something. They said they spend a lot of their time blasting through rock, so it would be right up my alley."

"So you haven't seen your father for three years either?"

"Even longer. He went out west five years ago. He came back at Christmas the first year, but after that he always said he had to work. He's up in the oil sands now, in northern Alberta. He says he can make double time working through the holidays, but I know there's more than that keeping him there. My brothers didn't come home last Christmas either.

My mother wasn't too happy about it. She thinks we should all be together at least once a year. I think so too, but you can't tell my brothers what to do, or my father."

"How come you didn't all move to Alberta?"

"My father wanted us to, but my mother wouldn't go. She said she'd rather die poor at home than rich in a strange place."

I stare out at the ocean, thinking about Jim's mother, determined never to leave the place she was born, even if it meant seeing half her family go away. That must have been hard.

"Does your mother work too?"

"She used to, when the fish plant was still running. That's been closed a decade now. She used to slice and gut – she could do thirty cod a minute in her prime. Now she knits sweaters with Newfoundland scenes on them, like whales or fishing boats, row houses – the kind of stuff tourists love."

Every time Jim says the word tourist he gives it a bit of a kick, like he has to fling the word out of his mouth, like it bothers him that people want to come here to see the province and all its natural beauty. I guess it's because he knows the other side of it, the side that made his dad leave home.

"Should we keep going down?" Jim asks and I nod. He takes my hand and pulls me up. I am wondering if he'll keep hold of my hand, but the pathway is so narrow he has to let go.

We continue on, stopping every now and then to look back at the water. Jim shields his eyes with his hand and stares intently, as though he's hoping to see some mythological creature, like the Loch Ness Monster, spring up.

We can now see the harbour and all of St. John's behind it. It's a really neat view. I hold out my palm and make as though the entire city is sitting in it. At the bottom of a series of steps, we come to a curve in the path, which at this point is no more than two-feet wide. Below it is a dead drop, straight down into rough water. Bolted into the rock above the path is a chain that hikers are supposed to hold and use for leverage as they pull themselves along. I watch a few people do it. I hope the chain is bolted in with a deep rivet because with each person it takes a real yank. I don't know if I can do it.

"Look inwards, at the rock. Don't look down. Just take it slow and hold on. You'll be fine. I'll be right behind you. Don't worry," Jim says. I look behind me and see that my only choice is either to do it or go back up the way we came, which would be a huge climb.

I grab the chain and do as Jim said. I stare at the pink rock and place one foot gingerly in front of the other. It only takes about twenty steps to get around the curve. A couple of tourists waiting to go the other way actually clap for me.

Now it's Jim's turn. He starts off nice and slow, like me. Then halfway around the curve he starts doing this high-wire routine, going all wobbly like he's trying to balance, hanging out over the cliff with one hand secure on the chain, his legs flailing about behind him. Even the tourists look scared. My heart is beating hard. I'm not ready for this.

"Jim, don't be an idiot," I call out, but by then Jim is around the bend and standing right beside me, in one piece.

"I had you going, didn't I?"

"Yeah, well ..." I'm too furious to speak. I try to think what the equivalent would be if Jim came to Montreal and, on his very first day, I took him somewhere dangerous and did this I'm-about-to-die act that would leave him stranded god knows where – like jumping across the metro tracks to the opposite platform, dodging the high voltage rail, the one that can kill you. How would he like that?

"Hey, I didn't mean to scare you, Cheryl," Jim says, reaching for my shoulder. I pull back, so that his fingers only graze me.

"When I was a kid and we came to visit my aunt, my mother and father had to practically carry me past that spot, one of their arms on each of my shoulders, inching me along. I guess I've just gotten so used to it, it's like nothing now."

"Forget it," I say. "Let's keep going." I turn and Jim follows me.

We walk the rest of the path in silence, until we hit this section of pretty flat rocks that leads down to a section of houses that seem to be built into the rock.

"This is the Battery," Jim explains. "Used to be where they stored the arms and stuff, but now people live here." What stretches ahead of us are the most unusual houses I've ever seen. They're made of strange shapes as the wood bends around, over and under the rocks. Even the road – if you can call it that – has to widen or narrow, according to the rock's design.

At one point we come to somebody's front deck. I stop, but Jim says not to worry. It's all part of the pathway and people are allowed on it, like the Parks Canada sign says. Then he points up to a house whose walls and wooden railings are covered in cartoon cutouts, like Bugs Bunny, Tweety, and Yosemite Sam. Another tiny yard has a collage of dolls sitting at a tea party, with tiny porcelain cups on tables in front of them. A few pottery and artist studios are sandwiched between the houses.

This place is funky. Most people in the smaller towns I lived in were so square you'd get in trouble if your grass wasn't cropped at exactly two inches. And even the so-called funny stuff that decorated lawns was kind of ordinary, like all those wooden cutouts of old ladies' bums leaning over in the garden and pink flamingoes. Stuff anyone could buy at Zellers.

We continue, hiking narrow paths up and between people's houses, close enough to reach out and tap their windows. Then we hit a more open section. I look straight up and see nothing but tall grey stone hovering above me, a few stunted trees clinging to it. I can't help thinking that if this wall were in the city, some developers would already have turned it into a rock climbing park and there'd be colourful plastic nubs sticking out all over it.

"Here we are," says Jim. "Standing under eons of history – something that might have existed before dinosaurs even walked the earth. It makes us totally connected to everything that was here before us. Isn't that awesome?"

"Yeah, it's pretty amazing," I say.

"I knew you'd like it."

"You did? How?"

"I don't know, I just did." Jim looks right into my eyes for a few seconds. His eyes are hazel in this light, reflecting the copper colour of the sun. I'm not used to being stared at like this, especially by a guy. So, I turn back to the rocks.

At the end of the Battery, we emerge at the base of the hill that we started to climb so many hours earlier. Jim seems impressed that I could do it.

"I never thought you'd make it," he says.

"Yeah, well, you obviously thought wrong," I answer.

"Too bad the trip was a failure though," he says, hanging his head and shaking it exaggeratedly. My heart stops for a minute. Not that I care. But why was this a failure? I'm too scared to ask. Maybe I am horrible company. Maybe he has done this walk with other girls — girls who actually made him laugh every now and then. Girls who know how to talk to guys and make them feel all warm inside, or who find his acrobatic stunts amusing instead of terrifying.

Ones who might have the nerve to squeeze his hand in return.

"Yep, a real bummer," he continues. Now I'm getting angry. I thought our afternoon was pretty good, even though it started off rough. At least Jim seemed to be enjoying himself.

"Well, drag somebody else to the top of a bloody rock next time!" I snap. "I can find my own way back." I start to turn away.

"If only we'd seen whales," Jim says, in a dreamy voice, letting the word "whales" linger in the air like a whisper. "Yep ... with whales this trip would have been ... perfect."

Then something happens to me that hasn't happened in
a long time.

I feel it like a flame on my cheeks, the prickling heat of a
full-fledged blush.

***

My parents stop talking when I walk into the kitchen. I
have a feeling they were discussing me, which they often do
when they think I'm not listening. They examine my situation,
as they call it, and try to figure out why I don't fit in. Their
theories are that I just don't try hard enough, that it's just my
age, and that it's hard to break into new groups. That pretty
much covers the whole range of possibilities, I guess, and the
one they emphasize just depends on their mood.

I can tell by their faces that they want to pump me full of
questions, but they don't want to appear too eager.

"We saved you some soup, sweetie," my mother says. "Do
you want me to warm it up for you?"

"It's okay. I can do it," I answer. I stand over the strange
pot, waiting to see little bubbles pop up through the carrots
and potatoes. I can almost feel my parents at the table behind
me, holding back. As I stare at the soup, I think about saying

goodbye to Jim. We lingered outside, between our houses, then I just said something stupid, like "thanks for the walk." And he said "no problem, anytime." If we'd stayed there any longer, we might have shaken hands. So I just said "see ya" and came in.

"Well, Cheryl, aren't you going to tell us how your walk went?" my father finally asks.

"The walk was long and hard," I say, plunking my bowl onto the table. I'm glad the steam is rising to hide my face.

"Oh, I see," responds my father, kind of sadly. "Did you go anywhere interesting?"

I know my father would love to hear all about Signal Hill and Deadman's Pond and the Battery, anything that helps him get to know the place and blend in. The more he knows, the easier it will be for him to mingle and seduce people into sharing their stories. So I won't tell him. I have no reason to help him with his book. I guess this place will be Chapter Four: the Collapse of the Cod Fishery.

"Nope. We just walked around. That's all," I say, shoving some bread in my mouth.

"Well, I got to meet some of my new colleagues today and see my new office. It's a really modern building, you'd be surprised — it even has an open glass elevator. I can take you there tomorrow, if you want." I just shrug, wondering if my father realizes how snooty he sounds sometimes. "And I found out what courses I'll be teaching. It'll be a pretty heavy load, but I should have some time to travel around a bit and do some research for my book."

I picture myself burning my father's book when it's finally published, holding it over a flame in whatever backyard we're living in. When we left Montreal for Murdochville three years ago, I didn't know he was planning to write a whole book. I thought that was going to be a one-year stint, so that he could study the effects of the mine closure on the community. They never told me it would be the first of many places, at least not explicitly. Even if they had, I probably wouldn't have believed them. It would have sounded too incredible, like they were making it up, just to tease me.

"Jim seems nice," my mother pipes in, after she sees that I'm not offering any unsolicited information. Then she studies my face for a reaction. I hold real still, blowing on a spoonful of hot soup. I can feel how badly they want me to admit to liking something here, so that they're off the hook.

"Jim is a nutcase," I say. I could back this up by telling them how he pulled this stunt hanging off a chain that was bolted into some rock over a deadly drop, how I thought he was going to die. But then they'd know where I went.

"Oh, Cheryl," they say together, disappointed. I finish my soup, wash my bowl and tell my parents I'm going to bed early. Luckily, they don't try to stop me.

Now, finally alone, I close the door to my new room and lie on top of the bed and allow myself to replay the hike over Signal Hill. I go over the whole thing slowly, again and again, lingering over the part where Jim ran his finger along my cheek.

I fall asleep with the sun high out over the water in my head.

***

I'm sore, I'm in a hole. It's rocky and deep. When I tear open my eyes, I discover it's not that at all. It's just this damn mattress. I forgot to flip it.

CHAPTER 3
hard as rock

I'm trying to eat my breakfast in peace, but my father is blabbing about this beach the guy at the car rental place told him about. *It's called Middle Cove and it's only twenty minutes from here. Supposedly it's a really beautiful spot.* He has said the same thing every morning this week. I thought he'd eventually give up, but here it is Friday and he's still at it.

I know he's gearing up to ask me if I want to go, again, so I don't look up. Making eye contact would be fatal right now. I concentrate on my peanut butter toast instead.

I don't want to sightsee with my parents. It'll just give them the impression that I'm resigned to staying here. It occurred to me when I woke up Tuesday morning, still seeing Signal Hill in my mind, that I can't get attached. Sure, it was pretty, but it's just scenery. I have to detach myself from the walk with Jim and reduce it to a postcard, a paper object that I can just take with me, maybe tack up over my bed in Montreal.

That's why I've been avoiding Jim, staying in my room and reading.

I've seen him a few times, leaving for his nightly walk with Boss. The first two nights, he looked up at my bedroom window, as if he was wondering whether he should ask me to join them, but I stood back, nose squished into the dusty curtain.

Last night, he didn't bother.

My father's managed to reel my mother in already, which isn't hard to do since she's game for anything, anytime. They're talking over my head at the kitchen table. "Well, I've got to go register Cheryl at the school board sometime today, but we could work around that? Do you want to come with me?" It takes me a minute to realize that my mother's question is directed at me. I look to the side, at her hands. They're wrapped in hot towels. She only does that when her rheumatism is bothering her. So far, she hasn't even bothered to unpack her quilting supplies.

The silence at the table tells me she's still waiting for an answer.

If I tell her not to bother, she'll just trick me into a discussion that I'd rather not have. Silence is the best defense with my parents. If I protest about going to school here, they'll have a quick response, and before I know it I'll be drawn deeper and deeper into an argument that I have to climb my way out of. I need to stay calm and aloof.

"It's called Holy Heart," I hear my mother say.

"What?" I call out before I can stop myself. I shouldn't have said anything. I should've pretended I didn't hear. But that name really jabbed me.

"Your new school. That's what it's called – 'Holy Heart of Mary.'"

That name implies that the school will be full of open arms waiting to embrace me, lovingly. But that's never been my experience. It'll more likely be full of kids staring me down as I walk by, my eyes straight ahead, trying my best to look like I couldn't care less. And I'd die if what happened in Saskatchewan ever happens again. I had refused to take the school bus so my mother drove me to town, forty kilometres away. I was late and had to walk into the classroom after everyone else had already settled in. The silence was deafening – no rustling paper or shuffling feet, just thirty pairs of eyes following me as I walked to the back of the class, clunking down the aisle in my heavy boots. I'd worn the boots even though I knew they'd make noise, because I liked the fact that they were black and hard and would at least give some part of my body a shell to hide in. I'd have encased my whole self in a suit of armour if I could have.

"You can register me at 'Holy Heart' or 'Holy Lung' or 'Holy Whatever.' I couldn't care less," I blurt out. "I'm not going to a new school." Then I turn and stamp back up to my room, my footsteps booming in the silence. So much for calm and aloof. I just hope no one follows me. I'm in no mood for another long discussion. We said everything there is to say back in Saskatchewan. That's when they first announced that we'd be coming here instead of going home. There is no argument left to make on either side, for or against. We left a whole field of words behind us, stretching out along the endless prairies. My mother and I also cried enough to fill the entire rain barrel that sat beneath the eaves of the old farm house. Enough to keep our angry field watered for a whole year, in spite of prairie droughts.

***

Even though I said I wouldn't see Jim again, that I'd put our hike on Signal Hill out of my mind and just hole up in my room until I could find a way home, my mother's plan to register me at school has me panicked. I'm not going to find a way back to Montreal sitting here. I need to be "proactive," one of my father's favourite words.

Who else can I ask for help but Jim?

Maybe he can show me some places where I might find a job. I figure a one-way ticket back to Montreal can't cost more than three hundred bucks. Even if I work for minimum wage, I could save that in a few weeks, I think.

As for what I'll do when I get there, that's another question. I suppose I could see if the family renting our house would let me have the basement. Or maybe Janna's family would agree to take me in for the year.

As I'm getting dressed, I think of sitting on that rocky plateau halfway down the path on Signal Hill. Everything seemed so far away and unimportant up there, with nothing but the ocean stretching all the way to Ireland in front of us and everywhere else like a loose jigsaw puzzle behind us. I wonder if it would seem that way again if we went back up there today.

When I step outside, I almost choke. The entire street is covered in fog. I can barely see the other side. It's as though everyone in St. John's is exhaling smoke at the same time, except the fog isn't thick and grey, like cigarette smoke. It's white and wispy, like cotton candy that has been stretched between the houses, thick in some places and thin in others.

It's actually kind of neat, in a freaky sort of way.

I take the few steps to Jim's front door cautiously, using my hands to guide me. I probably don't need to, but I ring the doorbell. I could never just walk right in to somebody's house, especially the first time going there. It wouldn't feel right. I was raised in a city where people keep their doors locked at all times and only speak to strangers with the door opened a few inches and fastened by a chain.

"I might've known it was a mainlander," Jim says with a wide smile on his face. If he's surprised about finding me on his doorstep, he's not letting it show. "How do you like walking in the clouds?"

"What?"

"The clouds − that's what fog is. You really don't know much, do you, city girl?" Now Jim's got something to put next to rocks on the list of things I know nothing about. "It's okay. Nobody knows fog like Newfoundlanders. Our veins are probably filled with it. Anyway, what's up?" He tugs my arm and pulls me inside. "Gotta close the door or it'll roll in."

"I need a job," I say.

"Are you asking if we need a maid?" he asks.

"Very funny. You know what I mean. I was hoping you could take me around, show me where to apply for jobs."

"And what is it you'd like to do? Type, sew, cook?"

"Very funny again. Where do other kids work around here? McDonald's, Burger King, Famous Players, the Bay ... you know, that kind of thing?"

Just then a woman's voice calls down the hall. "Jim, who is it now?"

"It's Cheryl. From next door."

"The girl you was talking about?" the woman says. "The one you took up the hill? The one with the blue eyes?"

"Yes, Nanny," Jim says, a faint hue of red riding up his neck. I wonder what else he told her.

"Well, bring her in, b'ye. Where's your manners to?"

Jim turns and I follow him down the narrow hallway into an equally narrow living room. A woman who looks like an older version of Jim — same narrow face and dark eyes — is sitting on a flowered sofa. She has white hair like an old lady, but smooth skin like a young one. It's kind of jarring. Boss is curled up at her feet, covering them, like a fur blanket. The dog gives me a lazy glance, then goes back to snoozing, her snout between her paws.

"This is Nanny," Jim says. "My aunt."

"Cheryl, love, have a seat," Nanny says, pointing to the cushion beside her on the sofa. "Jim, make us some tea." Jim doesn't argue or answer back. He just disappears into what I guess is the kitchen. Jim's aunt smiles at me. "Right, my dear. You make yourself at home," she says. Then she turns her attention back to the television, where a talk show is on. Three men and one woman are sitting on a sofa, trying to talk over each other. I have no idea who anyone is and I can't tell what the topic is either. Jim's aunt is staring at the screen, nodding her head the whole time, as if she agrees with what's being said, even during the commercials. Above the TV, a picture that looks like a stained glass window is hanging. Some guy in a long blue robe is standing behind an X-shaped cross, his right hand hanging over the middle where the two beams intersect. Underneath him are the words: "St. Andrew, Patron Saint of Fishermen."

"They're all on fire today," Jim's aunt says when the show comes back on and the arguing continues. I simply nod. Jim finally returns carrying a tray that holds three delicate-looking teacups on saucers, and a matching teapot, milk and sugar set in a floral pattern. The whole tea thing should look out of place in Jim's big hands, but it doesn't. He seems so comfortable holding it. He sets the tray down on the coffee table then pours us each a cup, all without spilling a drop.

"Here, Nanny," he says, handing his aunt her cup and

saucer. He places it very carefully in her hands, securing it with his own until he's sure she has it. "Watch out now, it's hot."

"Thanks, love," Nanny says. Then she takes a sip of her tea, lifting the cup slowly to her mouth. That's when I notice the shaking. Her fingers are vibrating so much that the tea sloshes around the rim of the cup, but miraculously stays inside. When she returns the cup to its saucer it continues to rattle, but doesn't spill. Jim looks over at me and winks, as if to say not to worry.

"Is it okay, Nanny?" he asks sweetly. This must be his at-home voice; all the sarcasm vanished. I think about my own home-voice. It doesn't sound at all like Jim's. My parents were still huddled over the breakfast dishes when I left, like my refusals had paralyzed them.

"You makes the best cup of tea in St. John's, Jimmy," she says, laughing. When she laughs, her head nods and shakes all at once. "And what are you up to today?" she asks, rattling the saucer back onto the table.

"I'm going to take Cheryl to the village," Jim says.

"That's lovely," says his aunt.

The village! What village? Didn't he hear me? I want a job, not more sightseeing.

"I'm taking the car, if that's okay," Jim says. Well, at least we're not hiking out to this village, wherever the hell it is.

"Of course, but drive safely, that's all I ask," says Nanny.

When I say goodbye to Jim's aunt she presses my hand warmly between her two shaky ones. "See you again soon, my love," she says. "Mind yourself on the road, Jim."

"You know I always do, Nanny," Jim responds affectionately.

Boss follows us down the hall, until Jim orders her back to Nanny.

"Not today, girl, not today," he says.

***

"Where are we going?" I ask when we're settled in the car, an old long four-door with a big steering wheel.

"You want a job at some fast-food joint or store or something, so that's where I'm taking you. To the village."

"What village?" I try to keep the impatience out of my voice. After all, Jim is doing me a favour. And I have been ignoring him for days. He could easily have said no.

"It's a mall. The Village Mall." Then he laughs. I wonder if Jim toys with everyone this way.

"You're just too funny," I say. But Jim's not kidding. A few minutes later we pull into the parking lot of a big shopping mall. "This is it – see? The Village Mall," Jim says, reading the sign slowly, enunciating each letter, like a grade one teacher. "Stores galore. Teenagers in every one."

"Perfect," I reply. "Just what I wanted."

We spend the rest of the morning walking from store to store. I ask the same question in each one: "Are there any jobs here?" Almost everyone says sorry. A couple of places give me an application to fill out. Jim doesn't say much. He looks uncomfortable at the mall and he barely glances at any of the merchandise in the stores. He just stands behind me as I ask my questions, his shoulders slightly hunched. I keep expecting him to point out that I'm probably scaring people off because I'm all in black, although I didn't put any black around my eyes today, and I'm not wearing any chain jewelry around my neck. I think I look pretty tame.

"I'm dead," I finally tell him around lunch time. "I can't take another step. Want to get some pizza?"

"Lead the way," he says. "I'm sure you'll find it faster than I can."

We find a pizza place – I knew there'd be one – and settle at a tiny table in the food court.

"The thing is, Cheryl," Jim says between bites, "it's too

71

late in the summer. All the jobs are taken. If you'd come a few weeks earlier, maybe." Jim actually sounds sympathetic. He's probably right, but it's not what I want to hear.

"But sometimes people quit or they don't work out and get fired. You never know."

Then Jim starts to laugh.

"What's so funny?" I ask.

"It just struck me as funny all of a sudden. You, coming to Newfoundland to find work. Just so you could get out of Newfoundland. Don't you know this province has the highest unemployment rate in the whole country?"

"Well, it's not like I chose it, right? My parents did."

"Last year someone tried to open a strip joint downtown. When they advertised for dancers so many girls came to apply it floored the owners. They came from all over the province, young and old, skinny and fat. Some were grandmothers for Christ's sake, desperate to make a bit a money for their families."

"Really?" I respond. "Do you think they're still looking?"

"Could be, but you wouldn't get in."

"Oh, really. And why not?" For some reason it bothers me that Jim thinks I couldn't get a job stripping. I'm in pretty decent shape and I have big boobs. At least that's what Ewan

72

and his dumb friends said. Ewan told me his friends referred to me as "the big-boobed girl in black." I used to think it sounded like a great name for an all-girl rock band – Big Boob Babes in Black or something.

"Keep your shirt on, Cheryl. Only 'cause you're too young. In every other way you'd probably be okay," Jim says, looking down at his pizza, a grin on his face.

"Gee, thanks," I say, staring at the table. You don't have to be psychic to figure out where Jim's mind is wandering.

"Anyway, how come you don't work?" I ask to distract him.

"Well, I do, kind of. I play in a small band, with two other guys from school, Ned and Steve. I'm on the tin whistle. We usually set up down on George Street."

"Are you any good?"

"We're okay. We can pull in a fair bit of money most days. We do even better on foggy days, when us musicians aren't visible to the crowds. It makes it seem like the music is coming from fairies or ghosts. The tourists love it. They gobble up all that mystical stuff the tourism places really peddle. Did you know St. John's is called the City of Legends? They make it sound like we're all changelings or something."

"You're all what?"

"Changelings. You know, kidnapped by fairies as babies

and replaced? Aren't there any changelings in Montreal?"

"Not that I know of." Actually, if I am a changeling, it would help explain why I haven't inherited any of my parents' enthusiasm for new adventures. All those genes are sitting inside the girl who now lives with the fairies, probably up on Mount Royal.

"Nanny's full of stories about all that old stuff. She comes from a small place where they used to believe it all. Stupid superstitions, that's what my father called the stories and whatnot. In a way, I think he was glad to get away. My mother and Nanny would just talk about fairies and things to get him going and he always fell for it. Nanny's never been anywhere else. I can't even imagine it. Her health's not too good, you may of noticed," he says.

"Did something happen to her?"

"Yeah, but nothing physical. It was when her husband, my uncle, died. It happened twenty-five years ago this February. She never got over it," Jim says.

"How'd it happen?"

"He was working on an oil rig out in the ocean when it collapsed. It was big news around here, the collapse of the Ocean Ranger. I wasn't even born yet. He was my dad's best friend too. He started dating my dad's youngest sister, Nancy

— we call her Nanny — when she was fifteen. His body was never even found. I think that's the part that drove my aunt over the edge. The thought of him becoming fish food."

"Wow," I say, shaking my head. Imagine loving someone so much that a quarter-century after their death you're still shaking? That seems incredible. Beside me, Jim is nodding, as though he's saying hi to someone. I turn around and see a group of teenagers staring over at us. The girls are giggling, the guys grinning.

"Friends?" I ask.

"Nah, just kids from school," Jim says. "Nobody I give a crap about." I look back and see that they're walking toward us. Jim shifts in his seat.

"Hey, Jim," one of the girls says. She's pretty, in that plastic kind of way, with lots of makeup, streaked blond hair, and huge hooped earrings. "What are you up to?"

"Not much," responds Jim. "You guys?"

"Just hanging out," the same girl says. She's looking at me now, checking out my hair. "Who's your friend?"

"Cheryl," Jim says flatly, like he doesn't really want to tell her.

"I like your hair," says the other girl, who's obviously trying to be a clone of the first one, but can't quite pull it off.

The tight pink spaghetti-strapped top that she's wearing, with "Princess" written in glitter across her boobs, keeps riding up over her stomach. And the streaks in her hair are more pinky-orange than blond.

The two guys standing behind the girls are shifting their weight and laughing.

"Yeah, how do you make it stand up like that? You must use a ton of gel," the pretty girl says. "Either that or stick your fingers in a socket."

I just glare at the two girls. I can't believe they think they're funny. They remind me of some of the girls who gave me a hard time in my last school. Girls in the popular clique who probably would have been mean even if I hadn't been a complete stranger. They never passed me without saying something nasty, something they thought super clever. Like, if they saw me drinking something at lunch they'd want to know if it was blood. And what was in my sandwich? Crushed spider? Then they'd crack up.

"Hey, way to go, Jim," one of the guys says suddenly, wrapping his arm around the bigger girl.

"Yeah, way to go," the other guy joins in. Then they all crack up. I suppose the "way to go" is a reference to Jim being with me. They make it sound like he just won me at some carnival booth or landed me on the end of a fishing rod.

The way they say it also implies they've never seen Jim with a girl before, which means he doesn't have a girlfriend. I figured he didn't, but you never know.

"Didn't know you'd know where it goes," says the first guy, at which the entire gang cracks up.

"Let's go," Jim says, keeping his cool.

"Sure," I say. I get up slowly and deliberately, so they don't think they're scaring us off. I let my chain-belt clink hard against the back of my chair as I push it under the table.

"See ya," Jim says. I nod in their direction, and Jim and I head back toward the car.

"Who were those guys? What jerks," I say.

"I'm used to it," says Jim. "When I first showed up at Holy Heart they made fun of my accent all the time. I worked at toning it down. Now they just think I'm a loser 'cause I'm into getting good grades and stuff. I got a bit of that in my old school too. Lots of my classmates just gave up when our school closed, but I wasn't going to do that. I have goals, like going to Horton Bluffs and other stuff. That'll just be the start. And I'm trying to get a scholarship."

Did he say Holy Heart? That means Jim goes there too. I never thought to ask him. Then those loser kids would be at

Holy Heart also, part of my welcoming committee, which is all the more reason to get out.

"Thanks for bringing me," I say as we wind our way through the parking lot. "I know you probably had better things to do."

"What could be better than taking you to the Village," Jim says, "and running into a group of assholes?"

"You could be out looking for whales, I suppose."

"Oh yeah, whales. Don't worry. We'll see whales. They'll be here all summer."

All summer? I guess I should remind Jim right about now that I won't be here all summer. And what's with the *we*? Maybe I've given Jim the wrong idea by hanging out with him today.

"Anyway, you wouldn't want to come to the mall every day, would you? All those stores squished up together under those artificial lights," Jim says as he turns the key in the ignition. "I get lost in there."

"Are you serious? This mall is tiny compared to the ones in Montreal. We have the biggest underground shopping complex in North America. You can walk and shop for miles through connecting tunnels. It's really neat."

"Sounds horrible to me. I'd suffocate. Can you believe the town I'm from has only one store? But you can buy everything at it, from seal sausage to underwear."

"Wow. How practical," I respond. "The two things people are always running out of." Jim laughs. I have an image of men's underwear hanging next to a string of sausages. It's not exactly pretty. I don't dare tell Jim because he'd crack some joke about me being perverted.

***

"How 'bout seeing a real village now?" Jim says when we're back on the main road.

"Where?"

"It's not far, but it's really cool."

"Sure, why not? Any jobs there, you think?"

"Probably not. It's really small." Jim gives me a sympathetic look, as if he's really sorry I had such crappy luck today.

As we drive, I think about how different Jim was with those kids from Holy Heart. I can't imagine him joking around with them like he does with me. It's like the mall and their presence changed him, like he couldn't be himself, or at least the self that I've seen both times I've been out with him. I guess that means Jim is comfortable with me, which is strange. My mom's always telling me I have the opposite effect on people, with my dark clothes and attitude. I guess they don't seem dark to Jim.

"The fog's still in," Jim says, as we drive along. "I'll turn down and drive along the harbour. I like seeing ships in the fog, don't you?"

"Oh sure, I do it all the time. All that fog we had in Saskatchewan, 'cause of all the low-lying clouds and cold sea air."

"Ha. Very funny," says Jim. "And I thought you said you lived in B.C."

"I did, but then we moved to Saskatchewan."

"You guys sure move around," Jim says, as though it's a good thing. I don't respond. I'd rather watch the fog, which is nowhere near as thick as it was a few hours ago. It just covers the ships that line the harbour with a thin veil of mist, like they've been in a long steamy shower.

"Are these all fishing boats?" I ask.

"No. Different kinds. The big ones behind us are container ships. That's where all the island's supplies come in."

"Like sausages and underwear?" I ask.

"Yeah, except seal. Those are homemade, on the island. I don't think mainlanders would go for seal sausage, do you? They'd think they were eating the world's cutest animal or something."

I think of those white baby seals, the ones with big blue eyes, that you see on posters to protest the seal hunt. I'm not sure I'd want to eat them either.

"I knew they were killed for fur, but I didn't realize people ate them," I say.

"They've been eating seal on Newfoundland for hundreds of years. Kept a lot of people alive."

I turn around and look at the giant cranes that are lifting containers way into the air. One of them might actually be carrying the rest of the boxes that we had shipped from Saskatchewan.

"These smaller ones are fishing boats, skiffs and schooners," Jim says. He drives slowly so that I can read the names scrawled across their sides and backs – the Darling Dora and Little Lizzie III. If my father fished, I guess his boat could be called the Cheery Cherry, or something embarrassing like that. Or the Elegant Ellen, after my mother.

"Look at that big one from Russia," Jim says. "We've always got a couple of foreign vessels here. Or navy ships, even submarines at times. Always something different to look at." He points to the high masts of a large wooden sailing boat. The oak-coloured wood looks like it's been polished, it's so shiny.

"Isn't that one a beauty?" he asks. I nod. It looks like the same boat we watched come in from Signal Hill, the one Jim said was a tour boat.

As we approach the end of the harbour, I can see the Battery and all its quirky houses jutting out toward the Narrows. Across the water, just visible through the fog, is the lighthouse. "What's that place?" I ask, pointing.

"Fort Amherst," says Jim. "I'll take you over there sometime. Well, that was our harbour. Time to hit the village." Jim makes a sharp turn left and we climb a steep hill. I settle back and watch the houses go by. After a while, they go by pretty close, the road is so narrow in parts.

"We're here, mademoiselle," Jim says, pulling into a parking lot beside some more water.

"Already? How could we be in a whole new village? We only left the harbour five minutes ago?"

"Take you even less than that to drive through my hometown. There's basically one road that winds its way around the bay and past the two dozen houses. And there's no traffic signs anywhere, not unless you count the one the government put at the foot of the wharf to warn people about drowning. They did that cause some tourists slid off the wharf driving onto it to get a closer look at an iceberg. Thought they'd drive to the end of the wharf, take a couple of pictures, but that never happened. They just rolled off the side and into the water, which luckily isn't deep at that point. The whole town came out to help push the car back up. They were so embarrassed, sitting there all red in the face, thanking everyone."

"I bet you enjoyed that?"

"Who me? Of course not. It was very tragic."

Jim gets out of the car and walks to the edge of the parking lot. I follow and stand beside him.

"Where are we?"

"It's Quidi Vidi Village."

"Kiddy what?"

"Quidi Vidi, and that's q-u-i-d-i, not what you're probably thinking."

I look out at the oval pool of water, surrounded by wharfs and small fishing boats. The building we're parked at is a big white restaurant.

"Hey, think I could get a job in there?" I ask. "Or there?" I point to the only other big building, a green one with a "Brewery" sign on it.

"Probably not. Why not forget about jobs for today? If we go up this road, around the bend, we'll be able to see the opening to the harbour. We can even watch the boats come in

… if you want." I remember Jim's face watching the ships come in through the Narrows, the way it kind of lit up. I wonder if every time he sees one, it reminds him of home, and of his father.

"What do they fish here? I mean, according to my father there are no more fish." I don't tell him that that's why we're here.

"They do lobster and snow crab, I guess, and some cod, but not as much as before. There's a look-off sort of thing you can get to up there, too. It's got an old cannon and stuff. We can drive up later."

The word "later" hits me. Jim is making so many plans – with me. Even those kids at the mall thought we were together. They're probably spreading gossip already – they look like the type. I can see them labelling me and Jim "the Geek and the Goth," saying we were spotted together at the Village Mall. In my old towns, I laid low and, except for my black clothes last year, didn't do anything to attract attention. I can't believe I might already be the subject of gossip here.

I have the feeling Jim would like to show me the whole province. In a way, I'd love to see it, especially where he's from. I'm forming a pretty good picture of it in my mind. I can see Jim heading us in that direction – he keeps making plans, talking about "later". No one's ever done that before, except my parents. And I always resist their plans and try to escape them.

"Hello, Earth calling Cheryl ..." Jim is waving his hand in front of my face, drawing me back.

"Sorry, I was daydreaming."

"Obviously. Anything exciting?" Jim moves closer, a flash in his eyes.

"No, not really."

"Too bad. Ready to see Quidi Vidi? I mean, it's not Times Square or the Taj Mahal or anything, but those sheds up on stilts are kind of cool, don't you think?"

Jim's hand reaches toward mine. I know that if I let it connect, everything will change, tipping the balance in favour of staying and seeing what Jim wants to show me. But I told myself I'd stay disconnected. I'm not sure I'm ready to change that.

Jim's fingers are brushing against me, ever so lightly, like a gentle brush of wind.

"Cheryl," he says softly. My name sounds sweet on his lips, sweeter than it should.

"I think I have to go home now," I say, pulling back. Jim turns around and puts his hands on his hips. I can't tell if he heard me.

"I mean, I should get back," I say.

"Is it that black cloud that's scaring you?" Jim asks, pointing up. I look up and see a huge black cloud in the distance, floating rapidly toward us. I didn't even notice it before. "'Cause if it is, don't worry, Cheryl." Jim turns back to me, his eyes boring straight into mine, hopefully. "You know what they say around here – if you don't like the weather, wait ten minutes. It's always changing." I can feel Jim's brown eyes drawing me in.

"It's not that. It's just that I have to get back." I have to get back to a place where Jim can't draw me in with his chocolate-brown eyes.

"Okay, if you have to." Jim shakes his head, as though he's erasing a thought. We retrace our steps back to the car, slowly. I try not to look around at the fishing shacks that Jim wanted me to see, standing across from us on their high posts over the water, painted different colours. But it's hard to resist taking a peek. Suddenly, I wonder what life would have been like here a hundred years go. What if Jim and I were married and he was going off every day in his little boat to catch fish. And I stayed home with the women, to "make the fish," as Jim called it.

The black cloud is now directly overhead. The minute we

step into the car it opens up, raining huge drops that hit the car so hard I'm sure the metal will be pockmarked.

Neither of us speaks the whole way back. I concentrate on the windshield-wipers slapping back and forth on high speed, barely able to clear our view before it's watered up again. I can't help feeling like I've ruined the day more than the rain has, even though I think I made the right decision. A few minutes later, Jim parks the car outside Nanny's. The second he slides the key out of the ignition, the sun bursts through the cloud and the rain stops.

"See, I told you," Jim says. "The weather around here is always changing. It's like it can't make up its mind." Jim stares at me, like he's hoping I might change mine, but I open the door and get out.

"Thanks for taking me to the mall," I say, standing between our two houses. "And Quidi Vidi."

I move to put my hand on the doorknob and am about to turn it when Jim says, "I'll be walking Boss tonight, around eight. If you want to come."

I really want to say yes, but I just shrug and say "I'll see" before going in.

Jim keeps standing there for a minute before going in. I know because I watch him through the porch window.

***

The first thing my mother tells me when I step into the kitchen is that she registered me at school today.

"Whoopity-doo," I whisper under my breath. I see the Britney Spears wannabe and her sidekick clone laughing down at me and Jim. Holy Heart's finest. "I'm so thrilled."

"Everyone seemed really nice and helpful," my mom continues. She's trying to draw me in. I don't participate.

All through supper my mind keeps drifting back to the harbour and the big boats bobbing gently in the fog. There is something about them that makes you want to jump aboard and sail away, out past the Narrows and into the vast ocean. Jim had that look in his eyes too, when he saw them.

Maybe Jim will come crashing in here tomorrow morning to whisk me off to Fort Amherst.

But he probably won't. After the way I acted at Quidi Vidi, he must think I'm a complete idiot.

I take off to my room, leaving my parents to discuss my new school without me. At eight o'clock, I look outside, to see if Jim is walking Boss. I probably won't join him, even if he is. I want to see Jim, but I wish I didn't want to. It's that wanting to do things that's confusing. It's not a feeling I'm used to.

A minute later Jim comes out with Boss on her leash, tugging and excited. Jim looks up at my window. I pull back, hiding behind the dusty curtain. He stands there for a few minutes, watching. Boss is turning circles, tangling her leash around Jim's legs.

Eventually, he shrugs and walks off, his shoulders hunched.

***

I go to bed early, like an old lady, and fall into the hole, curling my body to fit its shape perfectly. I might regret it later, not flipping the mattress, but tonight it just seems like the right thing to do.

CHAPTER 4
how to be impervious

$\mathcal{L}$iving on a farm last year knocked the habit of sleeping in out of me. Up with the birds isn't just an expression to a farm family, it's a religion. Ewan turned it into a form of torture. He'd clash buckets against the back wall of the house, right under my bedroom window as he was doing his chores. Or he'd spray the hose through the screen, sprinkling me in my bed. In winter, it was snowballs – smack against the glass.

So this is getting weird. Yesterday, I slept right through lunch. When I woke up, I was sure I'd just heard my door clicking shut. It was probably my parents, coming to check that I was still alive. My mom told me she used to do that a lot when I was a baby, tiptoe into my room and place her hand in front of my nose to feel the little puff of baby breath, just to check that I was still breathing. I was one of those wasn't-supposed-to-happen babies, or so my parents had been told by several specialists. Something about the shape of my mom's womb. She said it took her ages to believe I was really here.

Today, it's almost noon when I go downstairs. My father has a wide, eager grin splashed across his face. I don't look away fast enough and our eyes catch. "Come on, Cher, I'd really like to go find this beach with you."

That's when I notice a picnic basket full of food on the kitchen counter, packed and ready to go. I can't stand it when he tries so hard. Then I feel crappy if I let him down. It's another one of the great traps my parents set to pull me in, to make me part of their excited team of travelers. I'm about to protest and hold my ground when the kitchen door opens and in walks Jim, all smiles, followed by my mother.

"Jim said he'd come. Isn't that great, Cher," announces my mom.

"What?" My mouth falls open and Jim's smile vanishes. He must have thought I asked my mother to invite him and here he is, all eager. I haven't seen him since we went to the two villages, days ago. I haven't really done anything since then, except hole up in my room. I know Jim's been trying to see me. He's looked up at my window just about every night, before walking Boss. It's odd. It's like he knows I'm there, watching him. Otherwise, he'd ring the bell, or just barge in, to see if I'm home.

"Jim says it's a great spot," my mother continues, blabbing on to cover up my lack of enthusiasm.

"Yeah, it is," Jim says, looking at me. "I mean, there are better, but for a twenty-minute drive, it's pretty good."

The entire house is holding its breath. Every creak is like a crack of thunder. I don't respond.

I can't believe my parents have gone and done this. They're going to use Jim to get me interested in being here. I can just picture them discussing strategies to turn me around and settling on Jim, the one contact I've made here. They probably even decided that my mom should be the one to invite him, since he'd be less likely to turn her down. I can't believe my mom actually had the nerve to go next door and ask him to come. I wonder if she knocked first, or did she just walk in? Maybe Jim's aunt ordered him to make her some tea, then they had a nice chat about dying cultures while they were at it.

"Now you can't say no," my father adds, looking quickly at my mom in that conspiratorial way they both have.

Of course I can't say no. Wasn't that the plan? I push back my chair, hard, letting it hit the wall behind me.

"I'll get dressed," I mutter.

Upstairs, I put on the darkest, most unbeachlike clothes I own. Hardly one centimetre of skin is showing when I'm done. All I can think about is how glad I am that I turned Jim down at Quidi Vidi, that I didn't let him hold my hand. That means I haven't been won over at all. I'm still just on my side. They can do their best — all three of them.

I know how to be impervious.

***

I don't speak the whole way to Middle Cove. I'm like extra cargo, or a spare tire. My mother, on the other hand, can't ask Jim enough questions. She wants to know where he grew up, what grade he's in, what he plans to do with his life. If this keeps up, she'll know him better than I do by the end of the day. But why should I care? I had already decided that Jim has to be like the rest of this province — part of the scenery that I'll take in, then leave behind.

Every now and then, from the corner of my eye, I catch Jim smiling at me, trying to draw me in, but I don't let him.

He's telling my mom about his mother's knitting business. "She can whip up a sweater an evening and never even take her eyes off the TV. She's got my two younger sisters helping out. They do the sleeves or the pockets, the parts without designs. It's a real assembly line, just like the fish line at the old plant. When I was still at home she tried to get me into it. She thought I could do the sewing up. She said she'd seen me with a needle, mending my dad's nets in the winter. "Just think of the sweater as one of them nets," she said, "and go in and out the same way." But there's no way I'd do it. I'm happy to help out and all, but I've got my pride and I put my foot down at knitting."

"Isn't that fascinating," says my mother. "Did Cheryl tell you I do needlework too? I quilt. I'd love to see some of your mother's sweaters sometime."

"Sounds like your mother has managed to be resourceful in hard times," my father says. I want to gag. I can see him mentally taking notes: knitting versus dying. Poor Jim has no idea he's being studied and that even his mom's sweaters are grist for my father's mill. I should warn him about my father's book, but it would require too much talking. I feel like my mouth is full of stones.

Besides, I'd have to find the right words. I remember when I told Ewan about my dad's book. It didn't go over too well. I wouldn't have told him at all, but he had overheard my dad talking to his. My father was going on about the future of farming, sharing some grim statistics. Ewan had even heard my father ask whether he thought Ewan would carry on the tradition, and his own father admitting he didn't know. That seemed to really bother him.

"How does your dad know so much about it?" Ewan asked.

"It's his job, Ewan. That's what he does."

"What? What does he do? Does he have a crystal ball or something?"

"No, he studies change in cultures."

"What changes? We're not changing."

I didn't dare tell Ewan what my dad had said about the number of lost farms in Saskatchewan. According to him, there were more than a hundred and forty thousand farms in the nineteen thirties. Now, there were less than fifty thousand.

"Whatever, Ewan. Just forget it. It doesn't mean anything. It's just what anthropologists do. It's stupid." I tried to throw him off, but he wouldn't let it drop.

"But my dad's working really hard to make this farm successful."

"I know, Ewan. My dad knows that."

"But that's not what it sounded like. He made it sound like we were all doomed." Ewan's face was now red and his cheeks were puffed out, like a gopher's.

His whole attitude toward me changed after that. He still hung around the back of the farm house and brought his dumb friends over to gawk at me, but he was cooler, more aloof.

Finally, Jim points out where we need to turn to hit the beach — a sharp right at the bottom of a hill.

Ours isn't the only car in the parking lot. In fact, every tourist in Newfoundland must be here. There are even a couple of big tour buses. I'm glad. My parents will hate that. They refuse to think of themselves as tourists. *We're tourists of the mind*, I've even heard my father say, as if our bodies stay behind.

"Is everything okay, Cheryl?" Jim asks me while my parents are getting stuff out of the trunk.

"Never mind. It's complicated," I say.

Jim helps my parents carry the basket and blankets down to the beach. He's wearing jeans cut off at the knee and a black T-shirt with a Led Zeppelin logo on it. I wonder if he wore black just to keep me company.

"Wow! The guy was right. What a great beach," my father says in his big isn't-this-exciting voice.

I take a quick look around at this so-called beach. It's not exactly white sand and palm trees, more like black sand and no trees. It's also missing girls in bikinis and guys trying to impress them with beach volleyball. Thick, coarse sand stops a ways down and is replaced by a strip of rocks about ten-feet deep. The rocks are a mixture of off-white, light grey, rain-cloud grey and the mauve of unripe plums. They remind me of my mother's hair, which has that same mottled pattern, with a shock of white around her temples. She even once had plum-coloured streaks put in her hair, much like the purple of these rocks. It's like she somehow had this beach in mind when she went to the hairdresser to get the streaks done. If I were speaking to her, I could ask her about it.

Past the rocks, there's a mound of black stuff near the water's edge, like an oil spill has washed up on shore.

"Capelins in," Jim says, pointing to it. "Or, as my dad would say, 'Fish are eating the rocks'."

My father laughs. "Capelin, you say?"

"Yeah, capelin. They're little fish."

I move a step closer and see that the black stuff really is fish, a whole heap of them, piled on top of each other.

"They're late this year. Global warming or something, I guess," Jim says. "We usually have our capelin weather in June, all that rain and drizzle – that tells us they're coming. They come close to shore by the thousands to spawn, then the poor suckers get spit up onto the beach by the waves. They're so exhausted from all the effort of spawning, they can't resist."

My parents laugh. Jim looks at me to see if I find him funny. I do kind of find the thought of fish knocking themselves out with reproducing amusing, but I won't join in the laughter. I'm still too mad.

"Anyway, they're what bring the whales in," Jim continues. "But it's all happening later and later now. People come down and catch the capelin by the bucketful when it comes in. Some smoke it right here, over the rocks. It's a real delicacy. But that might not last much longer. Stocks are diminishing. Too much over-fishing."

"No kidding," responds my mother. "How sad! They're really quite beautiful, with their silver streaks glinting in the sun."

Whenever my mom talks colour, it can only mean one thing. She'll be whipping up a capelin quilt next week, if she ever unpacks her stuff. No doubt she'll pepper the background of this one with the grey-mauve rocks.

"Not to me," I say. "They look like rotting bananas."

"Oh, Cheryl. It's a matter of perspective, I guess," my mom says.

I let it drop, or else she won't give up.

We continue along the beach until my parents stop and set up our picnic on some low rocks that reach toward the water like a series of dark, bony fingers, cut and bruised from too much hard work. I'm amazed by the way the cuts on the fingers are perfectly straight, like someone took a hedge-trimmer and randomly sawed off a piece here and there, leaving flat ridges and deep vertical lines. How could that happen?

"You say the capelin bring in the whales, Jim?" my father asks.

"They used to bring the cod in too, when we had some," Jim adds.

"Now that's interesting, Jim. I didn't know that. Was your family affected much by the loss of cod?"

Here we go. The interview has begun. Once my father has finished with Jim, he won't want to get to know me anyway. I won't have to keep dodging him. He'll avoid our house like it contains the plague. My dad thinks his job brings me closer to people, but it's just the opposite. I should have warned Jim in the car, but what was I supposed to say? *Oh yeah, by the way, my father will want to study you. Just ignore him and go about your daily business. He's assessing how you cope with losing your job, your home, your heritage – and, in your case, your family. Nice weather we're having, eh?*

I tune out by thinking of the capelin flying out of the water, like some kind of species-wide suicide pact, only it's more like a mass-murder, since they didn't exactly want to be flung out of their natural habitat like that. I wonder if some of them try harder than others to resist being tossed.

"... government up in Ottawa, the big chiefs, the ones who know what is and isn't good for us," Jim is saying. This won't be what my father wants to hear. He wants to know about Jim's family, about the personal pain. "Most of them bureaucrats never been out on a fishing boat. Probably turn green after the first five minutes in some of the swells we get."

"Isn't this an outstanding view?" my mother asks suddenly. I bet she wants to spare Jim the interview as much as I do, or at least help make it seem more natural. My mom is a huge supporter of my dad's project. She's working on indexing his book for him. I wonder if Jim will get an entry, maybe under "Jim's story."

Basically, we're in a cove. On either side, rocky cliffs jut out into the ocean. The one on the left is lower, with a strip of evergreen trees sitting on top, looking like they're fighting hard not to fall down. The cliff closer to us is pretty high, with perfectly vertical sides where birds perch on the tiniest of footholds, or clawholds I suppose. Foamy water is crashing at the foot of the cliffs and each time the spray comes up my mother gasps. It's not even touching her, but she points her chin up as though it is. When she shields her eyes, I notice that her fingers are quite swollen today. She suffers when it's damp, which, if you asked me, is another good reason for us to have gone home instead of coming to Newfoundland. I mean, it *is* an island in the middle of a cold ocean.

"Pretty, eh Cher?" my mother says.

I just shrug. Jim is smiling over at me. I can tell he wants me to like the view too, but I'm working on seeing it as a picture on a tacky calendar, the kind you can buy at the drugstore.

"There's lots more coves like this one all around the Avalon," Jim says. "If you're looking."

"Well, we'll have lots of time for exploring before school starts," my father responds. I can feel three pairs of eyes on me now. Thank god a man walking his dog cuts in.

"Seen some whales here yesterday," he tells us. "You best come early in the day or in the evening if you want to see them." My father thanks him. *See*, I want to tell him, *we do look like tourists.*

"What d'ya say we stick our feet in the water before we eat? We can't live by the ocean and not at least stick our toes in," my father says. "You gals game?"

"Sounds good to me," my mother responds. She's already rolling up her pants and kicking off her sandals. I'd have to take off my black boots and socks. Just to stick a toe in the water? I don't think so. I watch my parents run to the far end of the beach, where it's quieter. They're holding hands, inching their way into the water. Whenever a wave rolls in they let out a squeal. Jim must think they're nuts.

"Your parents are fun," he says to me.

"They're fun*ny* all right, as in 'should be locked up' funny," I answer.

"Nah, they're all right," Jim says. "I can't remember the last time I was together with both my parents."

Jim is building a round tower of rocks as he talks, doing a pretty good job of balancing smaller ones at the top. He keeps going down to the water's edge to choose more. The rocks are shiny, shaded purple and blue, some with stripes in them, others speckled.

"We used to do this all the time when we were kids, collect the saltwater rocks. We'd make these towers as high as we could, then kick them over, see whose could make the most noise."

"That sounds like so much fun," I say.

"We had to amuse ourselves somehow, Cheryl. It's not

like we had a megaplex in town, with movies and bowling and laser quest, or whatever crap they have inside."

Jim starts another outside wall to the tower so he can make it even higher.

"Is that when you first started liking rocks?" I ask. I probably shouldn't, since I said I'd keep my distance, but I am curious and this seems like a good time, with my parents gone.

"Could be," he says.

"Didn't you ever want to fish when you were older, like your dad?"

"No way. I fished with my dad when I was younger, but I never really took to the water, not the way my brothers did. I always knew I'd do something different," Jim says. "When I was in the boat with my dad, my favourite part would be hugging the coast, studying the cliffs. My dad couldn't get me to focus on the fish at all. And then my mom would catch me digging way down in the ground, trying to chip away into the granite."

"Wow, you must have been an exciting kid."

"Sure was," Jim laughs. "Forget about dragons and wizards. I liked to read about rocks and fossils and stuff. I remember reading a story about these kids, Plinius Moody and Mary Anning. I was dead jealous of the pair of them."

"How come?"

- lori weber -

"They both stumbled on these great finds when they were really young, like ten or so, same age as me when I read about them."

"What did they find?"

"One of them found dinosaur tracks in a cliff near his house, somewhere in Massachusetts, but the girl found tons of stuff, starting with a huge fossilized sea monster on some cliffs in England."

"Whoa. Did they get rich?"

"No, but Mary got a tongue twister. You know 'she sells sea shells'? That's about her."

"That's cool. She's immortal then."

"Yeah, like all fossils. That's partly why I like 'em. They last forever. They might change a bit over time, but the changes are small and they take millions of years. Nothing else in life is that solid and nothing else on earth can be counted on in such a sure way."

Suddenly, I'm aware that Jim has stopped building his tower and is sitting right next to me. He has this uncanny ability to get close to me and draw me in, without my even noticing. I said I wasn't going to talk and here I am, in the middle of a conversation — about rocks, again.

"Boss and I were real sorry you couldn't join us for our

walks," he says.

I can feel Jim's deep brown eyes on me and the pressure of his arm leaning against me, heating me up.

"Yeah, well ..." I'm trying to think up an excuse for why I've been ignoring him, one that doesn't make me sound insane, when I hear my parents squealing. They're running toward us, their pants wet up to the knees.

"You have to feel it, Cher," my mother says. She is holding her hands out like a cup in front of her. "It's incredible." There's a pool of water in her palms.

"Go on, girl. Don't be scared," Jim says.

"God, I'm not scared, it's just stupid," I say, but I dip my finger into the well anyway. Then I gasp. The water is colder than a tub of ice cubes. I can't believe my mother's holding such freezing water against her swollen fingers. Is she crazy? I have seen her cry when her pain gets intense.

Jim is laughing. He was probably baptized in water this cold, or else he fell overboard a couple of times, fishing with his dad, reaching out to pluck some rock from the water. He'd be immune to it by now.

"Very funny," I say. My parents are laughing too. I look at the three of them. They're having such a good time, like one big happy family. I know I could be laughing too, joining in.

That's just what my parents want me to do. I can feel how eager they are, their arms around each other, thinking how smart their little plan was, how well it's all working. I have a sudden flash of this game going on forever, my parents moving me around and trying to rope me in, with no end in sight. After all, there are all kinds of dying cultures my father could study. Even next year, he could decide to document some Innu community in Labrador. And he'd insist that we stay in an igloo, to have the real deal. How would I even tack my portable room décor into ice?

"What do you think, Cheryl?" my father asks.

"I think the smell of rotting capelin is making me nauseous," I say, standing up.

"Oh, Cheryl," my mom says, studying Jim's tower, taking in its shape and colours.

"It was nicer before," Jim says, following her gaze. "The rocks have gone dull in the sun. The water really makes them shine. Take them out and they go a bit flat."

He's right. At first, the stones were deep purple and blue. Now, they're all murky grey. I walk toward the water, feeling three pairs of eyes following me. I stand there for a minute, until I can hear them starting to unwrap sandwiches and occupy themselves with eating.

Then I bend down and grab the rock that caught my eye moments ago, lying in a shallow pool of water that seems to be part of a small stream coming down from the parking lot. On one side, it's speckled grey and white – the other is as purple as eggplant. A white stripe slices it in half. Jim's right. Rocks can be pretty amazing.

I slip the rock into my pocket, feeling its cold wetness soak through, against my skin.

Behind me, my mom's calling my name. When I turn around, she is holding up a sandwich – egg salad, my favourite. My parents and Jim are sitting around Jim's rock tower. I have an incredible urge to run over there and kick it down, to see how much noise it would make.

But I don't. I control myself and take a seat on a rock behind them, letting the wind tear the plastic wrap from my hands and lift it high over the water like a transparent bird.

***

Lying in bed that night, I keep seeing hoards of capelin leaping out of the water. It's like the whole ocean is emptying out, layer by layer, giant waves of fish, their silver backs flashing.

Their only purpose, it seems, is to be food for something else. What an incredibly pointless existence.

Jim tried to pull me into a conversation the whole way home, but I couldn't talk to him, not with my parents listening so hopefully. Jim's hand kept inching toward mine on the back seat, but I could see my father checking us out in his rearview mirror, so I kept my hands closed in my lap, curled up like crabs in their shells.

Jim must really think I'm a nutcase. He probably wouldn't understand, even if I could explain the effect my parents have on me, and how much I want to be able to go home, to decide what happens to me, for a change, instead of being dragged around. I guess if Jim were in my shoes, he'd just get up and go home, on his own. That's because things are easier for guys. If I were a guy, I could just hit the road and stick out my thumb. There's a ferry about an hour from here that could take me over to Nova Scotia. I could hide in the trunk and come out once the boat was moving. What would they do if they found me? Make me walk the plank like Wendy in *Peter Pan*? Then I could hitchhike from Nova Scotia to Montreal. I'd probably get lifts with truckers who overdose on coffee in all-night truck stops. But try doing that when you're a sixteen-year-old girl. Even if I dressed in my blackest clothes and wrapped a forty-pound chain around my waist I'd be asking for trouble.

I'm just about to get up and finally flip my mattress when someone knocks at my door. I can hear my parents downstairs, watching television, but I've hardly said a word to them since we got home. It's possible one of them wants to talk to me about what happened today at Middle Cove. Or maybe they want to take me to another beach, to see the waves at night.

"Cheryl?"

Oh my god! It's Jim. What the hell is he doing here? I'm not even dressed. I can't believe my parents let him in.

"What do you want?"

"I want to see what you've done with my old buddy's room."

"Yeah, sure."

"Okay, I confess. I want to jump your bones," he says, laughing.

"Oh, that's charming," I answer. I can feel my cheeks burning.

"Seriously, Cheryl, open up. I have something to show you."

"It's like ten o'clock at night," I snap back through the

closed door. In the meantime, I grab a sweatshirt and throw it over my old nightgown, a white lacy thing that I've had since I was twelve.

"No it's not. It's ten-thirty," Jim says, turning the door handle. "Remember? Half an hour later in Newfoundland. Besides, your parents said you were still up."

"Whoa! Only I open this door," I cry, turning the handle from the inside. Jim walks in confidently, as though he's stepped into this room a thousand times.

"Hmm, looks good, very artistic," he comments as he scans the walls, taking in my scarves, postcards, and fans. Then he strides straight to the desk.

"Come see," he says, laying something on the desktop and shining the lamp down on it.

When I look into the circle of light, I see two flat rocks sitting on top of Africa.

"Rocks! You crash into my room at night to show me rocks?"

"Not rocks, Cheryl. You have to look closer, beyond the surface." Then Jim bends closer to his rocks and stares at them intently, as if to show me how to do it. He's acting like there's some action going on down there that I'm too dumb to see.

I bend down closer, staring intently like Jim did, but I

don't really know what I'm supposed to see. There *are* some lines etched into the rocks, but they don't resemble anything, to me.

"What the hell are they?" I ask.

"They're fossils, of course."

"Fossils! Fossils of what?"

"Some kind of spiny sea creatures," Jim says. I just raise my eyebrows. As usual, I don't see what Jim is all excited about.

"Do you have any idea how old these are?" he asks me. "And rare."

"No, I told you, I don't know a thing about fossils."

"Oh yeah. I forgot, you're a townie, a city girl, right? Well, I'll tell you. These could be about half a billion years old. I found them myself, on a field trip to Fortune Head, last year. Mr. Wells was dead impressed. They're my best fossils, 'cause they're articulated, which makes them even more special. The grooves in them from the spiny fish are pretty obvious. Fortune Head's a really special place cause it's one of only three places in the world where these kinds of fossils exist. The other two are in China and Russia," Jim says, pointing to the last two countries on the desk map, as if I wouldn't know where they are.

"Wow! You weren't kidding. You really are a rock expert."

"I told you, Cheryl. I want to become a geologist. I've wanted to since as far back as I can remember, but I'm not sure it'll ever happen. It costs a lot of money to go as far as I want to go."

"Your father must make good money in Alberta," I say.

"Sure he does, but he sends a lot to my mom. Things are expensive where I'm from, and she's still got my two sisters at home. He sends my aunt money too, for taking me in. And then he's still got boat payments. He'd just bought a new one a few years before the fishery shut and of course he couldn't sell it off. What good's a fishing boat without fish? There's not much left after all that."

I don't know what to say. I've always just assumed that one day I'd go to university. I thought everyone else just assumed the same. I can't imagine worrying if I could afford it or not. My parents have been talking to me about university forever now and I grew up hanging around anthropology departments. I never really stopped to think that might be an advantage.

Jim is still studying his fossils. I wonder how many hours he's spent in this same position, his hair hanging over his eyes.

"If we do go on that field trip to Horton Bluffs this summer, I might get lucky and find a rare fossil," Jim says, straightening up.

"What's so special about the Horton Bluffs?"

"They're world famous for having the first amphibian footprints. A guy named Logan found them back in 1841. Some pretty impressive bone fossils have been found there too, probably of an ancient fish called a *Rhizodus*. Scientists think it could walk on land, too."

"Oh. That's impressive, I guess." I look down and it hits me that I'm in bare feet. Jim's never seen my feet before. They've always been encased in black boots.

"Feel this," Jim says suddenly. He places his palm right over the back of my hand and moves my hand around, as though it's a computer mouse. He guides my fingers over the fossils, his index finger pressing down on mine as we trace the spiny lines together, slowly.

"The lines are so delicate," I say.

"That's because they've been washed over by millions of years of elements. You're feeling sandstone and limestone when you touch these things," Jim says. "All the layers that once covered them, even ice from the last ice age, ten thousand years ago."

I try to picture the bony little creatures pressing against the stone, all those years ago. They were probably being chased by predators and their only option was to burrow between some rocks. And now, Jim and I are feeling these etchings together, our eyes closed and our breath mingling.

"These are kind of neat," I admit softly. Jim doesn't speak. He just squeezes my hand, like he doesn't want to let go. Then he lifts his hand ever so slightly and begins to trace the back of my hand with his fingers. His touch is light and delicate on my skin. His fingers brush down the raised cartilage, then dip into the hollows between. My whole hand is tingling, as though Jim is drawing all my blood to the surface.

"I can read you too, the same way," Jim says, bending toward me so that his face is really close to mine. I can feel him staring into my blue eyes, his breath on my skin. I'm not used to being studied up close like this.

"You can?" I say, pulling back a little. "Why?"

"I don't know. It's just like that with some people. Like you meet them and you feel you've known them your whole life. You connect. Do you know what I mean?"

I nod. I do know. But the knowing feels so strange.

"Cheryl," Jim says. "About today. I got the feeling I did something wrong, coming along. But I couldn't say no to your mom, could I? Not when she came over and invited me. I was being neighbourly."

That's a word I haven't heard in eons. I used to know

what it meant, when I actually had neighbours that I knew. In Murdochville, the two mining families on either side of us had already left the town. In Osoyoos we were in an apartment building with mostly old people who were trying to nurse their bone trouble, and at the farm house in Saskatchewan our nearest neighbour was miles away.

"Yeah, well, my parents and I aren't really getting along too well at the moment," I say.

"I could see that. Is it just because they brought you to Newfoundland?"

I realize that sounds lame. It doesn't seem like much of a crime. I'd have to explain so much to Jim for him to understand, but I have to try.

"I just really wanted to go home. I thought we were finally going home this time. They said it would just be a year, and then two, then three, and now four. I just want to go home, you know?"

Jim nods, as though he gets it. I guess he might, in a way. After all, he's away from home too. He probably left friends behind and his family is all split up – in three different places. At least mine is still together.

"I'm playing with the guys tomorrow afternoon. But maybe I'll see you after, okay?" He looks at me intently.

I start to say "Maybe," but that's what I said when Jim brought me home from Quidi Vidi. He deserves a better answer this time. "I'll try."

"Well, that's better than a no," Jim responds.

Then he picks up his fossils and leaves.

***

My hand is on fire, where Jim touched it. It's like I never really felt my hand before. It's just been there, inconspicuous.

If it weren't so dark in here, I'd be able to see whether his strokes have left marks on my skin.

CHAPTER 5
on the rock alone

I am awakened by rain, lashing against my window with incredible force, like a million tiny fists pounding to be let in. A pool of water is collecting on the sill then spilling over, creating a small waterfall. I'm sure it's not the first time this has happened, judging by the yellow streak on the wall and the blackened wood, the size of a plate, on the floor under it.

Across the room, the lamp on the desk is still lit, casting a circle of light on the map where Jim's fossils lay last night. I guess I forgot to turn it off. The rest of the room is grey, with no hint of sun, even though the radio clock says 11:00 a.m.

I lie here thinking about the fossils, and it strikes me that they are kind of yin and yang too. The rock they're embedded in is hard, yet they contain something as delicate as those etchings, thin and wispy as silk. Maybe that's why Jim likes them, because they're a mixture of so many things – hard and soft, past and present.

My dad says he's only interested in the present. That's why he's an anthropologist and not an archaeologist. If he were, we'd be going around living on dig sites. Here, he does his digging in disguise, camouflaging himself as a normal person. I guess my mom and I are part of the disguise – his normal family, following the working husband around.

Downstairs, I find a note on the kitchen counter, in my mother's shaky handwriting: *We've gone to the university. Be back later. Have a good day, Mom and Dad.* I know my father wanted me to go see his office too. They probably waited a while after breakfast, then figured it was best to let me sleep. They're probably hoping that rest will put me in a better mood.

I fix myself a grilled cheese sandwich and take it into the living room. Of all the rooms in a house, this one is the hardest to feel at home in. Our last place was also furnished, and I always felt like I was intruding in the living room. I guess because it's the *living* room, the place where people gather together and live. I can just imagine hundreds of birthday and Christmas celebrations taking place in here over the years, for Robbie and his family. They didn't leave any family portraits lying around, but they didn't have to. I can feel their presence everywhere.

I plunk myself down on the brown plaid sofa. Across from me sits a matching chair, with a pop-out footrest. The bookshelf against the back wall is practically bare. I guess Robbie's family boxed up all their personal stuff, except for a row of Encyclopaedia Britannicas and some other big hardcovers, to give us space. On the bottom shelf is a stack of board games, including Monopoly, Clue, and Risk, stuff I used to play when I was ten. On top of the bookcase sits a row of pictures that they forgot to hide. What's odd is that there is a bridge in each one, with some member of Robbie's family standing in front of it. Then I remember my dad saying that the mother was an engineer. Maybe her specialty is bridges. If so, she sure lives in a strange place.

Our laptop is sitting on the coffee table, but it's completely useless without an Internet connection. If we were online, I could check my email and catch up with Janna. I haven't had any contact with her since the day she met me downtown in Montreal, on our way here. My parents had gone to visit the family that was renting our house, just to check things out. Janna came downtown and we walked around, soaking up the city and catching up. I could've cried on Sainte Catherine Street, I was so happy to see concrete, tons of it, piled up to the sky. Later, we hung out in the hotel room and she talked non-stop about Stephan, her new boyfriend. She kept wanting to know if I had a boyfriend too. She assumed I'd have a string of them across the country. It was hard to explain that that was so far from the truth. She didn't seem to get that when you're trying to fit into a new place it's all kind of awkward. Then, as if she couldn't wait to show me, she pulled out a round case of birth-control pills. She even took one there, in the bathroom, making a point of telling me how easy it was to forget.

I finish my sandwich and put my dish in the sink, balancing it on top of a stack of plates, bowls, and pots that are still sitting there from last night. My mother usually likes to do dishes because the hot water is soothing on her fingers. She always ignores the dishwasher, if there is one. I wonder why she didn't do these. Maybe her fingers were so sore she was afraid she'd drop something. It's happened before.

That pool of ice water in her hands yesterday couldn't have helped. I can't believe she'd hurt herself like that, just to get me to feel the ocean. It's like that time in Osoyoos, when she hiked far up into the mountains to collect rare wildflowers that grew there, in bright purples, pinks, and oranges that were so lustrous they looked like they'd been coated in lipstick. We'd seen them the day before, from the car, when we drove up to the look-off on Anarchist Mountain, a name that made my mother laugh. She said that name was totally unjustified, because even an anarchist would have to be impressed by the beauty of the view – the Rockies, the lakes, and desert cacti. Anarchists liked chaos, but this, according to my mom, was proof that a higher power was trying to make some order in the world.

After her hike, she made up a big bouquet, just for me, and left it in my room. The colour exploded when I opened my door, as if the flowers had an interior flash. It almost made up for the hard day I'd just had, trying to find my way around the new school. The classes were going apple picking the next day and we had had to organize ourselves into groups of six. I ended up in the group of stragglers, or leftovers, all the kids who were either too shy or unpopular to get chosen by anyone else. The apple picking itself was kind of fun and mindless. A tractor pulled us into a huge orchard and the farmer ordered each group off at different spots and gave us canvas bags to hang over our shoulders. We couldn't eat the apples in the field though, because they'd been sprayed. My arm muscles ached the next day.

I decide to do the dishes. I haven't done much to help out since we got here, so I guess it's not going to kill me. Scrubbing and rinsing will also help kill time. Jim said something about getting together later today, after his band plays.

Before last night, I had decided that all the places Jim has shown me can't mean anything. And neither could he. But it's all different today, and all because of those fossils.

***

Nunnery Hill is not quite as charming by day, without the lights of the ships shining on the harbour. It's still pretty though. The rain has stopped, leaving a veil of mist around the water and the Narrows. I decided I didn't want to spend the day waiting for Jim to show up. I also didn't want to be home when my parents returned, full of excitement about my dad's new office and questioning me about when I was going to come see it. So, I decided to walk around downtown on my own, something I haven't done yet. I figure I might even see Jim.

Another cruise ship is in port, which will be good for Jim and his band. When I hit Duckworth I turn right. The street is full of people, going in and out of gift shops where wooden ships and sun catchers, with colourful row houses or puffins, decorate the windows. I see lots of wool sweaters too, with fat stitches depicting ocean scenes and I wonder if any were made by Jim's mother. I pass the cafés that Jim described, where people are sitting outside, reading newspapers and sipping coffee, even in the mist. It's true that I can't picture Jim here. He'd be too restless without rocks or whales to look for.

A sign on a huge grey stone building across the street reads "Court House." Beside it, a long staircase runs down to the street below. A group of tourists are on their way up, huffing and puffing, their cameras bumping against their chests. As I pass them, I wonder if they see me as a tourist or not. It's possible that I'm actually blending in. I've seen a couple of people dressed like me, but more punk, with purple hair and safety pins in their ears. On Water Street I find more of the same – gift shops, restaurants, a few music stores, some banks. It's busy down here too, but nobody seems to be in a great rush. People kind of meander, as though they don't really have a destination. It's sure different from the way people walk on Sainte Catherine Street in Montreal – like their destination might vanish any minute. And nobody waits for green lights to cross, so each corner is a tangled web of pedestrians and cars, competing for space.

I come to a corner where artists are selling jewelry and other crafts at kiosques that wind around a corner onto George

Street. I think Jim mentioned George Street, when he told me about his band. It seems pretty lively. A blend of music fills the air, wafting out from all the bars. In the corner, a wide staircase splits in the centre and goes off in two directions to the street above. In the middle, on a sort of landing, some musicians are playing folksy tunes on a violin, tin whistle, and banjo. A small crowd is gathered around, bopping along with the music.

When the music stops, the crowd disperses, still clapping. That's when I see Jim, holding his tin whistle.

I lean back against the wall at the bottom of the stairs, hoping I'm hidden. I'm a bit shy about seeing him, after what happened last night. The band starts up again and I watch Jim play, raising and lowering his instrument as he blows into it, tapping his feet. They actually sound pretty good. At the end of the set, one of the guys picks up a top hat and passes it around. Almost everyone tosses in some money. It would be hard not to, with the musician standing ten inches away, staring you right in the eye. I'm thinking all this when it dawns on me that Jim is looking straight down at me. It's like he knew all along that I was here, watching. Now he's waving me up.

"Hey guys, this is Cheryl. Cheryl, this is Steve and Ned." They both nod in my direction. Steve is scooping out the change and counting it. He drops a handful of coins, including a bunch of twoonies and loonies, into Jim's hand.

"See you tomorrow, okay?" Ned says. "Nice to meet you, Cheryl." They wave goodbye and walk off, leaving me and Jim alone.

"You were right. You guys are pretty good," I say.

Jim winks. "We're all right. There's lots better, but we do okay."

"Do you play every day?" I ask.

"Try to. But it doesn't always work out. Sometimes I have better things to do," he says, staring at me.

"Like forcing girls up Signal Hill?" I ask. Jim laughs.

"Or being suckered out to Middle Cove by their parents," he says.

"Where'd you learn how to play?"

"We had a great music department in my old school. Lots of people are surprised by that 'cause it was such a small place. Holy Heart's not bad either. Ned and Steve had the idea and asked me to join. They're okay. They were pretty curious about where I'm from and stuff, more than most guys. They have plans to get to Europe next summer. They want to see the world, but I just need the money for Horton."

"Do you actually make good money doing this?"

"You'd be surprised. Hey, do you play anything?"

"Just the flute … a little, but really elementary. I wouldn't have the nerve to play in public like this anyway."

"Too bad. Girl in a band, helps draw in the guys," Jim says. "Especially if she's …"

"All dressed in black," I cut in.

"No, I was going to say pretty," Jim says.

I look down at the ground, at my black boots, so Jim won't see my face. Luckily, he starts down the stairs.

"So, what d'ya think of our great big cosmopolitan downtown, big city girl?" Jim says when we're back on Water Street.

"It's not as bad as I thought it would be," I say.

"Oh, well, I'm so glad it meets with your approval. We're a bit short on skyscrapers though. Unless you count that one," Jim says, pointing to a modern building that rises about seven floors into the sky.

"That is definitely not a skyscraper. It's barely a tree-top scraper," I say.

"Yeah, but remember I told you fog is low clouds. So, technically, that building does scrape the sky. In fact, all our buildings do. Ergo, we have more skyscrapers than you do in Montreal."

"Okay, you win," I say, laughing.

"Hey, are you doing anything for the rest of the day?" Jim asks.

"Nope."

"Good. Let's go home and get Boss and my aunt's car. We could go somewhere if you want."

This is my last chance to keep Jim in the background, like that lighthouse in the foggy mist, but I want to go.

"Why not?" I say, shrugging. "It's not like I have anything else to do."

"Gee, thanks. Try to hide your enthusiasm," Jim says.

"No, I meant, that sounds good."

We walk back up more hills, through narrow lanes, and over streets that connect like a jigsaw puzzle. I could never memorize this route, no matter how many mental snapshots I took. Every now and then Jim blows into his tin whistle, letting out a high note as he turns to see if I'm still with him. I feel the calf muscles in my legs straining. No wonder Jim looks so fit.

"I just need to go tell my parents," I say, when we finally reach Gower.

"Okay. Meet me at my place. I'll probably have to get my aunt some tea first. I'm like Pavlov to that lady. She sees me and she salivates for tea."

My parents aren't back yet, so I leave them a note on the kitchen table. I have no idea where we're going so all I say is *I'm out with Jim. See you later.* I grab a hooded sweater, a bright red one with UBC written on the front. I usually don't wear it outside, but I remember how windy it was on Signal Hill. Knowing Jim, we'll be going somewhere near water.

At Jim's, Nanny asks me to sit beside her while she drinks her tea. Jim has a cup ready for me too. Once again, Nanny's eyes never leave the television, but she turns to smile at us every few minutes as though she's really enjoying our company.

"Me and Jim's father was born on Fox Island Harbour," she tells me suddenly, as though I've just asked her where she's from.

"Oh, that's nice," I say.

"It was nice, until we all had to leave. Pulled our houses across the bay to Burgeo. It looked like a house regatta," Nanny chuckles. "Michael and I wanted to stay inside and row out the window, but of course we couldn't. Some houses didn't make it to shore."

I look at Jim to see if I should actually ask Nanny questions to continue this story or not. He's nodding slightly, as if to say go ahead. "Why did you have to leave?" I ask.

"Government, of course," Nanny says forcefully, as though that was the most obvious answer in the world. "Said we were too small, not enough people to keep us going. There were only fifty of us left in the end." Nanny's hands seem to be shaking harder now.

"It's all right, Nanny. We'll tell Cheryl all about it another time, okay? We want to catch more of the day." Jim gathers up the tea stuff on the tray. "I'll try to be home for dinner."

"You be careful, Jim," Nanny says as he bends to kiss her cheek. Nanny closes her eyes and smiles, as though the feel of Jim's lips on her skin is the most precious thing in the world to her. I think how, if I didn't know better, I'd swear they were mother and son.

"Come back again, Cheryl, love."

At the door, Jim clicks his tongue and Boss runs down the hall, bouncing around in circles while Jim gets her leash.

"Nanny likes you," Jim says when we're in the old car.

"How can you tell?"

"By how much she was talking. She only talks to people she likes."

"And what about you?" I regret it the minute I say it. He'll think I'm fishing for a compliment. "I mean, I bet you talk to everyone."

Jim smiles. "Would you believe at school people think of me as dead quiet?"

"Yeah, I do find that hard to believe."

"You're going to love where I'm taking you," Jim says. "It's Boss's second favourite place. Look at her. It's like she knows."

I turn to see Boss spread out on the back seat, her tail wagging ferociously, her tongue hanging out, like she doesn't care if the whole world knows how she's feeling.

***

Jim heads over a bridge, straight for a wall mural that depicts old-fashioned people sitting on fences and wharfs, and a string of jumping dolphins, all of it in peachy-browns. It reminds me of one of my mother's quilts, except she'd have to add more colour.

"Where are we going?" I ask.

"Ah, it's a surprise. First, I'll give you a lovely tour of Shea Heights."

"Chez? As in *chez moi, chez toi*, that sort of thing?"

"No. Shea, s-h-e-a, as in the place where Joey Smallwood grew up."

"Joey who?" I say.

"Smallwood," Jim says, loudly. "You mean you never heard of him?"

"I guess you can just add that to rocks, capelin, fossils, and fog," I say. "Things that I'm completely ignorant about."

"Joey Smallwood, for your information, was this province's first premier. In fact, if it wasn't for him, we'd probably be living in two different countries. He brought us into Confederation."

"Oh yeah?"

"I bet you don't know when that happened, either?"

I shake my head.

"Didn't you learn anything about Newfoundland in school?"

I shake my head again. "Sorry. The Plains of Abraham, the Métis, the building of the great railroad. But so far, no Newfoundland."

"Well, don't worry. You'll learn about Smallwood here, at school."

Jim doesn't know that my mom registered me at Holy Heart, his school. For some reason, I don't tell him. I can't actually admit that I might be staying here for school, not to myself, and not out loud. It would make it all final and real, in a way I'm not ready to accept.

"I bet I know a few things you don't know. I have been around, you know? I'm not a complete ignoramus."

"Okay. Like?"

"Like, do you know how they blow up old grain elevators?"

"No, but I can guess. With dynamite, right?"

"No. Well, not the ones I saw anyway. They come in with these huge shovels that claw at the old wood like giant paws, tearing huge holes in the bottom. Eventually, the whole thing caves in. People wait for the dust and debris to settle and then carry off old pieces of wood for mementos. My father even interviewed somebody who turned it into works of art, to preserve it. He has tons of pictures of elevators, before and after the explosions."

"What for?"

"For his book."

"For a book about grain elevators?"

"No, his book about different cultures. Didn't I tell you he was writing one?"

"I don't think so. You just told me he was here to teach."

"Yeah, well, he'll probably work on his book too." I turn to look out the window so Jim won't ask me any more about it. I shouldn't have mentioned the book. I don't want it coming between us, just like it's come between me and everything else in my life.

"My mom would cry when the elevators fell," I say finally. I didn't mean to share that detail. It just slipped out.

"Why?"

"Because she thought they were so beautiful. She said they were tall, elegant pieces of history just being destroyed, changing the landscape. When we'd drive around my mom would let out a gasp whenever she saw a grain elevator in the distance. The roofs stick up first, kind of like little steeples. You can drive toward the same one for hours."

"Guess lots of other people are losing their history too," Jim says. "Not just us."

If I could, I'd tell Jim that that's exactly what my dad's book is about. Maybe it wouldn't be so bad if he knew. Maybe he'd understand what draws my dad to dying cultures. I've never been able to get it, but just now, describing the colourful grain elevators to Jim, I think I almost did.

We keep driving until we hit the end of the road. The sun has blasted through the clouds and mist, turning everything golden yellow. You'd never suspect there'd been so much rain this morning. Jim and I get out of the car and Boss jumps out behind us, unleashed. There are lots of other cars in the parking lot. The wind is ripping here, and I'm glad I brought my sweatshirt along.

"What is this place?" I ask.

"It's Cape Spear," Jim says. "The most eastern point in Canada."

In front of us, ocean rolls forever toward the horizon. Way off to the left, past several inlets, the cliffs around the city are visible, with Cabot Tower sticking up from Signal Hill, small as a tooth. We follow a worn pathway in the grass that leads toward the rocks. Jim looks for whales as he takes big steps around the marshy spots, encouraging me to do the same. At the end of the grass, the huge red rocks begin a gradual incline to the water, stacked in uneven layers, like giant wood chips. The waves below are gentle but steady, gathering force near the shore where they crash and spit up white foam.

We hook up with a wooden walkway which we climb, passing a much steeper mass of reddish rocks, sharp and jagged and stacked in spikier, more menacing layers all the way to the foot of the ocean. Several tourists are climbing down the rocks, toward the water. One group is a family – parents and two kids. The father stops and lines his kids up against the backdrop of ocean, then climbs back a few feet to take their picture. I guess he can't read the huge "Danger: Hazardous Coastline. Stay On Trail" sign on the path. We keep climbing and winding around the cape. The sun is low in the sky behind us, casting a sharp light out on the water, tinting it gold. Boss is leaping and tumbling ahead of us. Jim stops at the lookout and gazes toward the water.

"What are you looking for?" I ask.

"They gotta be out there," he says.

"What?"

"Whales," Jim replies. "I haven't seen one all summer. It's not natural, especially since the capelin are in."

Way out in the water sits an iceberg, the first one I've seen since I was on the plane. It looks only inches high from here.

"Hey, an iceberg," I call, pointing. "Almost as cool as a whale, for me, anyway."

"Late in the year for an iceberg," Jim says. "Must've been a huge one."

"Maybe it's the one I saw from the plane, on the way in," I say. "Looks like it could be."

"They'd all look the same from up there," Jim says. "You gotta get close to see their shape. Each one's unique, just like snowflakes."

I look up at the ridge at the top of the path and notice that a bunch of tourists are also looking at the iceberg through binoculars.

"You're not going to quiz me on how old the iceberg is or anything?" I ask.

"Nah, I'll let you off the hook this time," Jim says, a faint smile playing around his lips. "Come on, let's keep climbing," he says, brushing my hand. "I love it up there."

We climb a bunch of stairs to a red and white lighthouse. Jim leans against the fence that separates us from a high cliff and I stand beside him. The fence looks old, as though if everyone leaned against it at once it might collapse.

"Bet you don't have anything that compares in Montreal," he says.

"Nope, we don't. But we do have a pretty neat look-off," I say. "It's on Mount Royal, our mountain in the middle of the city. At night the lights below are really cool."

"But no whales, right?"

"None here either, as far as I can tell." Our hands are close on the railing. I wish he'd put his hand on mine like he did last night. This time, I'd touch him back. It looks like he's about to when a noisy group of people comes out of the lighthouse, which is also a museum. I try to block them out, but it's hard. They're talking over each other about what a hard life it must have been, so cut off, such cold weather, hard to get supplies. They must be talking about the lighthouse keepers long ago. I'm starting to think there isn't any way of life that wasn't hard in Newfoundland.

"Come on, I know a place that's more private," Jim says. We go back down to a concrete clearing, where a rusty old cannon is sunk into the ground. Behind it, a square opening is cut into the hill, also made of concrete. Jim stoops into it and calls for me to follow. I step into a dim space that smells of wet stone and cold earth. We wander through the curving tunnel whose walls are covered in white wavy patterns, sort of psychedelic. I'm sure whoever did all the drinking thought so too. The tunnel is littered with broken beer bottles.

"Know what this is?" Jim asks.

"The deep hole of Cape Spear?" I say, shivering.

"Ha! It's an old World War Two bunker. There were actually soldiers here at one time, because of all the U-boats, the German subs."

"Really? Something else I obviously didn't know."

"Yeah, they came pretty close. We even took a direct hit by the Germans. Well, a ship moored just off the coast, at Bell Island, did. Come on, let's go deeper," Jim says. He grabs my arm and pulls me further into the tunnel, where the light is extremely dim.

"Far enough," he says, stopping so suddenly that I smack into him. He flicks on a pocket flashlight and holds it up to his face. His mouth is wide open like he's screaming and he's shining the light into his mouth to light up the red of his gums.

"You must be a blast at Hallowe'en," I say.

"Stick around and you might find out," Jim says. I'm thinking how to respond when something furry rubs against me. I scream and jump at the same time, then remember Boss. But I find myself standing even closer to Jim.

"I'd like it if you stayed," Jim says. He's using that soft voice, the one he uses when he talks to his aunt. I'm shaking like her too.

"You would?"

"Sure. I find you intriguing."

"Ah! You mean I'm an enigma," I say.

"A what? An enema?"

"Shut up!" I punch his arm, hard. He grabs my hand. I can feel his breath getting closer to my face. I've never actually kissed a guy before, not unless you count the time Josh Kreiger kissed me at our graduation dance in grade six, my last year in Montreal. But that was totally disgusting. Jim's not disgusting, just the opposite. I close my eyes, which is dumb because it's dark anyway.

Jim's lips brush against mine ever so softly and my mouth opens. The anticipation is like a million helium balloons cut loose as Jim's tongue touches the tip of mine. My whole body moves against his and I lose all my edges, melting into the space around me.

***

The scream cuts the air, chopping it in half. Jim and I freeze, his mouth suspended on mine, his hands on my back, mine around his neck. Within seconds, the tail end of the scream whips through the bunker, like a gust of strong wind, blasting us apart.

"Holy—" exclaims Jim, jumping back.

Boss takes off, barking like crazy. Jim and I follow, running back to the entrance. When I emerge I am momentarily blinded by the late afternoon light, but Jim is already on the path, running down to the big rocks we passed earlier. Boss is way ahead of him, leaping and barking.

When I reach the rocks, I see the family that was out there earlier, gathered together about halfway down. All I can hear is crying and screaming. I know the sounds are human, but they don't seem to be. It's like a sound that might come from some strange mythical creature from another world.

Suddenly, I hear Jim yell, "Run up to the lighthouse and get the park rangers!" The father turns and takes off, as though Jim has switched him on. The mother, on the other hand, is still hysterical. Her arms are wrapped around a little boy and she is smothering his head against her belly.

Then it hits me – the little girl is missing. The realization is like being knocked over by a giant boulder, making it hard to breathe.

Boss is nowhere in sight. If the girl is in the water, Boss is probably in there with her, pulling her in. I remember Jim telling me about her special paws and tail, but I never thought I'd actually get to see her use them.

Jim is running back up to the wooden stand on the pathway, the one beside the warning sign the family obviously ignored. He grabs the life saver and rope that are hanging there, then heads back out. More people are here now, gathered beside me on the wooden look-off, the one people are not supposed to venture beyond. I wonder if I should run down to Jim and offer to help, but I don't know what I could do. Besides, my feet feel completely paralyzed.

"Come help me," Jim calls out and several of the men run down to join him. I can see Jim pointing below, but I can't see what he is pointing at. I suppose it must be the girl, but I don't have the nerve to move closer to look.

I watch Jim organize the group of men into a line and get them to hold the rope. Then he carries the life saver to the edge and tosses the orange ring into the air. That's when I start to move closer, slowly, just to the edge of the first ridge. I lean over as far as I can until I can actually see the little girl. She's fallen pretty far down, past several of the jagged layers, to land on the lower rocks. She is splayed out, her legs twisted in a weird way in front of her. The rest of her body lies perfectly still. She isn't right at the water, but close enough. The life saver has landed on a shelf above her.

"There's only thirty feet of rope," a man says. "Not enough. What in god's name was she doing so far out?"

By now two of the park rangers have come down with the girl's father. They're carrying lots of rope and another tube. "We've called the emergency," one of them says. "They'll be here soon." Some of the tourists, mostly women, are inching their way to where I'm standing, and they're shouting down encouragement to the little girl. "Won't be long love, hang in there." I wonder if she can hear any of it in the whipping wind. That's if she's even conscious. I don't call anything down because I don't think I'd have any voice right now. I'm way too freaked out. I've never been this close to such a dangerous situation.

"We have to get her up," one of the rangers says. "I don't like the look of the waves coming in. When they start cresting that way there's always the danger of a rogue one."

That's when Jim steps up. "If you can get me closer with a rope I can go down there and tie her on," he says. "At least that would hold her."

"I can't let you do that, son. It's too dangerous. We have to wait for the rescue crew. Regulations."

"It might be too late by then," Jim says. "Look at those waves. Put me down. I'll be fine."

The officials look at each other and shrug, as if they're not sure, but they agree to do it.

"You tie yourself on too, young man. Not just the girl."

"Will do," Jim says.

I watch Jim climb down toward the cold spray, the end of the long rope looped over his shoulder. I can't believe he volunteered to do this and I can't believe they let him. I remember that day on Signal Hill when Jim was fooling around on the chain above the swirling water, how my heart slipped into my mouth. And he was only doing that for fun. I am so scared right now my heart is racing, beating like it's trying to be let out. Every part of me wants to scream at Jim to stop, to come back up. But I still can't find my voice and wouldn't have the nerve to use it anyway. This is obviously something Jim wants to do. Who am I to try to stop him?

I am relieved when I look down and see that Boss has somehow managed to wind her way down to the girl. She is nudging the girl with her giant paws, as though she's trying to shake her awake. Everyone gasps as the girl's arm lifts and her hand clutches Boss's black fur, showing us she is still alive.

Jim jumps from ledge to ledge, sometimes sliding down carefully to the next one when they are farther apart. The rope stretches out behind him like an umbilical cord, tethered to the wooden post of the life saver stand. It doesn't take long for him to reach the girl and tie the rope around her. Then he loops it around his own waist and signals upward, his thumb in the air.

"He's got her," one of the rangers calls out. "Let's hope everything's good now until the emergency comes."

Jim tries to lift the girl, but she doesn't seem to be able to put much weight on her feet. He puts her arm around his neck and supports her, finally getting her upright. He moves her as close to the rock wall as he can, so that she is no longer out in the middle of the landing.

We all see it coming, but we are completely helpless to do anything about it – a giant wave that gathers like a ridge in the ocean, rising and cresting, as if some angry sea monster has unleashed its giant breath. Instead of screaming, we are all stunned silent. The women around me are pointing and gasping, the men grabbing the rope along its length. When the wave jumps up, we all fall dead silent – one giant intake of breath. My breath catches on the salty air, as though it's the last breath I'll ever take. I cover my mouth with my hand, even though no sound was coming out, as the wave leaps onto the rock, scooping up Jim and girl. It seems like they are vanished inside the spray for ages, like everything is happening in slow motion, like I'll never be able to see Jim again. I feel as though I'm tumbling down the angry rocks, scraping and cutting myself as I fall.

I don't want to look, to see what's at the end of the rope below. I want to turn and run back into the bunker and curl myself into a ball.

Slowly, voices start up again, nobody speaking much above a whisper, as if people are afraid of angering the sea monster below. I pick up the snippets around me without trying to, without really wanting to. I gather that the girl and Jim are still there, but they're no longer standing.

And Boss? No one says anything about Boss. I tell myself that if she was washed away, she'll be able to swim back with those giant paws.

I know that I have to look. I have to force myself. I open my eyes slowly, deliberately, ready to shut them again fast, the way you look at a roadside accident. Way below, two bodies are lying on the rock, completely drenched. Jim is no longer holding the girl, but they are still tied to the rope, dangling there like fish that were caught but never reeled in.

That's when it hits me. If Jim hadn't gone down there, the girl would be floating out to sea right now. And if he hadn't tied himself down, he'd be floating out too. In my mind, I see the girl, Jim, and Boss floating out into the middle of the ocean, past the most eastern tip of Canada into no-man's-land, the three of them clinging to each other like a raft. The image makes me shiver.

The girl's mother, who is standing not too far from me, must be seeing even worse. She is totally still. She isn't even crying anymore. It's like she's turned to stone. Her husband is standing a few feet back from the men who are holding the rope, as if he can't bring himself to participate. I remember him earlier, telling his kids to back up so he could get them in the frame with the ocean behind them, probably telling himself that the sea was beautiful and calm today. What could happen? He didn't know the rocks would be slippery. He had never heard of rogue waves. Neither had I, before today.

I suddenly picture Nanny here, her beloved Jim crashed out below. She'd be shaking so hard the rock below her would crack.

"The dog!" someone calls out, snapping me back to life. I look down and see Boss, dragging her black fur through the water toward the shore. A minute later she's pulled herself up and is leaping across the rocks to where Jim is lying. I wait for his hand to dig into her fur, to show us he's okay, but it doesn't. I don't dare think about what that could mean. I just tell myself that everything will be okay, now that Boss is with Jim. It almost makes the lump in my throat loosen. As if Boss knows what I'm thinking, she curls her huge body up at the foot of Jim and the girl, creating a buffer between them and the unpredictable water.

If Boss were right in front of me, I'd wrap my arms around her huge neck and squeeze. That's if I could move. I feel like I might never move again, my body is so rigid with fear.

Just then, the sound of sirens fills the air. I hold my

breath and cross my fingers, only letting go when I actually see the trucks and ambulance pull into the parking lot. A huge gasp erupts on the rock. Some people actually clap, like it's the end of a play, or the safe landing of a plane. Down below, Jim and the girl are being tossed, still attached to the rope, on the back of a smaller swell of water. When the wave subsides, they slide back against the rocks. It's as though we all feel the slam, vibrating under our feet.

Finally, there's some action with the rescue crew. A whole team of men in orange jackets is running toward the rock, carrying ropes and other equipment. It seems like no time at all before they are away over the edge. Another team is leading the parents and son toward the truck. They lead them away slowly, tenderly, as though they know they are on the point of breaking. The mother looks back over her shoulder a few times but doesn't resist.

Minutes later, the young girl is carried up by one of the rescuers, followed by Jim with another orange-suited man. Jim seems to be using his own legs, but the rescue worker is lending him a ton of support, backing him up like an extra body. Boss runs up after them, leaping and barking. I stand back and watch the crew wrap Jim and the girl in blankets, then lay them on the stretchers and carry them toward the ambulances. It's like I am watching things from a great distance, one I don't know how to close. As if I'm part of things, but not, at the same time, like the rescue had nothing to do with me. Which it didn't, except that I'm here with Jim.

Suddenly, Boss is barking around my feet. She jumps up and pulls at my arm, spraying me with the water that soaks her fur, as if she wants me to be wet too, just like her and Jim. It brings me to life and makes me realize I have to do something, fast. Then Boss takes off toward the parking lot, doubling back a couple of times, to make sure I'm following.

I see the men loading Jim into the ambulance. Boss is going wild at their feet. I start to panic again. If I don't make a sign, they'll leave without me. Not even my parents know where I am. I picture myself curling up on the stone and waiting for rescue myself, my red sweatshirt glowing like a flare.

"Wait," I call out on top of my lungs. A few heads turn to look at me. I'm running now, as fast as I can, down the path and toward the parking lot.

"I'm with him," I say when I reach the ambulance.

"Why didn't you say so? Hurry up, get in, we have to get to the hospital." I jump into the back of the ambulance and Boss jumps in after me. I dig my fingers into her wet furry neck. Jim is wrapped up in blankets across from us, his eyes shut and one side of his face swollen.

The ambulance starts to speed along the windy, twisty road, past Blackhead and Shea Heights. I can see the first ambulance up ahead, its red light flashing. Inside it, the little girl must be wrapped up like Jim, fighting for her life.

I reach out gingerly and touch the blanket, over Jim's chest. It's there, the steady beat of his heart.

Relief gushes out of me, so strongly it startles Boss.

CHAPTER 6
pangaea

"*I* just don't know it," I say again, for the third time. "I know it sounds unbelievable, but it's the truth."

"Not even a phone number," the nurse at the Emergency desk asks. "Or a last name?" Jim has been taken away and I'm supposed to be giving the hospital some information on him. The trouble is, I don't know much. Poor Boss is on a rope outside, drying on the lawn. I hope somebody thinks to bring her some fresh water. I never understood the irony of people lost at sea dying of thirst, but now I do. The ocean water is so heavy with salt, the whole ambulance just reeked of it and Boss's fur was matted with it. She'll need to be hosed down.

"I just moved here," I say. "A few weeks ago. All I can tell you is he lives in the house next to mine, on Gower." For days I tried not to notice the brass numbers nailed into the wood outside our house. I either closed or diverted my eyes whenever I passed them. Now I realize that the address has sunk in anyway, without my knowing it. But I really don't know what number Jim's is. It could be higher or lower.

A police officer comes up behind me. "This her?" he asks. The nurse nods.

"And this is the young man's wallet. No address. And his car keys." The nurse hands a large envelope over to the cop.

"I guess you and I'll take a ride, young lady, and see if we can't find out where your friend lives."

"But I really shouldn't leave him here all alone," I protest.

"He's fine," the nurse pipes in impatiently, twisting her pencil around a single curl that has escaped its bun. "You can come back later, but we really need to let his family know. I'm assuming your family would want to know too if you'd nearly drowned." She glares at me for a second, challenging me to deny this.

We're about to get into the police car when I remember Boss. "Wait!" I call out. "Jim's dog. She's here, tied up. Can we take her home?" I fully expect the officer to say no, that we don't have time to worry about some dumb old animal, but he doesn't.

"Sure, good idea," he says. He even goes over to get Boss, untying her and scratching her gently under the chin. As we drive along Gower, I think how this is just great. I've only been here for two weeks and I'm being driven home by a cop. My parents will flip if they see the car pull up and me getting out. They'll probably think I tried to stow away in the cargo hold of a plane or something. I only hope they're not sitting out on our stoop, like they've taken to doing, waving across to the neighbours, establishing ties.

"That's mine," I say, pointing to our house. We no sooner pull up to the curb than my parents are rushing out the door. They must've been sitting in the living room, their eyes plastered to the front window. Maybe they wanted to stay near the phone, in case I called.

"Cheryl, what happened?" My mother is already fussing over me on the sidewalk, smoothing down my hair and running her hand over my damp sweatshirt.

"I'm okay, Mom. Don't go nuts."

"What happened, Cheryl?" asks my dad.

The police officer steps forward. "Slight accident out at Cape Spear. Your daughter's fine. It's a young lad named Jim who got the worst of it. We're trying to locate his house. Is this it?" He points to where Boss is sitting, panting up at Nanny's door.

"That's Jim's," says my dad.

The cop knocks loudly, but there's no answer. Jim's aunt

is probably blaring the volume on her television, she's so hard of hearing. Then I remember what happened to Nanny's husband. She'll get the scare of a lifetime seeing a police officer at her door.

"Wait," I say, before he knocks again. "Jim's aunt is not really well. Can I go in first? She'll be scared if she sees you." When he doesn't protest, I open the door and call out. "Hello? Are you here, Nanny?" I hear slippers shuffling, then Jim's aunt appears in the hallway. She looks so little standing up. Her shaking body makes her seem even more scared, like a frightened bird.

"Yes, my love?" she says, looking up at me. "Cheryl, is it?"

"Yes, Nanny." Nanny comes to the threshold of the house, squinting as though the daylight hurts her eyes.

"Where's Jim to?" she asks, looking around.

I look over at my mother. Now I wish she knew the story. Then she could help me tell Nanny.

"Well, he kind of got hurt out at Cape Spear, rescuing a little girl. He's at the hospital." At that last word Nanny's face falls and her cheeks and jaw start to quiver. She raises a shaky hand to her mouth.

The officer steps forward and cuts in. "Hello, Ma'am. I'd like to take you up to the hospital now, if that's okay? See your nephew. He's doing real well, no cause for worry."

I don't know how the cop knows this. He hasn't even laid eyes on Jim. Maybe he just senses that it's what Nanny needs to hear. Nanny starts to move forward then pauses.

"Do you want me to come with you, Nanny?" I ask. She looks up at me and her eyes widen.

"Oh, would you, my dear?" she asks. "I'll just change my shoes." I steady Nanny as she kicks off her slippers and slides her feet into brown loafers, holding the backs open with a very long shoehorn. I'm glad she doesn't have to tie any shoelaces. Her hands are so shaky, she'd never manage the bow. Then I take her arm and lead her toward the police car.

Before getting in, I turn to my parents who are right behind us, looking worried.

"Are you sure you're okay?" my mom asks. She has that about-to-try-to-hug me look in her eyes, so I nod quickly.

"What can we do? Let us come with you, honey," says my dad. "We can follow in our car."

Then I remember Nanny's car. I had completely forgotten that it's still out there.

"If you want to help, maybe you could go out to Cape Spear and bring Jim's car back. If they'll let you." I look over at the police officer.

"I have the key. If you want to, you can do it. We'd have sent someone over later," he says.

My parents look at each other and nod.

"How do we get there?" my dad asks.

"Water Street over a bridge to Shea Heights, then follow the signs. It's about half an hour," the officer says.

"Okay, sure. We can do that," says my dad. I knew they would. My parents always jump right in, without hesitation.

"We better get back to Jim," I say. My mom's eyes are full of tears as she steps forward to help me lower Nanny into the back seat.

"Thanks, Mom," I say. The tears in her eyes start to spill over.

We wave to them as we pull away, and they wave back, then I watch them grow smaller in the rear window.

I reach over and hold Nanny's hand.

***

Nanny doesn't let go of my hand the whole ride to the hospital. Her skin is so thin, it feels like the top layer of an onion, the one you can practically blow off. I look down at the brown spots that mark her age and wonder what her life was like as a child in that town she mentioned, Fox Island Harbour. Jim told me Nanny's sixty. I quickly calculate when she would have been born. Maybe she was a teenager in the sixties, when the whole British Invasion thing hit. I wonder if it ever hit Newfoundland. And if it did, was Nanny a Beatles fan? Did she actually scream at the TV, watching their famous stint on the Ed Sullivan Show. That's if they had TV where she lived back then.

The nurse at the Emergency desk is happy to see that I've come back with someone. I'm sure she thought I was a complete basket case and that I was just going to run off and abandon Jim to his fate.

She asks Nanny a bunch of questions, ones I couldn't answer, like Jim's full name, address and phone number, and date of birth. It seems they couldn't find his health card in his wallet. "When he comes round, you tell that young man he should carry it at all times, understand?" Nanny just nods. I'm not convinced she understands much of what's being said to her. When she has to sign the bottom of a form, I hold her wrist to help steady it. It's like there's nothing between her skin and the bone, one rubs right up against the other. Her handwriting is so shaky, I can't make out her last name. If I didn't already know her first name was Nancy, I wouldn't recognize that either. I can't make out the last name and the nurse doesn't give me time to look.

"He's in 564," the nurse tells us finally. "Take the elevator at the end of the hall if you can find it." She stares right at me when she says that, emphasizing how hopeless she thinks I am. Then she flashes Nanny a very wide and comforting smile.

I wonder what the nurse meant by "when Jim comes round." But at least she didn't say *if*. That would be worse. I keep telling myself that as the elevator takes us up to the fifth floor, stopping on each one to let people on and off. Nanny is leaning against me, as if she would fall without me there to hold her up.

When we enter Jim's room another nurse is standing by his bed, taking his temperature. "Oh, hello," she says. "You're Jim's relatives? He's resting. We gave him something to help him sleep. You can't stay too long. He's pretty groggy. The doctor will be along shortly."

The minute the nurse is gone, Nanny calls out, "Jimmy, my son." She holds out her arms and approaches his bed. She's about to touch him when she stops dead. I look down too and see why. The whole left side of Jim's face is bruised and swollen, the colour of rotten cantaloupe. I can't believe that bruise darkened so fast. I mean, I was in the ambulance with him for twenty minutes. I didn't notice anything then, except for the swelling.

Nanny plunges right in anyway and hugs him. Jim doesn't wake up, but I think I notice a slight wince on his face when she touches him. "What in God's name are you after doing, my son, jumping into the ocean?" Nanny asks.

"I don't think he can hear you, Nanny," I say, noticing that Jim is hooked up to an IV tube. His bed is slightly raised and he's leaning back on a couple of pillows. "And he didn't jump into the water. The water jumped out at him."

"Tell me, Jim, why would you do such a thing? Don't you know what the water can do?" Nanny is sniffling now. It's like she didn't get what I was trying to tell her. I know I have to answer for Jim, to make Nanny understand.

"He was really brave, Nanny," I say. "He didn't even hesitate. No one else would go down the rock. You wouldn't have wanted him to leave the little girl stranded there, would you, Nanny? She was just a young girl ... only about eight or nine years old, I think." I feel a lump forming in my throat when I mention the girl.

Nanny straightens up then and looks at me very closely, as though the whole scenario has finally made sense to her. "A young girl, only nine? My, my, my! The same age as our Joannie, Jim's younger sister." Then she looks back down at Jim. "No, you did the right thing, Jim," Nanny says to him, ruffling up his hair, which is sticking to his forehead, a great deal of pride in her voice. Then she just stares down at Jim for a while. I wonder if she's thinking about her own husband, lost at sea after the oil rig collapsed into the storm. Maybe she's wondering what would have happened if someone had been able to rescue him, how different her life would have been. Nanny's legs give out on her a little and she leans into the bed railing.

"Here, Nanny," I say, sliding over a chair and helping her into it. I pull up another one for myself and sit beside her. "We just have to wait for the doctor to show up, to find out about Jim."

Nanny nods and leans toward me, as though she wants to be as close to me as possible. If I reached out, I could pull her tiny head onto my shoulder. It occurs to me that this is like a scene in some hospital drama, but the odd thing is that I'm not just watching it – I'm totally part of it. I suddenly remember the funeral I attended in Osoyoos. Two teenagers from our school had been killed on the highway that runs between Osoyoos and Penticton. That stretch of road was known in the

Okanagan Valley as a teenage death trap. They were coming back from an all-night bush party, where groups of kids meet on deserted logging trails and burn the bottoms of apple crates and get completely wasted. You'd hear all about them at school on Monday mornings. One of the guy's sisters was in my homeroom class, so we all had to go. Everyone else was bawling their eyes out, but I just stood there feeling really stupid. I just felt sad in a general way, like you do when you watch the news and people are being blown up or crushed by landslides. But I couldn't feel connected in any personal way. They all probably thought I was heartless.

No one would accuse me of feeling heartless now. I reach out and pull Nanny's head onto my shoulder. She fits just perfectly into the crook of my neck.

A few minutes later, a young doctor steps into the room. Nanny's head springs up.

"Hello, I'm Dr. Patel. You must be Jim's family." Dr. Patel shakes our hands. "We want to keep Jim in, just for observation. He doesn't have hypothermia — he wasn't really in the water long enough — but he did catch a good chill. We need to make sure he's thawed out, so to speak. We also need to keep an eye on his lungs for a while, just as a precaution, because he probably took in some water. His spine looks fine, but we'll double-check tomorrow, just to be sure."

Dr. Patel pauses, as though he knows we need a minute to take in all the information. But then he takes a deep breath and continues. "Now, as for the rest of him ... Jim will be fine ... but he did suffer some rib damage. In fact, six of his ribs are broken. It's not uncommon for what he's been through. The force of the water throwing him back against the rocks, especially since he was hanging on to the girl, could easily break ribs. No punctured lungs though, which is really lucky. He's also less respondent than we'd like him to be, so there's every possibility that he has a concussion."

"Can he come home?" Nanny asks after a minute.

"Not today, of course, but we'll see how things develop. It shouldn't be more than a few days." Dr. Patel flashes a brilliant smile and I sense Nanny relaxing. That smile must come in very handy in his profession.

"We'll speak again tomorrow, okay?" Dr. Patel places his large hand on Nanny's shoulder and squeezes. I imagine her bones collapsing.

I want to ask about the girl, but if the news is bad, this wouldn't be the best time to hear it, with Nanny beside me. There's a good chance that girl is in much worse shape than Jim.

Dr. Patel leaves and we continue sitting and staring at Jim's bed. There's nothing either of us can do, but it doesn't seem right to just leave.

"Like a seal sausage," Nanny says finally.

"What?"

"He has to thaw out, just like a seal sausage. When you takes them out of the freezer, they have to thaw before you can cook 'em."

Now I'm afraid Nanny may be losing it and I won't know what to do. Maybe I should call my mother.

"Ever had seal sausage, my love?" Nanny asks me. I shake my head.

"I'd never even heard of seal sausage ... until Jim mentioned it."

"Jim gets out, you come on over and I'll fix you some seal sausage. You'll never get anything like them anywhere else but Newfoundland. When Jim comes home we'll have some, right?" Nanny looks at me. I just nod.

Nanny walks up to Jim's bed and leans over the railing. "Make sure the old hag doesn't sit on you tonight, Jim," Nanny says. "Nobody will be here to call your name backwards, to make her leave you alone."

Then Nanny laughs, quietly. Nanny loves Jim like a son,

maybe the son she might have had if her husband hadn't died. It's clear there's nowhere else on the planet Nanny would rather be than right beside Jim.

And, it hits me, the same goes for me. I can't even imagine anywhere else. All there is is here.

Nanny kisses Jim on the cheek, the one that isn't bruised. I stand behind her, watching. I can't exactly do the same, not in front of Nanny. I look at the sheets wrapped tightly around Jim's chest and think of his broken ribs and all that they mean – no hiking up hills, no walking dogs, no driving cars, no blowing into tin whistles. No searching for fossils.

No trying to kiss me again.

"Bye, Jim," I say. I want him to hear my voice at least, so that if some part of him is conscious he'll know I was here. "See you tomorrow."

Then Nanny and I leave.

We take a taxi back to the house, each of us staring out the window in silence. The sun has gone down and the streets are quiet. I notice right away that Nanny's car is back in its spot, which means my parents had no trouble finding Cape Spear, like I suspected. I can't just leave Nanny on her own, so I go in with her and settle her onto her spot on the sofa. Even if I hadn't seen her sitting there a couple of times, I would've known it was her spot. There's a deep indentation in the brown cushion, just the right size for Nanny's bum.

"Can I make you a cup of tea, Nanny?"

"No, no, I'll be fine, no need to fuss, Cheryl, my love. You get on home. Your parents will be worried. Don't leave them waiting any longer."

"Are you sure?" Just as I'm saying it, Boss jumps onto the sofa and settles her huge head in Nanny's lap. Nanny buries her fingers in the dog's fur, which still looks a bit damp and smells like salt water.

Nanny doesn't seem to mind.

"Okay, well, see you later, Nanny."

Nanny nods and waves. Somehow, I picture her staying in that exact spot until tomorrow, when she can see Jim again.

***

I find my parents sitting at the kitchen table, my father drinking a beer and my mother a mug of tea. Her hands are wrapped around it, soaking in its warmth.

The minute they see me they both rise out of their chairs, like they might need to catch me. A minute later they're all over me.

"Cheryl," my father says, "we were so worried. The police are still out at Cape Spear. They've put yellow tape up all around the rocks, just like at a crime scene. It must have been horrible." He puts his hands on my shoulders and steers me into a chair.

"It was, Dad, but I'm dead tired. It's been a really long day. I just want to crawl into bed."

"But Jim? Is he all right?" my mother asks, standing over me. "Can't you tell us that much at least? Everyone was still talking about it. They said a young girl was swept into the water by a rogue wave. I can't believe you had to witness that."

"She wasn't exactly swept out. People are exaggerating the story already. But she would've been if Jim hadn't gone down to help her. And then they both kind of got battered around by one."

"Oh, Cheryl." She takes a step toward me.

"I'm okay, Mom, really. You don't have to go ape." My mom's face pinches and she looks down at her feet. I remember Nanny's head on my shoulder. What would my mother say if she'd seen me like that?

"What about Jim?" my dad asks.

"He has a few broken ribs and maybe a concussion.

That's all they know for now. But he definitely doesn't have hypothermia."

"Thank god for that," my mother says, sitting back down. "Hypothermia can be serious."

"Yeah, he just needs to thaw out," I say. "Like a seal sausage."

My parents give each other a what-the-hell-is-she-talking-about look. I know this isn't a funny situation, but it suddenly strikes me as amusing that my parents are the ones in the dark, for a change. It's usually the other way around.

"It all must have been so scary for you, honey." My mom's hand reaches out for mine, holding it. Her fingers are so swollen, but she squeezes anyway. I remember how I felt out on the rock, so small and helpless. Even my loudest voice turned silent in that wind.

"Yeah, it was," I say. "Completely." I don't pull back my hand.

Then we're all just quiet. My parents are probably trying to picture the scene out at Cape Spear, but they can't really. You had to hear the panic in that mother's scream and then, later, witness her stone-cold silence. Just remembering brings the goose bumps back to my skin.

"Is the little girl okay?" my mom asks finally.

"I don't know. I was too afraid to ask."

"People out at Cape Spear seemed to think she would be," says my dad.

"Let's hope. Her poor mother," says my mom. She has stopped holding my hand now and is concentrating on her swollen fingers, spread out before her like a fan, as if they might help her imagine the mother's pain.

"I'm really tired, you guys. I need to go to bed. I'll see you in the morning, okay?" I can feel my mom and dad sending each other sympathy across the table. They want so desperately to be useful, to be involved, but I've let them in as much as I can for one night.

"Oh yeah, I see you got Jim's car. Thanks. He'll appreciate it," I say. Their faces brighten a bit. Then I disappear upstairs.

I put on a Marilyn Manson CD, loud, with my earphones on. The music invades my brain, washing out all my thoughts and images, which is exactly what I wanted. Except suddenly Manson is singing about someone being crippled and their spine turning into a spring – words that take me right back to Jim. Dr. Patel said Jim's spine was probably fine, which is lucky, considering the force of the waves hitting him against that massive rock. He could have fallen out of the tube into the water and died out there.

I lower myself onto the mattress, feeling for the shape that I've learned to mould myself into. I don't try to fight it. It wouldn't be right to be comfortable tonight, not with Jim in the hospital with so many broken ribs, unable to move.

I wonder if he's dreaming about rocks and expeditions to different parts of the world. What did he call that old continent ... Pangaea – linking Newfoundland, Europe, and Africa in strange and unseeable ways.

Just like me and Jim and Nanny.

CHAPTER 7
this perfect family space

I drift in and out of sleep the next morning, dreaming of fossils that turn to skin — *the soft skin on the underside of my arm — suddenly laced with etchings. In a flash, the etchings turn hard and scabby. The scabs lift off in a solid piece, twisty like a snake. But there's no blood, just a deep fault line in my arm, as if it split open in a quake. The skin is dry and hard, like an African desert.*

Finally, I tear myself awake, not wanting to sink back into the dream.

The desk lamp is still lit, shining on the map of the world. I look over at the door and remember Jim bursting in with his rocks and then trying to impress me with the ancient scratches, using the fossils to draw me in because I'd been so miserable out at Middle Cove. I remember how I wanted to kick his rock tower and send it crashing down.

I wish Jim could walk through that door again today. I'd

love to see that teasing grin on his face as he works up his next plan for us. But then I hear Dr. Patel's words: broken ribs, possible lung damage, concussion. Jim won't be barging in anywhere for a while.

The house sounds really quiet. My parents are probably still sleeping. Or else they're sitting at the table, waiting to hear more about what happened yesterday. I replay the scene out at Cape Spear in my mind. I see Jim throw the tube over the water, only it's like he's attached to it, sailing out over the waves. The girl in the water is a little dark smudge, bobbing up and down like driftwood. And Boss is treading water with her huge paws, keeping the girl from sinking.

Out of all the people who could have climbed down, why did it have to be Jim? Even the girl's father didn't play such a big role. All he did was run up to the lighthouse, and only because Jim told him to.

Downstairs, in the kitchen, I'm surprised to discover another note on the table. I didn't think my parents would want to leave me alone today. Maybe they've gone back to the university, to finish setting up my father's office or to meet some new colleagues.

Have taken Mom to the hospital to see about getting some shots for her hands — all flared up. Should be back soon. Please don't go off anywhere until we get back. And stay away from the ocean! Love, Dad.

My mother's hands must be pretty sore if my father's taking her to the hospital. He's done it before, but only when they get unbearable. The only year her hands didn't bother her was when we were in Osoyoos, because it was so dry. Osoyoos is on record as having the hottest weather in Canada. The summer we left, the Okanagan area was ravaged by huge forest fires. We watched them on the news from Saskatchewan. Whole sections of forests were burning up, leaving black scars on the mountains. The images made my mother cry, but not me. She said she couldn't understand why I didn't feel anything. After all, some of the spots that were scorched were places where we'd gone for hikes and bike rides, along the old rail lines.

Her rheumatism wasn't too bad in Saskatchewan either. She was able to work on a huge quilt that won a prize at a country fair in Saskatoon. People were amazed that someone from a big city could capture the land and its colours the way she had. She even included the northern lights, floating in colourful ribbons across the top. But it seems to me that her rheumatism has done nothing but flare up since we stepped off the plane in St. John's.

When her hands get really bad they remind me of ginger root, all gnarly and crooked. Come to think of it, they did look like that last night, clutching her mug. I suppose I could've asked her about them. A good daughter would have, even under the circumstances.

I carry a cup of tea into the living room and look out the front window. Nanny's car is still there, which means she hasn't gone to the hospital. I'm not even sure she can drive on her own. It's kind of hard to picture, with her shaky hands and bad hearing. When I'm finished with my tea I'll go over and see if she wants me to take her to the hospital, although I can't drive us there either. We'll have to take a cab.

It takes me a minute to notice that a modem is now sitting on the bookshelf, its green lights flashing. That means we now have Internet access. It must have happened while I was out yesterday. I guess I could check my emails from Janna and catch up on what's happening with her and Stephan. I suppose I could tell her about Jim and how he kissed me in the bunker. I could describe the whole rescue scene, the way Jim tore himself away from me and scaled down the rocks, his strong muscles pulling in the frightened child, me in the ambulance kneeling beside him, wondering if he'd live or die. I could make it seem like a TV script.

Janna would love that.

But when I think of Jim lying in his hospital bed with his broken ribs, I know it's not something I could use to score points with.

***

I don't knock because Nanny wouldn't expect me to. She's not in her spot on the sofa and the house is really quiet. The only noise, I realize, is coming from the backyard. It's Boss, barking like mad. When I open up, she jumps all over me, licking my face and practically knocking me off my feet. She's acting like she hasn't seen me for years.

Boss follows me around as I peek in the kitchen and dining room, looking for Nanny. I don't go upstairs, but call up, in case she's still sleeping. There's no reply and no sign of life anywhere in this house, expect for Boss.

I feel really bad about leaving the dog alone, but I can't stay. Nanny's obviously gone off to the hospital without me. She must have put Boss out to pee and then forgotten about her. Nanny must still be in a state because of Jim. It's odd that everyone I know is suddenly at the hospital – Jim and Nanny and my parents.

Back home, I decide to call the hospital, to check on Jim and see if Nanny is there. If she is, I'll ask her if she wants me to come over. She might need help getting home, even though she got there on her own. I wonder why she didn't wait for me. Maybe she thought it would be bothering me, asking me to come so early.

I'm about to grab the St. John's phone book sitting on the shelf facing me, when a car pulls up outside the house.

It's my parents – with Nanny! I can't believe it. My parents took Nanny to the hospital. A minute later, they're all coming through the door.

"Hi, honey," my mother says. "We thought we'd see if Nanny needed a lift to go see Jim, since we were going to the hospital anyway."

"Have a seat, Nanny. We'll make some tea," my father says, leading Nanny to the kitchen. "Cheryl, you want to put the kettle on?"

I know my first thoughts should be about Jim, but I want to scream. Seeing my parents with Nanny makes me feel the same way I did when my mother walked through the door with Jim, the day we went to Middle Cove. As if they're taking something away from me.

I want to take Nanny home and help her to her spot on

the sofa and make her a cup of tea over there, not here. Jim and Nanny were *my* friends, people I met on my own, not people my parents tried to force on me, like some of the kids in Saskatchewan who were sons and daughters of the farmers my father interviewed. My mother would always try to get me to go to the school dances with them. She said it would help me fit in, but I always refused. I pictured myself plastered to the gym wall watching the farmers' kids dance up a storm.

Without thinking, I slam the kettle on the stove. Nanny's whole body jumps.

"Cheryl," snaps my father. "Easy, honey." He nods toward Nanny, who is holding a balled-up tissue in one fist. She's obviously been crying. My heart clenches.

"What is it?" I ask.

"The doctors said Jim will have to stay at the hospital for a few days, at least until Sunday. He does have a concussion after all."

"Sorry, Nanny," I say.

"But he's a real local hero today, isn't he, Nanny?" My mother jumps in, as though it's her job to cheer Nanny up. She flips over the newspaper lying in the middle of the table. A picture of Jim being hauled over the lip of the rock by a rescuer covers the entire front page. Under it, the caption reads, *local boy rescues young girl.* There's a picture of the girl too, smiling in her hospital bed.

"So, I guess you know the whole story?" I ask.

"Well, the reporter's version anyway," says my father.

"Oh, Cheryl. You must have been terrified," my mother adds. She moves toward me, her arms open.

I'm in the corner of the kitchen, nowhere to run.

So it happens – she hugs me.

The last time I let my mother hug me was three years ago, in Murdochville, the day I found the mice. It was early spring and I was helping my mother rake the yard. We were removing all the debris that emerges once the snow has melted, the rotten leaves and soggy litter. In the corner of the yard, where the ground was soft, my rake sunk in too far. When I pulled it back, a big chunk of earth came with it. I flipped it over to find a nest of baby mice, each one no more than an inch long. There were eight mice, all curled into each other in perfect symmetry, like a pink jigsaw puzzle. I didn't know what to do – fit the chunk of earth back into the hole and hope the mice survived, or take them out and give them shelter elsewhere.

"What should I do with them, Mom?" I asked.

"Put the earth back where you found it and let nature do

her thing. Nature's the big healer," she said. My mother often told me that nature could take care of just about anything, if we let it. It was the strongest force on Earth. I believed her then, when I was younger, but I don't anymore. Now I know that nature can't heal everything. What about my mother's rheumatism that's inflaming her joints and locking her fingers into warped positions? Or Nanny's shaking, caused by heartbreak?

Two weeks later I dug up the earth in the same spot. My curiosity was killing me. I had to see what had happened to the mice. They were still there, in the same place, but they were all dead, hard and grey, more like stones than mice.

It was that day that my mother hugged me, telling me it wasn't my fault.

The whistle on the kettle blows and my mother lets go of me.

I'm glad I have the tea to turn around and focus on. That way, she won't be able to see me cry.

***

An hour later I'm back from settling Nanny at home. I left her with the television on and another cup of tea in her hand. My mother is going to bring her some dinner later on.

My mother puts down her book as I walk into the kitchen. I automatically look down at her hands. They look bad, as though someone inflated them, like balloons. I'd forgotten that that was the real reason for their trip to the hospital.

"So, what happened with your hands?" I ask. My mother looks at my father and they lock eyes, as though they're communicating by telepathy.

"Cheryl, there's something we're going to have to talk about," my father says. He's using his serious we-have-to-have-a-discussion voice. I wonder what I've done wrong this time.

My mother picks up the kettle, but she can barely grasp the handle. I take it from her and fill it.

"Thanks, honey," she says. My parents sit down at the kitchen table and my father points to the empty chair, indicating that I should take it.

"Well, it seems we have some decisions to make," my father says to me. "We saw a doctor at the hospital this morning. Even though he wasn't a specialist, he could see that your mother's hands are looking pretty bad." My father lifts my mother's right hand into his, cradling it as he speaks. He strokes it gently, as though it's a delicate and injured bird.

"He gave me a referral to a specialist, Cherie, but he warned me that I could wait up to a year just to meet with her," says my mother.

"Up to a year? But we're only supposed to be here one year."

"The thing is, Cheryl," my father jumps in, "we were wondering if perhaps your mother should leave sooner. This damp climate is not doing her any good. I've never seen her hands this bad. And she's feeling it in other parts too, isn't that right?" He looks at her and she nods.

"Leave sooner?" I say.

"Well, we were thinking she could go back to Montreal. We've always had the option of getting the house back. And it's been no secret that you didn't want to come here in the first place. So, if you want to, you can go back with her. I have to stay. I know it will be really hard to be separated, even if it's only for a little while. It's not what I want, but I've signed a contract for a year and I can't get out of it. Besides, I really want to do this research. There's a little fishing village one of my colleagues was telling me about, right here, beside St. John's. I could start on it, then travel around on weekends."

"Do you mean Quidi Vidi?" I ask.

"How did you know?" my father asks, his eyes going wide.

"Jim took me there," I say. Jim! How am I going to tell him I'm leaving while he's in such bad shape. I pull the newspaper toward me and stare at his picture and remember how I felt when I saw him drenched on the rock so far below.

"What do you think, Cheryl?" my mother asks.

"About what?"

"Going home, sweetie."

I don't know what to say. I should be thrilled. That's what they're expecting. I can actually go home and I don't even have to find a job first. My mother will take me, for free, no scheming or begging. I can get back to my old life and my friends. I guess that means I'll have to get to know Stephan and Janna's other friends. And I can go to bars downtown with them, learn how to do the whole fake ID scene for the next two years, until I turn eighteen.

And I can finally sleep in my own bed, not a bed that's been moulded by someone else's body. Unless the girl who's been sleeping in my bed for three years has screwed it up.

"It's great ... I guess."

"We'll talk more about it later," my father says. "Mom and I are going to lie down for a while. We were up really early. Okay?"

All I can do is nod. And even that's not easy.

***

I have to see Jim. That's the only way I'm going to be able
to sort out my feelings. I'll know right away when I look at him,
whether I'm happy about going home or not. I'll have to walk
to the hospital, even though I don't know how to get there. I'll
just start out in the general direction and ask for help along
the way.

It's a misty day, again. The houses look faded, as if their
fronts have been spray-painted a faint coat of grey, their
bright colours barely peeking through. When I can glimpse
the water, it's the same colour as the sky. One kind of rolls and
tumbles into the other.

As I walk, I think about yesterday and how, maybe,
everything happened for a reason. Sure, Jim and I kissed, but
just for a few seconds. It was more like the start of a kiss, the
first spark. But since we didn't finish the kiss, I guess you
could say that, technically, we're still just friends. That'll
make it easier if I do decide to leave.

At least that's what I tell myself.

Three people point me toward the hospital and I find it,

no problem. My clothes are damp and clammy by the time I get there, like they were after hugging Boss yesterday.

I stop outside Jim's room and take a deep breath. It's going to be hard seeing him this way, on my own, but I'll have to try to be perky and upbeat, for his sake.

I can hear talking, but I assume Jim's roommates must have visitors. That's why I'm caught off guard when I turn the corner and discover three people standing around Jim, an older woman and two young girls.

I automatically pull back where they can't see me.

"You always were impulsive," the woman is saying as she strokes Jim's forehead. "But you had sense. I'd have expected your brothers to do something like this, but not you."

Jim's response is too faint for me to hear.

"Jimmy's gonna get a medal or something, from the Queen," one of the girls says. "For saving someone's life."

"Not the Queen, stupid. The Lieutenant Governor," the other one corrects her. "And it's not for sure either. It's just what the nurse said."

"So? It could happen." This must be Joannie, Jim's youngest sister, who's the same age as the girl Jim saved.

"I knows, Jim. I'm not saying you shouldn't of helped out, but my God, son, look at you."

Jim's mother is blocking my view of him, but when she steps aside to pull up his cover, I glimpse his face. The bruise is even blacker than yesterday. It's like the blood hadn't finished leaking into his skin yet. Yesterday it was a cantaloupe, today it's an eggplant.

I catch Jim saying "not as bad as it looks."

"You two go get your mother some tea from the caf, will you. I wants to see Jim on my own for a while. I've not laid eyes on you for months, only to see you like this."

She fishes around in her purse for change. I turn and head farther down the hallway, to make it seem like I'm here for someone else. I have no idea if Nanny told her sister-in-law about me. I suppose I could just walk in and introduce myself. "Hi. I'm Cheryl. I was with Jim when it happened." His mom might say, "Oh, you're the girl we heard all about?"

On the other hand, she might look at me like I just stepped off of Mars, or like I was intruding into this perfect family space.

When the girls have gone, Jim's mother moves to the other side of the bed, giving me a clear view of her face. She looks about the same age as my mother, but more worn out. There are lines around her eyes and her hairline is thin. I can see that perfectly because she keeps brushing her bangs back, as though they're preventing her from seeing Jim. Her fingers are constantly moving, either playing with her own hair, or Jim's. She pulls the blanket up to Jim's chin, then pokes up the corners of his pillow, again and again, like she can't keep still. Maybe it's because of the knitting. Jim said she's always got a pair of needles in her hand, stitching away.

Nanny must have called her last night to tell her what happened. Of course she would, that makes sense, it's just that I had forgotten that Jim had a real mother somewhere. Jim told me that, from his hometown, you need to take a ferry to a bigger town, then get the road that leads up to the Trans Canada. From there, it's a ten-hour drive to St. John's. That would mean his family left home at midnight to get here for two, which would be impossible, unless the ferries run all night.

The girls come back, carrying their mother's tea. The older girl looks sullen, like she'd rather be anywhere else. But Joannie looks excited, as if coming to the city to see her hero brother may be the biggest thing that's ever happened to her. There are three copies of this morning's paper lying on the bed. Joannie will probably show them off to her friends back home, then frame the picture of Jim and hang it over her bed.

"Looks like the old hag sat on you and crushed you, son,"

Jim's mother is saying.

"For God's sake, Mom. Don't start with that crap," says the older girl. Even though I can't see her face, I know she's rolling her eyes. I can feel the roll in her voice. Joannie is laughing. Jim's actually chuckling too, but holding his chest at the same time.

"Don't make me laugh, Ma. It hurts," he says slowly, as if he's drugged. "I'm all tight in the chest."

His mother takes his hand, the hand I might have taken if I'd caught him alone. His sisters stand on the other side of the bed. They're like a human shield. No need for curtains to give this family privacy. They've got it covered.

There's nothing for me to do but leave.

***

"Nanny said Jim's family is down," my mother says at dinner. She took a plate of her chicken stew over to Nanny a few minutes ago. "Isn't that nice?"

"Guess so," I say, without looking up. My parents were still asleep when I came home, so I never told them that I went to the hospital and actually saw Jim's mother and sisters. There wasn't much point. Plus they'd want to know why I didn't talk to them and that's not something I feel like explaining, even if I could.

"I wonder if his father will come home, too?" my dad asks. "What do you think, Cheryl?"

I shrug. "Don't think he'll bother."

"What makes you say that, honey?" asks my mother.

"Because he hasn't been home in years and he seems pretty happy to be away from this place. Jim said he never bothers coming home anymore, so why would he bother now?"

"Just because he had to leave to make money doesn't mean he doesn't care about his son, Cheryl," my father says. "People leave this province all the time to earn a living and ..."

I tune him out, but it occurs to me that it's perfect for my father that Jim's dad is in Alberta while his son is in the hospital. It'll highlight the plight of the former fishermen in Newfoundland even more. I can see the subheading in this chapter: *Jim's story: a homespun tragedy*, or *Jim: caught in the web of economic loss*.

My dad is still going on, quoting some statistics now about the number of people who've left the province. I can't take it anymore.

"You don't know anything about Jim or his family," I cut in

sharply. "And they're not just research material for your book."

My father finally shuts up.

"And for your information, Jim is real person. He has dreams of being a geologist one day and finding rare fossils, piecing together ancient history. He isn't just someone who's lying down and dying off, like you think. Even getting slammed around by the ocean didn't kill him, in case you hadn't noticed. So you can quit hoping."

"Cheryl! You make it sound like your father enjoys hardship." My mother's hands are still puffed up, clutching her knife and fork. I know stress adds to her condition. I should be nice. I should be sweet, but I can't do it.

"Well, doesn't he? Otherwise he'd have no material."

My parents give each other their what-are-we-going-to-do look.

"Well?" I ask again. I know they can't deny what I just said and they don't even bother trying.

"I'm going upstairs," I say, finishing my stew. "I'll see you tomorrow." If I stick around, I'll only say more things that I'll feel bad about later.

Marilyn Manson blocks out the thoughts in my head, singing about guilt and how it's something we try to beat, but can't. It grows inside us, squirming in our bellies, twisting in our guts and making our spines turn to jelly.

Touché once again, Marilyn.

***

Boss is barking. Jim's sisters are being pulled down the street by her, toward Nunnery Hill, their four hands clinging to the leash.

Is it my imagination, or did Boss look up toward my window, as if she wanted me to come along?

CHAPTER 8
some rock-solid place

*J*im's family sets off for the hospital early the next day, piling into Nanny's car. Nanny gets to ride up front, helped into her seat by Jim's mother and sisters. She's so tiny they practically lift her in.

"I'm sure they'd take you with them if you asked, Cherie," my mom says when she catches me watching from the living room window. She woke me up at the crack of dawn to try to talk me into going on the bird and whale tour at Witless Bay with them. When I said no she urged me to at least come down and have breakfast with them, to see them off.

I couldn't find a way out of it.

"No they wouldn't. They don't even know me," I respond, still sleepy, little pieces of my dream still heavy in my head, like bits of bone that need spitting out.

"No, but Nanny does. And the others must know about you by now."

I guess she's right, but I can't be sure. And I can't help thinking that if Nanny wanted me to come, she'd have found a way to ask me. I remember the way Jim's family surrounded his bed yesterday, his mother fussing over him – peck, peck, peck, like a mother hen. I don't see how I'd fit into the picture. I'd probably just hang out in the background, plastered back against the wall, and that's not where I want to be. I want to stand inches away from Jim and look directly into his brown eyes. I think back to that split second of our kiss, when I felt every cell in my body rush toward him. Neither of us is likely to forget the sound of that mother's scream, but I hope Jim has some memory of what happened before it.

"It's okay, Mom. Drop it," I say.

My mother hasn't said anything more about leaving Newfoundland, but I can tell she's thinking about it by the way she keeps looking down at her hands and sighing. Even this boat tour is a sign. She says she wants to do it now because summer is almost over, but that doesn't make sense. My mom usually acts like she has all the time in the world.

"You can almost feel fall in the air and see it in the light," she says, sipping her coffee at the front window. "I'd really like to see the seabirds at Cape St. Mary's too, and drive around Trinity Bay."

"Don't worry, Ellen. We'll get you there," my dad replies, stressing the "we," as if he and I have made plans to whisk my mother around the province. "Are you sure you won't come see the whales with us, Cheryl?" My father is loading his knapsack with binoculars, camera, sun hats, rain capes, a map, and other boat tour essentials. "I've heard they're spectacular."

"I told you. I don't want to go near the ocean for a while, after what happened Thursday."

I know that'll shut them up, even though it's not the real reason I don't want to go. That has more to do with how they'll expect me to be as excited as they are, as they pass the binoculars around and ooh and ah over everything that moves.

Besides, I'm hoping I might be able to see Jim today, in between his family's visits. Even the mother hens on the farm escaped the coop from time to time, to take a break from their chicks.

***

By noon, Jim's family is still not back. Maybe they're planning to stay right by Jim's side all day. I guess nothing is stopping them. If Jim's mom wanted to, she could sleep all night on the cozy chair in the corner of Jim's room. The nurses might even throw a blanket over her.

I could be waiting forever to see Jim again, sitting right here in this same spot, going nuts. I have to get out. If I don't, I'll go crazy.

Without planning to, I find myself walking toward Signal Hill. I'm so full of energy, I feel like I could practically run right to Cabot Tower. At Deadman's Pond, I sit on a huge rock. I can't help thinking that Jim might not have been kidding about the hangings and how the water behind me might be full of skeletons. It's like every place in this town has a story. I never did get a chance to ask Jim how Nunnery Hill got its name. I'm sure that would be a good one too. I can't decide whether I really want to go all the way up Signal Hill right now. If I did, I could hike down the trail again and sit on the plateau looking out at the water, watching the ships come in. But it wouldn't be the same without Jim.

I skip it and turn back to Water Street instead. At George, a girl with a guitar is singing in Jim's old spot. She's got a pretty good crowd listening to her sing a song about women watching the water for their men at sea.

The chorus is something about "roaring waves" and "watery graves," words that take me right back to Jim.

I decide to walk back along the harbour. The quay is full

of people, which isn't surprising. The weather is nicer than it's been in days, hot and sunny, the sky a solid sheet of blue way past the Narrows. The seabirds are circling and screeching like crazy, landing on the high masts and railings of ships, as if they're planning a takeover.

Across the harbour, out at the tip of the land, I see the red and white lighthouse of Fort Amherst. Jim had plans to take me there, but that might not happen now. I'll just have to remember it this way, sticking up from the rock like a giant candy cane.

I see them heading my way, but there's not much I can do to avoid smacking right into them, other than jump in the water. I can feel the exact second they see me. It's like they start to buzz, veering in my direction.

"Well, if it isn't Cheryl of the spiked hair?" It's the leader of the Village Mall goon squad, dressed just as tight and sparkly as ever. She drifts toward me and the rest follow, as though they're attached by a towline.

"Where's your hero?" she says next, laughing. The others laugh too, forming a semicircle around me.

"Yeah, we seen his picture in the newspaper," one of the guys says. "Didn't know he could swim."

And I didn't know you could read!

"Bet he was cute all wet, eh?" the other girl says. She blows a huge bubble that I'd like to see burst and stick in her bleached blond hair.

"Hey, if you're missing it while he's laid up, we got lots of friends," the other guy says, grinning.

"Yeah, but who could replace Jim? He's just so ... sexy," lead girl says. This has them all guffawing like crazy.

I remember what Jim said at the mall about how it was best not to play the game and provoke them, that that was what they wanted. That day, when these jerks were teasing Jim, I could feel him draw on some rock-solid place inside himself that helped him stay proud. They didn't crack him at all, even though they were trying just as hard as they are right now.

"Nice to see you all again," I say calmly. "Have a good day." Then I sidestep them and continue walking. I can feel them turn toward me, eager to continue taunting. When I'm a good distance down the quay, I turn back. I can't believe they're following me, or at least they're walking in my direction. Maybe I'm being paranoid and they've just turned back because they're going home. Still, I pick up my speed, making it seem like I came out to do some kind of power walk, for exercise. When I get to the end of the quay I cross

Water Street and look back. I can still see them, but they've stopped. They're in a little huddle, probably deciding what to do next.

I feel completely exposed all of a sudden. What could I have done if they had decided to follow me? It's not like I know people whose houses I could duck into, or call to come get me. There's no one but Jim, and he won't be doing any more rescuing for a while.

I can't believe the way they mock Jim and try to tear him down, just for fun. It makes me want to scream. I bet he's never done a thing to them. It's just because he's different, because he's serious about school and has real goals – goals that don't involve wandering around trying to act tough.

I should have done more to defend him back there. He'd have done more for me, I'm sure of it. I should have told them what he did out at Cape Spear, how the girl would have died if Jim hadn't jumped in. But the article said all that, if they had actually bothered to read it. It wouldn't have made a difference. If I do get to see him at the hospital, I won't tell him about what just happened. It would only upset him, which isn't what he needs right now.

All the way back up the steep streets, I can't help noticing the brightness of the houses, with their colourful fronts. I picture our house in Montreal – plain brown brick, like so many others in the neighbourhood. I wonder how it would look if we painted it red or purple, with bright yellow trim, to make it stand out, when we get back. Or, should I say if. All day I've been feeling the possibility, heavy as a chunk of granite, in my belly.

By the time I turn onto Gower, Nanny's car is back in its spot. I'm dying for news about Jim. Maybe my mom's right and I should just go over. I wouldn't even have to knock. I bet Nanny would ask Joannie to make me a cup of tea and pat the pillow beside her on the sofa. Then I could easily ask about Jim's concussion and his lungs. I'd even like to know about the bruise on his face, whether it's still purple-black, or has it faded to dark grey. Did he mention me at all, or am I as distant as the girl he rescued, floating out to sea?

It occurs to me that with Jim's family back home, I could easily head to the hospital, to see Jim on my own. I'm seriously thinking about it when Jim's sisters turn onto Gower, from the opposite corner. Two large grocery bags hang from Joannie's small hands, pulling down her shoulders. The bags are so heavy they're practically scraping the pavement.

If we keep walking at this pace, we'll run straight into each other.

I can hear Joannie whining about the bags. "They're too heavy – you take one."

"Forget it. Remember what you promised on the plane? I'm holding you to it."

"You're so mean, I hate you," Joannie spits.

We're just a few feet apart, outside our houses. Now's my chance. I take a deep breath and look straight into the older girl's eyes. I'm about to speak when Joannie pipes in.

"Hey, are you Jim's girlfriend?"

"Joannie!" her sister says, sending her a fierce look.

"I'm Cheryl, his next door neighbour. And no, I'm not his girlfriend."

"He asked if we met you yet," Joannie continues, stopping and putting down the bags. "I knew it was you because he said you had dark hair and blue eyes, and that you usually dress in black, but that it suited you. So it must be you. Right?" Joannie's voice soars higher and higher as she speaks, barely stopping for breath. She's got Jim's dark hair and eyes, with the same yellow sparkle, and the same long thin face and body.

"Ignore my sister. She's crazy. I'm Candy," the older girl says. "And she's Joannie." She points with her chin, as though her little sister isn't worth a finger.

"So, how is Jim? Is he getting better?" I try to sound casual, as if I haven't been dying to ask someone these questions for the past two days.

"The doctor says Jim's could've died out there," Joannie says.

"No, he didn't. He said the girl is lucky to be alive, thanks to Jim," Candy says, rolling her lighter-grey eyes. "Don't you ever listen?"

"But what about Jim? His concussion and lungs?" I ask, looking at Joannie to encourage her.

"He's fine. He's just a bit groggy and his ribs are all smashed up, but that's all," Candy says casually, as if she's used to people having bashed ribs and mushy brains. Or, like she's working hard at giving this impression.

"When's he coming home?"

"Tomorrow, probably," Joannie says. "But he'll have to stay in bed for a while, 'cause of his ribs. Did you know we took a plane to get here? I'd never been on a plane before. Neither had she." Joannie beams up at Candy, as if she knows Candy won't like her divulging that.

"She's not asking for our life story, Joannie. Going on a plane is no big deal, you know. Everyone does it."

"You never did," Joannie says.

"So? that's no big deal either." Candy avoids my eyes. I wonder if Jim told her that I've travelled a lot and that's why she's trying hard to act nonplussed in front of me, as if she thinks I'll gloat about it or something.

"Jim told me when he gets better he's gonna come home and take me to this place he knows – we'll have to go by boat – where you can find pirate's gold. It's really called pyrite, or something like that, but I don't care 'cause Jim said it can be really shiny and you can put it inside a piece of wire and hang it on a chain and no one'll know the difference."

"Joannie, for Christ's sake. No one cares about that stuff except you," Candy says. "I'm sure Cheryl doesn't."

"No, it sounds great. I've never seen pirate's gold," I say, shooting Candy a look. Am I ever glad I never had an older sister to demolish all my ideas. Candy's name suits her even less than mine suits me. At least I hope it does. "Are you going back to see him this afternoon?"

"No. The doctor said they were going to get him up walking with the physiotherapist this afternoon, to get him mobile again before he comes home," Candy says. "And then they're redoing all his x-rays, just to be sure."

"Oh." No point in trying to go see him then. "Well, I'll see you round, I guess."

Candy looks at her sister and points to the bags. Joannie sighs hard before picking them up.

***

My parents return from their bird and whale tour on fire with excitement. The boat took them out to huge rock formations that were plastered with thousands of puffins.

"The rocks were magenta. And the puffins' beaks glinted off them like burnt orange. I wish you had come," my mom says to me.

"And the whales," my dad says. "They were swimming beside, under, and practically over the boat. It was fantastic."

"And what colour were they? Cobalt?" I ask.

"Pretty close," says my mom, ignoring my sarcasm.

"Part of the rock looked just like a skull, with huge holes where the eyes and mouth would be. The captain cut the engine and let us drift under it. Then he ordered everyone to cover their heads, 'cause of the rainfall of bird droppings. It was so eerie, Cherie."

"So you got pelted by bird poop?"

"Pretty much," my dad says, smiling. Is there nothing that doesn't thrill these people?

"At the end of the trip the captain took out this huge cod. We thought it was real, but it was just rubber," my mom says.

"You'll never guess what he wanted people to do to it?" my dad asks.

"Let me guess. Kiss it?"

My parents look at each other, then deflate. They thought they were really going to get me with that one.

"How did you know?" they both ask.

"Everyone here knows that one, Dad."

Then they go off to clean the puffin crap out of their hair.

***

Later in the evening a taxi pulls up outside Nanny's. I watch from my bedroom window, my heart stopping. Maybe Candy was wrong and Jim is coming home earlier than expected. Maybe he walked so well and the X-rays were so positive, his bones milky white and fused together, that they decided to release him right away. And it would be just like him to do it alone, to prove that he could.

But it's not Jim. It's an older guy, who's as tall as Jim but a lot wider. He swings a duffel bag out of the back seat and onto his shoulder like it weighs only a pound. A few seconds later,

Joannie is running up to him.

"Davy, Davy, Davy," she cries. "You're here."

She jumps up and Davy catches her with his other arm, twirling her around, the duffel bag spinning out beside him.

"My lord, look at you. How ya doin', Candy."

"I'm not Candy, I'm Joannie."

"You're never Joannie!"

"I am too," Joannie cries, delighted.

Suddenly, Nanny's door opens. Davy stops spinning and places Joannie gently on the ground. He lets the duffel bag slide down his big arm and land with a thud, then he opens his arms and Jim's mother runs into them. He closes his big arms around her and the two of them stand there, rocking gently, her head barely reaching his tanned neck. Nanny is almost hopping up and down behind them.

A few seconds later, Davy lets go of his mother, scoops up Nanny and twirls her around too. She's just a wisp, her little feet flying through the air like birds.

"Go on with your foolishness. Put her down, Davy," Jim's mom says, laughing. "You're cracked, you are." When Davy does settle Nanny on the sidewalk, I don't think I've ever seen her look so happy.

"Hey, Candy," Davy says, lightly brushing her chin with

his fist. "All grown up, I see." This was exactly the right thing to say, because Candy smiles and her scowl disappears.

"Come on in, everyone. Don't be standing out on the stoop all day, the neighbours'll think I've got no manners," Nanny says.

Then I hear Joannie, in her high-pitched voice, say, "Speaking of neighbours, Nanny, can we go get Cheryl? We met her before. Can't she come over too? Please."

I automatically pull back. I wonder if she saw me watching, like some kind of Peeping Tom.

"Of course, Joannie, my love. I haven't seen that girl in days. You go on over and get her."

I zoom to the front door, so that Joannie won't have to have a long conversation with my parents, and find Joannie beaming on the sidewalk.

"Nanny said you could come over if you want to."

"Sure, I'd love to," I say. I call out goodbye to my parents, who are trying to hook up the computer to the new modem. To my surprise, Jim's family was waiting for us before heading in.

"For heaven's sake, we finally meet you," Joannie's mom says. "Nanny and Jim go on about you nonstop, but we were starting to think you were just a ghost, isn't that right, girls?"

Joannie laughs and Candy rolls her eyes.

Then I'm swept up between Jim's mother and Davy, with Joannie right behind, like she wants to close any gap that I might escape from.

***

"Davy, my love, why didn't you tell us you were coming. I'd have picked you up at the airport myself, instead of you throwing away good money on a taxi," Jim's mom says once we're all seated and Davy has come back downstairs. The living room seems incredibly small all of a sudden, the flowers on the papered walls pressing down on us. I'm on a hard chair, across from the sofa that now holds Nanny, Davy, and Joannie. Nanny's little body almost sinks into her spot, dwarfed by Davy.

"I wanted to surprise you, Ma," Davy laughs

"Surprise us you did. My god, you're some like your father at his age, my son," says Nanny. "'Cept, of course, you're better looking. Your father always looked stunned, like he'd just fallen overboard or something."

Davy looks around quickly, stopping at his mom's face, when Nanny mentions his father. His mom jumps up and offers to make tea, like she wants a diversion. I wonder if she feels funny talking about her husband with me here. I'm pretty much a stranger, even though Nanny and Jim know me. "Candy, you come and help," she orders. Candy sighs and follows her mother down the hall.

"Jim's gonna get a medal from the Queen," Joannie blurts out. "The nurses all said it, right, Mom?"

"They were just speculating, sweetie, but it might be," her mom calls down the hall. Joannie looks at me and shrugs, as though she wants to show me that no one in her family really knows anything. I smile back.

"No kidding. Our Jim, a hero?" Davy shakes his head. "He was always destined to be different. Funny thing is, he was the one to stay off the water back home, remember, Ma?" Davy is saying loudly. "He never once panned with us in winter."

"Good thing, too," his mom calls out. "A few have died that way. You're just lucky you never did yourself, jumping on the ice floes in that weather." Even though I can't see her, I imagine her shaking her head fiercely.

"And who's this then?" asks Davy, finally looking at me, making me squirm and blush all at once. "Jim's girlfriend, you said?"

"Candy got mad at me when I said that. Cheryl's Jim's friend, Davy, not his girlfriend. At least that's what she says, but I don't believe her," Joannie says. I can feel my cheeks burn even more.

"Cheryl was with Jim when it happened," Nanny says.

"And he jumped down those rocks, all on his own, without anyone pushing him?" Davy asks me. He sounds incredulous, as though the image of Jim that's fixed in his mind is of a shy ten-year-old, too scared to go near the water, his nose in a book. That's not the Jim I saw on Thursday, scaling those rocks like a pro.

"Yes, he did. He was the only one who even thought of it. If it weren't for Jim — "

"It was Jim for sure, my son," his mom cuts in, setting down a large tray that carries tea cups, milk, and sugar. "We saw the bruise and he has the sore ribs to prove it. You'll see. Don't you go up there teasing your little brother, like you used to back home. Show him some respect now, when you sees him. He's been through it, Davy, he has, for sure."

Candy comes in carrying a large teapot and sets it down on the tray. From a bag under her sofa chair, Jim's mother pulls out a half-knit sweater hanging on huge needles, and starts to knit. She's doing waves, in three different shades of blue, so that the water looks choppy. Her fingers move fast, click-clacking the needles like a machine.

"How's your brother?" Jim's mom asks, her eyes steady on the stitches. "He couldn't come?"

"No, Ma, we couldn't both come. They owed me some time, but he sends his love. Says he'll come home when he can, maybe in September."

"I guess in Alberta they don't think half-drowned brothers are as important as oil," Jim's mother says, still not looking up. She now has grey wool attached and is knitting a shape in the water.

"Ma, I know where you're headed. Let's not do it, okay, at least not yet. I just got through the door, right?"

Everyone stops talking, creating an uncomfortable silence in the air. The only sound is the clicking of knitting needles, like they are beating out time. Again I wonder if Jim's mom might not want me here, listening to her family's private conversation. It would be like a stranger sitting in when my family is talking about moving again and I'm all angry and my parents are all defensive. Maybe I shouldn't have let Joannie talk me inside.

"Tea's ready," Candy announces a few minutes later, without making a move to pour it. Nanny can't do it and Jim's mother is busy, so Davy gets up.

"So, tell me more about Jim," Davy says, pouring. "I

know what you told me on the phone, about the concussion and ribs. Is there anything else?"

"That's enough, don't you think?" says his mom.

"Those are big rocks out at Cape Spear. We used to climb on them ourselves, remember, Ma, when we came here when we were kids? It's a nasty spot. What the hell was a little girl doing out there?"

"People don't think, you knows that, Davy. It was a sunny day, the sea was calm, I suppose. Am I right, Cheryl?"

I nod, glad that she's actually including me.

"Lots of people from the mainland think it's all so charming, they just don't know the dangers, like we do."

Everyone's head turns slightly toward Nanny, whose tea cup is rattling. Considering I'm one of those ignorant mainlanders, I'm glad they aren't staring at me.

"And Jim just went right to it, to save that girl?" Davy asks again, shaking his head. It bugs me that he's having such a hard time fathoming how Jim could be so brave.

"Not only that," I say. "He got everyone organized, even the girl's father. He got a line of men to hold the rope that he went down on. Of course, Boss helped too." At her name, Boss perks up from her spot in the corner.

"I'm dead impressed. Didn't think that kid knew anything

but those stones he collects. Have you seen his room, Ma? I'm gonna feel like I'm sleeping in a cave or something tonight."

"He's got an idea of being a geologist, you knows that, Davy. He's wanted that since he was a boy. And I know he's got his heart set on getting out to Nova Scotia this summer, to look for fossils. I tell you, I'm all for it. If there's one thing we've got here, it's rocks. At least then he can stay home, not like the rest of you's."

"Ma, not again, please. You know why we all left. If we hadn't gone, you think you'd of had the money for three plane tickets to get here, especially last-minute like?"

Jim's mother looks uncomfortable when Davy mentions money, her mouth going hard, like she's trying not to let some harsh words fly. Maybe I should make an excuse to go. But I'm drawn to the grey spot on the sweater that she's knitting. It's fascinating to watch it take shape. Right now it's an oval, rising up over the waves that have ended and changed into a lighter blue sky.

"If Jim would come out too, he wouldn't have to be a geologist anyway," Davy continues. "He could make more money in a summer in Alberta than ten years rock-collecting here, I bet."

"Maybe it isn't all about the money, Davy," replies his

mom quickly. We all go quiet again, listening to the clicking of the needles and the rattling of Nanny's cup. Every now and then Candy sighs into the mix. I hold my breath, not wanting to remind anyone that I'm here.

"These girls haven't had their whole family around them since they were four and eleven. How's that supposed to be good for them?" Jim's mom finally asks in a much softer voice. If she actually starts to cry, I don't know what I'll do.

Davy doesn't answer her question. His sisters are oddly quiet, even Joannie has stopped bubbling beside him. It occurs to me that if she hasn't seen her father since she was four, she probably has no real memory of him. She'd just know him from pictures, almost like a stranger. No one has mentioned Jim's father directly, but this whole conversation seems to be about him. Jim said he's up in the oil sands, in northern Alberta. It can't be impossible to get home from there. There must be more to the story, probably things that can't be said aloud, especially in front of me.

I wonder how I'd feel about my dad if he had just gone off to do his research on his own, without bringing me and my mom along. If we only got the occasional phone call or postcard from new places. I don't suppose that would've been any better.

"Some nice partridgeberry cake in the fridge, Candy, my love. Go on and cut some up for us. I thinks we all need something sweet right now."

"Okay, Nanny," Candy replies, her voice almost civilized, which surprises me.

The knitted grey shape is now splitting in two. Jim's mother focuses on her knitting intently, as if it's the one thing keeping her steady right now. Then suddenly, she throws it down, jumps up and rushes over to Davy throwing her arms around him, like she's just noticed he's here all over again. She rests her chin on his head and strokes his short hair, her eyes shut tight. A small tear, thin as a hair, escapes the corner of her eyes.

"Davy, Davy," she says. "It's so good to see you. I just wishes you was all here. All of you."

"I know, Ma, I know," says Davy, patting his mom's back.

I don't know where to look while all this is happening. Nanny and Joannie are staring at their laps, as if they want to give Davy and his mom some privacy. I've never seen a mother hug her grown son so forcefully. And the odd thing is that Davy, when I peek at him, doesn't seem to be minding it. He looks relieved, and is squeezing his mother back softly. It makes me feel kind of sad but happy all at once.

Candy returns with the cake, all cut up on a plate. I expect her to roll her eyes at the scene, but she doesn't. She's squeezing her eyes tightly, as though she's holding something in.

Jim's mom sits back down and resumes knitting, even faster now, row after row, giving shape to a picture that must be so imprinted on her mind, she doesn't even have to look to see if she's got it right.

"Can I go up now, do you think?" Davy asks. "To see Jimmy?"

"No, son. It's too late. We'll all go in the morning, right, Nanny?" Nanny nods. I wonder if the "we" includes me. Jim's mother seems to desperately want her family around her, and I'm not family, even though she swept me right inside tonight, with no hesitation. Maybe witnessing all these sentimental moments has made me more likely to be included.

"Hey, I'm not tired at all. It's only six o'clock for me. Who's up to walking down to George with me? You, Candy?"

Candy's whole face brightens.

"Can I, Ma?"

"Oh, all right, but you keep an eye on her, Davy. She's underage, remember that."

"What about you, Cheryl?" Davy looks over, startling me. I thought he had forgotten I was here. "Game?"

Candy and Joannie both glare at me. Neither of them wants me to go along, I can tell, but for different reasons.

"No, it's okay, thanks. I think I better go home now anyway. It was nice to meet you all. Thanks for the tea, Nanny. And the cake."

"Never you mind, Cheryl. You come over any time you likes, you knows that," Nanny says. "Jim's that fond of that girl," Nanny says to Davy beside her. I blush again.

"Will you come back tomorrow? She can, can't she, Mom?" Joannie says, jumping up.

"Of course, honey. See you soon then, Cheryl," says Jim's mom. I can't tell by her voice if she regrets that I was here tonight or not. She stops knitting for just a second, pulling her work straight under her, to reveal that what she's knit are two whale fins, sticking out, upside down, in the water.

It figures that a mainlander would take forever to recognize them.

***

My parents are huddled around the laptop. My dad will do a lot of his research online, scouting out places to "visit" and researching what resources are available to all the poor people who are losing their way of life. He told me that, in his book, he's going to argue that technology has helped people cope with change, by making them feel less isolated. He said there's a chat room for everything today. Miners losing their jobs in the Gaspé can contact miners as far away as Siberia and find they have lots in common. Farmers on the prairies facing drought or insects can connect with farmers in Africa experiencing the same challenges.

You'd almost think those continental plates had shifted together again.

When I peek over their shoulders, I see travel information: flights to Montreal, in August.

"What are you doing?" I ask.

"Just checking out flights home," my mom says.

"Does that mean you've decided to leave for sure?"

"No, but it's still a possibility. I want to see what's available, just in case, honey."

Part of me is surprised. I thought that the excitement of today, with all that magenta and burnt orange, might have changed her mind. But her hands are as swollen as ever, maybe more from all those hours in the spray.

My parents just assume that I'll go too. That's the usual pattern. But, who could blame them this time?

***

Marilyn Manson is singing about wanting to be outside of society. In Saskatchewan, this song was my mantra. I sung it all the time. I especially loved the part about wanting to be outside of absolutely everything. That was me, feeling like my life was just waiting for me somewhere else. It suited my dark clothes and scary persona, designed to keep everyone away. I told myself that was how it was going to be anyway. If there's no way inside, you might as well put yourself on the outside – on purpose. And pretend that's where you wanted to be in the first place.

But everything is different here. Now, the lyrics are just confusing.

CHAPTER 9
bird rock

The house is dead quiet when I wake up, and it takes me a minute to remember that my parents are off to the bird sanctuary at Cape St. Mary's. They had to leave really early because it's quite far, on the other side of the Avalon. I've seen pictures of the giant bird rock. It does look incredible, rising straight up out of the sea like a tower, every square inch given over to seabirds.

They didn't try to talk me into coming today. I suppose they've given up on trying to convert me, now that my mom and I might be leaving. Maybe we'll be birds soon ourselves, taking off from this giant rock, over the tumbling water.

Jim's family piles into the car at about ten. I'm pretty sure they're going to get Jim. I wish I could go with them, but there wouldn't be room for me. Even Joannie and Nanny are hanging back. Joannie is standing with her arms folded across her chest on the sidewalk, staring angrily at the taillights. She stays out there long after Nanny has gone back inside. I decide to step outside and join her.

"What's up, Joannie?" I ask.

"They couldn't take me, 'cause they need to leave space for Jim, in case he comes home. It's always me who gets left behind, because I'm the youngest. It's not fair. They don't even ask me, they just tell me."

"Yeah, I know how that feels. I can hang out with you if you want." Joannie's face lights up.

"Can we put up some 'welcome home' decorations, for Jim? My friend Shannon did that when her brother came back from the army. He was away in another country, where there's a war going on. We made a banner that he really liked. It almost made him cry."

"A banner, eh? I guess we could do that. Let's see what we can find at my place."

Joannie and I rummage through the drawers in the cabinet under the stairs and find a box of crayons, so old they're all stubs. Robbie's probably had these since he was a baby. We also find a package of "Happy Birthday" balloons, not exactly appropriate for the occasion, but they'll have to do.

"Do you know if Nanny has any paper next door?" I ask. Joannie shrugs, so I grab a stack of my dad's computer paper.

He has a whole box of the old kind, all struck together with holes in the side, perfect for a banner.

"Can we do it over at Nanny's?" Joannie asks. "That way, we'll be around if Jim comes home today."

"Great idea," I say, trying to sound excited, for Joannie's sake. It's not that I'm not excited about seeing Jim, it's just that I'm kind of worried about it too. I know he must be wondering why I didn't go visit him in the hospital. I just hope I get the chance to explain it properly, to make sure he understands how I felt like I couldn't cut in on his family. I'd at least like him to know I tried.

We pop next door and set up all our stuff on the living room floor. We work while Nanny watches her talk shows; we make a colourful banner that reads, "Welcome Home, Jim – Our Hero." Joannie has the idea to decorate it with things from the ocean, like rocks, shells, seaweed, fish, octopi, anchors, coral, and other treasures from the deep.

"This way he won't just think of the bad parts when he thinks about the ocean," Joannie says.

As we work, Joannie chats about her family, sharing details as they come to her. "Davy sneaked Candy into some of the bars on George Street last night. My mom's mad and now Candy's snobbier than ever. She has lots of boyfriends at home. My mom's always mad about that too. They're all really ugly, but Candy thinks they're cute. I've seen them do stuff I'm not supposed to see," Joannie giggles. I don't ask her to explain, but it's not like I can't guess. It's probably stuff Jim and I would be doing if we had the chance.

At one point she says, "My mom cries a lot, at home. If she's knitting, the needles squeak when they get wet."

"Wow, Joannie. That's really sad. What's she crying about?"

"Her boys," Joannie replies, short and simple. I wonder if the boys include her husband. Joannie never talks about her dad.

"Jim said he'll come home when he's better, maybe for the rest of the summer. My mom made him promise yesterday."

I don't respond. All I can think about is how much I don't want that to happen.

"Candy's mean to me," Joannie says suddenly, a few minutes later. "She treats me like her slave."

"I saw that with the grocery bags yesterday. What was that about?"

"She said I could have the window seat if I'd let her boss me around for two whole days when we got here. I really wanted to see the clouds and she bosses me around all the time anyway, so I didn't see the difference."

Nanny tells us where to find some tape and we hang up the banner across the archway in the hall. It'll be right in Jim's face when he comes in. I wonder how he'll feel about being called a hero. He doesn't seem like the type of person to boast, not even about something as big as this.

"Jim was my best friend at home," Joannie says as we work. "Always teaching me things and taking me places."

Joannie is quiet for a few minutes, a lonely look on her face. Then we start blowing up the balloons.

"Hey, why don't you come home with Jim? I could show you around. You'd love it. There's a swimming hole in a river. We have a rope that you swing out on to jump into the water. And maybe you'll see some moose, there's lots of those around."

"Sounds good, Joannie. Maybe. You never know." There's no way I'm going to tell her we might be going back to Montreal. I can't believe it myself. I'm trying not to think about it.

We rub the balloons on our hair, then stick them to the walls in the living room, the "Happy Birthday" side facing inward. Boss barks up at the balloons, like they're alien creatures invading her space.

Every time she does it, Joannie cracks up. It's nice to see

her laughing. She looks just like Jim when she does, her mouth wide and mischievous.

***

Jim steps out of the car slowly, leaning on Davy. Joannie takes off, running into the circle of her family. When she hugs Jim, she does so lightly, not pressing too close to his chest, as if she's been given careful instructions.

"Cheryl's here!" Joannie declares, coming back to the door to grab my hand.

I can feel Jim's eyes on me instantly, locking with my own. The entire street is silent, except for the sound of my thumping heart.

"Told you she'd be here, Jimmy-boy," Davy says, play-punching his brother lightly on the arm.

"Shut up, Davy," Jim says. He takes a few steps in my direction and I move toward him, dropping Joannie's hand and meeting him halfway.

"Hey, Cheryl," he says. The bruise on his face is still dark, covering his entire left cheek and eye with a patch of navy. It makes him look tough, like he's been in a brawl.

Standing this close to him, the day at Cape Spear comes

rushing back, like a wave. I see Jim clinging to the rope down on the rocks, the wave rolling in. Then in the ambulance, wrapped up like a sausage in those blankets. I remember bending close to hear his raspy breath and smelling the seaweedy salt water on his skin.

"Are you okay?" I ask. I have an urge to smooth back his bangs, out of his eyes.

"He's fine, he's tough. Right, little brother?" Davy says, still hovering around Jim, as though he might need to catch him.

"I'm fine, especially now," he says to me. I guess he's not angry that I didn't visit him. He takes another slow step toward me and I want to throw my arms around him, but his entire family is watching us. It's like we're in a freeze-frame.

"Let's all go in," Jim's mom says finally. "I could murder a cup of tea."

In the hallway, everyone stops to admire the banner. Just as I suspected, Jim's cheeks flush when he reads the word "hero." But he looks touched, his mouth curling into a smile.

"Joannie's idea," I say.

Jim flashes his little sister a thumbs-up signal that makes her beam.

Jim's mom helps him lower himself onto a high-backed hard chair. I look away while she's doing it, because I have the feeling he wouldn't want me watching.

I sit on the far end of the sofa, beside Joannie. Jim and I keep looking at each other. I'm almost bursting with things I want to tell him and ask him, but can't. It's like I've also got a thick bandage wrapped around my chest, holding me in.

"Well, Jim's home, I'm going to get those seal sausages on. I took them out of the freezer this morning, just in case, before you all left," Nanny says.

"Candy, love, go help your Nanny with the dinner."

"Mom, why me? Why can't Joannie?"

"'Cause I asked you. Now go."

"I'll come too," says Davy. "I want to watch those sausages sizzle." That makes Candy change her mind real fast. I get the feeling she'd follow Davy anywhere.

"Now Joannie, me and you'll go get that dining room fit for humans. I don't suppose it's been used in years. Nanny, where's your dust rag to?"

Joannie wriggles with protest. "Jim said he'd show me all his rocks when he got home, Mom."

"Yes, my love, and I'm sure he will, but not right this minute, so you come with me."

"You'll show them to me later, right, Jim?"

"Don't worry, Joannie. I won't forget," says Jim. Then his

mom pulls Joannie up and they disappear down the front hall.

Suddenly, Jim and I are alone, but we're miles across the room from one another.

"Do I have to throw you a life saver and rope you in?" Jim asks, smiling.

"Nah, I think I can manage."

I move into the chair vacated by his mom. We're close enough now to touch. Jim reaches for my hand. I don't pull it back this time, like I did that day out in Quidi Vidi, under the black cloud. I wonder if Jim remembers much about that, or about what happened at Cape Spear.

"Jim, the concussion," I say. "Did it wipe out your memory?"

"No way. My memory is perfect. All of it." He doesn't have to say it, but I know he's thinking about the same thing I am. If we were truly alone, like we were in that bunker, we might try again. But the clinking of dishes and banging of pots reminds us that we're not. Beside, I'm not sure Jim could lean forward to reach me. And then there's his bruise. It looks so sore.

"It was really amazing, Jim. What you did out there."

"Ah ... well, I just did it, you know, kind of without thinking. It was weird."

"It was so brave. Imagine! You saved someone's life,

someone who'll grow up and have kids and grand-kids and tell them about you."

"Ah, knock it off. If it hadn't been me, someone else would've."

"I don't think so, Jim." And then, without thinking, I'm leaning toward him. I want to kiss him again, to be that close to him. The bruise covers part of his lips. I wonder if kissing would hurt. I guess there's only one way to find out.

"It's ready," Joannie bursts, practically jumping out of the dining room.

Jim and I sigh. This will have to be enough for now, Jim holding the hand that he traced, bringing those lines to life, as though they were just waiting to be unearthed.

***

The aroma of sizzling meat and frying onions fills the house.

Nanny calls everyone into the kitchen to help carry stuff down to the dining room. Only Jim is exempt. I whisk a steaming bowl of boiled potatoes past him and he winks. Davy helps Jim down the hall where we sit around an old-fashioned dining room table and eat. I never would have thought Nanny could put together such a meal, with her shaking hands. The seal sausage is dark red and juicy. I am a bit nervous about eating it. I try not to think of those white fluffy poster seals. I tell myself it's no different than eating chickens or cows. After all, they aren't exactly raised in humane ways — I saw that on some of the farms in Saskatchewan. And it would be incredibly rude to turn my nose up at the seal here and now, so I bite in. A sharp taste hits the roof of my mouth and the seal grease practically slides down my throat. But it's pretty good. Nanny tells us that as long as we have seals we'll never die for want of iron.

Jim and Davy eat their sausages the same way, taking small bites that they savour slowly, as if they have too much respect for the meat to desecrate it with their chewing. They ooh and aah through the whole experience.

"Oh, Nanny," Davy says. "You sure know the way to a man's heart. I can't tell you how many times I've had a craving for your seal sausage back in Alberta. Here's a confession — the guys started calling me fluffy, I talked about seals so much one night."

"Well, Davy, you knows where to get some, anytime," Nanny replies. The entire family turns to look at their mother, figuring she's going to make some crack about Alberta.

"I'll not say a word, my dears. I don't want to spoil this meal, for Jim's sake. He's not left home, not really."

"If I could fly you out to Alberta and set you up in your own little café you could make a killing whipping up home-cooked meals like this. I'm not the only one missing them," Davy continues.

"Davy said I could get a job out there real easy, Ma," Candy says. "I'm not going to school anyway, not really, so why shouldn't I go with him?"

"I told you, miss, you'll do the correspondence course and finish up. I didn't buy that computer and get all hooked up to that web for nothing."

"But it's useless and it's taking me forever." I figure Candy must be in the same grade as me. I wonder why she didn't come to St. John's with Jim in the first place, but I guess she would have been pretty young to leave home at the time, only fourteen.

"You tell her, Jim."

"Mom's right, Candy. What are you gonna do without high school?"

"You could come in to St. John's and go for nursing, or teaching," their mom tells her.

Candy scowls. I have to admit that the thought of Candy

doing either of those jobs is scary. I picture flying bedpans and blackboard erasers.

"I work with plenty of kids who dropped out," Davy says. "They're making good money, let me tell you. More than they'd be making even if they'd finished school."

"For heaven's sake, stop encouraging her," Jim's mom says. "You're setting her off, Davy. Those are guys you're talking about anyway. What about girls? What kind of work do they do out in the oil trade with no education? I think we can all guess."

That shuts Davy up and suddenly everyone is staring hard at their plates, which are now nothing but smears of black grease.

"I want to do what Jim does," Joannie blurts out a minute later, to break the silence. "Exactly what Jim does, finding rocks and stuff. He's even gonna help me find gold."

"Yeah, pirate's gold," Davy says with a smirk.

"Fool's gold," Candy laughs.

I look at Jim. For a quick second, his whole face darkens, but then he just shakes his head. It's like he's heard all this before.

"Laugh all you want, big brother," he says. "Not everyone wants to work in the oil. I know what I want. And maybe I'll find real gold one day. Then we'll see who's laughing because gold is worth more than oil."

I look over at Nanny. She was in the kitchen for an hour cooking up all this food, standing on her feet, chopping the onions with her shaking hands. And now she has to listen to all this talk about oil – not her favourite topic.

"Nanny, that was the best meal I've ever had," I say.

"Thank you, Cheryl, my love."

Jim taps my foot with his own, under the table. The phone rings at the exact same second, as though Jim's foot has set it off.

"I'll get it," says Davy. He's gone for a while. We can hear him talking and occasionally laughing out in the hallway, but we can't make out what he's saying. Finally he calls out, "It's for you, Jimmy." Unfortunately, it's not a cordless. Davy helps his brother up, then Jim takes slow, but fluid steps on his own to the phone.

"Who knows he's home already?" asks his mom.

"Maybe it's the lieutenant queen, calling about his medal," says Joannie, making Candy shake her head.

"Or more reporters," says Nanny.

Davy doesn't correct either of them. He makes a steeple of his index fingers and rests his chin in them, clamping his mouth.

We listen to Jim do the same kind of talking and laughing. A few minutes later he returns, his face flushed with a wide smile. "It's for you now, Ma. It's Sam."

"Davy, you rascal, you never said." Jim's mother jumps up and runs for the phone. I wonder if Sam is her husband, but Jim would hardly call him Sam. He'd say "Dad," I think.

"Sam's my oldest brother," Jim tells me.

Candy calls out to her mom that she wants to talk to him too, probably to ask him to convince their mother to let her go to Alberta.

"Me too," yells Joannie. "Don't forget me, like you always do."

"Lord, love a duck," says Nanny. "That's just about it. Just about the whole family." She looks happy and sad all at once. "Cheryl, be a love and go put some water on, will you?"

When I pass Jim's mom she has the phone cord wound tightly around her hand and she is trying to talk Sam into coming home. It's like she's negotiating a contract, taking Sam down from a week to a few days. "Surely the oil will wait two days," she says. "It's been there this long."

By the time I return from the kitchen, where I filled the kettle and rinsed out the big teapot, Candy is on the phone, with Joannie hopping up and down behind her.

"He's gonna try, but it didn't sound likely," Jim's mom is saying, back in the dining room. "It would be my dream to see you's all together again before we go home, all five of you. It's not too much to ask, is it, that I can see all my children together every few years?"

"Mom, don't start. You'll just get upset," says Davy. "Besides, where would Sam sleep. He's such a moose. Nanny would have to put him out in the yard in a tent."

"Remember the time you all took a tent up to Mary's Hill, you three boys? You wanted to be up early to see the whales. Then you got that crazy idea to hike down with flashlights, see the water at midnight. Little Jimmy was only two or three. You had him sleepwalking in the dark. He was terrified, especially when you told him all that stuff about the stick men with their powers from the devil. You had him carrying around a short stick of black wood, thinking it would give him magic powers and whatnot, like Superman. He looked out for stick men everywhere we went for about a year after that."

"Too bad he didn't have his stick last week, eh, Ma? He could've calmed the ocean." Davy and his mom crack up. Jim is shaking his head.

"I don't remember any of that."

"Ah, we're embarrassing little Jimmy," Davy says. "Especially in front of his girlfriend."

Jim and I look at each other. We haven't exactly used that word yet, or its male equivalent, but I guess it's kind of true.

"You always did take things too serious, Jimmy," says Davy. "But we shouldn't of teased you so much."

"Doesn't matter now," says Jim. "I survived."

Candy and Joannie return. "Sam said the same as Davy, Mom, that I should go out there. He could get me a job in a minute."

"I give up," Jim's mom says, putting her head in her hands. "I wants everyone together and you all just keep wanting to up and leave. I don't know, I just don't know."

"If we'd all stayed on Fox Island, none of this would've happened," Nanny says.

"What does that have to do with anything?" Candy snaps. Her mom sends her a biting look, which shuts her up immediately.

"Go get the tea, Candy," she says. "Take Joannie to help."

"If I have anymore tea, I'll drown," says Davy. "I'll help clear up though." Davy and his sisters carry the plates and bowls out to the kitchen. Around the table there is a heavy silence. Jim's mom and aunt seem to be miles away, back in a different place and time. Jim and I shrug across the table.

Suddenly the doorbell rings, startling Jim's mom so much her head snaps up.

"Now what?" she says. "If your brother was calling from a cellphone around the corner, I'll ..."

Davy flies to the door, probably thinking the same thing, and Jim's face is full of hope. But two seconds later, it's my father's voice we hear.

"Sorry to bother you," he says. "We were wondering if Cheryl is here?"

"She's in there," says Davy. "Glued to our Jimmy. Go on in."

My parents appear at the dining room door, smiling around, trying to tone down their excitement. Here's their chance to hang out with the locals and pick their brains. I want to crawl under the table.

"Come in, sit down. I'm Lucy, Jim's mom. We were just about to have some tea. Join us now?"

"Oh thanks, we didn't mean to intrude. We just got home from Cape St. Mary's and the house was empty. We worried a bit, you know, because of last time," says my mom. "I'm Ellen, by the way, and this is Kevin."

"Say no more. God gave us kids to help the white hairs

along. That's what my mom always said and it's so true. You have only the one – I've got five times the grey," Jim's mom says, pointing to her head.

My parents sit where Joannie and Candy were, my dad right next to Jim.

"It smells great in here," he says. "What did you have?"

"Seal sausage," says Nanny.

"Really? I'm anxious to try some myself sometime," he responds. My father always makes a point of eating the local food. It's like he thinks it'll soak into his blood and make him one with the land and people he's studying.

"Sorry. There's not a bit left," says Davy. "Not with me around."

"Oh, I wasn't fishing," says my dad, his voice trailing off, as though he's just realized his poor choice of metaphor. "So Jim, how are you doing? Feeling better?"

"Sore, but okay, I guess," says Jim.

"You're young, you'll heal quickly. Right? The resilience of youth," my dad says grandly, as though it's some well-known saying, looking around to see who'll agree with him.

Candy comes back in with the loaded tea tray, followed by Joannie who is carrying the cups.

"Got to be resilient where I work," Davy jumps in. "You

name it, it happens. Falling, cutting, stabbing, burning."

"Thanks so much, Davy, my son. I'll feel better now when you goes back to work. And about Sam too. I'll tell you. Sure, I'll be snow white by Christmas."

I watch my mom send Jim's mom a sympathetic smile, with a slight shake of her head, as though she can relate. But that's crazy. What do I ever do that compares to drilling for oil?

"I suppose it was all easier for you before the fishery closed?" my dad says. My heart thumps and my throat goes dry. If he starts interrogating Jim's family, I'll die.

"Oh yeah, lots easier," says Davy, pouring the tea. "Then all she had to worry about was us capsizing in storms or falling overboard."

"I'm not saying that fishing is without peril. I'm sure it was dangerous work, but at least you knew what it was. It was tradition. Am I right, Lucy?"

Oh God, I feel an index entry coming on: Lucy, fishing mother. Or Lucy, loss.

"Jim tells me you knit. I quilt. I don't know if he told you," my mom jumps in. I'm hoping they'll go off on that tangent, talking colour and patterns.

"I only knit so much now because I have to, since the

fishery closed up. I used to knit for the family. Now, I knit for strangers."

I can feel my father sucking that sentence out of the air and stamping it on his brain.

"Do you mind if I quote you on that Lucy?" he says. The dining room ceiling falls about six feet until it's almost on top of my head.

"Quote her? Are you a journalist or something?" Davy asks.

"No. I'm an anthropologist, as in *anthropos*, the Greek word for human being. I'm working on a book. You must know about it, Jim? Didn't Cher tell you?"

"She mentioned a book, but she didn't say much about it." I'm still fighting off the ceiling.

"What's it about? Knitting?" asks Lucy. Candy and Joannie laugh.

"No. It's mostly about dying cultures," says my father. That's when the ceiling comes down all the way, burying me in plaster dust and debris.

Jim's body snaps to attention across from me and his face pinches.

"Dying?" he asks. "Who's dying here?" He turns to face me. "You said he was here to study fishing culture. You didn't say anything about dying."

I don't respond. I just stare at my plate, holding in my breath.

"Well, as in the way of life, fishing life. That's dying, isn't it?" my father responds, even though Jim is still looking straight at me.

"Maybe, but the people aren't dying. You make it sound like we're all washed up, like the capelin."

"Not the people, Jim. The way of life. That's what I'm interested in."

"Hey, you know, Newfoundlanders can't be killed that easily," Davy jumps in. "Our ancestors survived with next to nothing, making fish out in the middle of nowhere for centuries. They didn't even get paid in cash, just supplies. And sealing. Let's not even get going on what's happened to sealers over the years, left to die out on the ice, crawling back to the ship on frostbit feet. And now, having to put up with all the protests from people who've never even been to this island. Trust me, we're pretty tough stock out here."

"I know, I'm realizing that. Look at Jim here. He's proof." My dad laughs, as though that was funny. But no one else does.

I look across at my mom. She looks as crushed as I feel,

in her way. I bet if she could wind the conversation back to knitting she would, reeling it in like a ball of yarn.

The dining room goes totally quiet. The table is so still, it's like some kind of still-life painting. And if mammals didn't have to breath to stay alive, the room would be dead silent too.

"The birds were amazing today," my mom ventures. "We saw gannets, murres, kittiwakes, and cormorants."

Jim's mom smiles at her, but it's like she's suddenly too tired to respond. She was hoping for a surprise visit by Sam, to add to the family portrait, but all she got was my dad, reminding her that the portrait might never happen.

"I can't sit any longer," says Jim. "I'm too sore. I got to lie down."

"I'll help you up, little brother," says Davy.

"Can I come too, Jim? You'll show me your rocks?"

"Not tonight, Joannie. Not tonight," says Jim, his eyes never leaving the table. Never once looking back at me.

Davy helps him up and we listen to them thump up the stairs, slowly and painfully.

***

I am running in the wheat again, only this time my feet keep slipping through the stalks and sinking way down into the earth. When I look down I see why. It's not earth, it's ocean. The wheat is growing on the water and the waves are loosening it, making clumps of it drift. I have to jump from clump to clump and my feet are unable to take hold. My hands grab the stalks of wheat and rip, until I'm holding nothing but a handful of seeds.

CHAPTER 10
rock museum

$\mathcal{M}$y parents are sitting on the sofa, a map of Newfoundland spread out on their laps. Behind them, a picture of Trinity Bay fills the computer screen — a big field of tall golden grass set against the ocean. A long line of laundry is hung above the grass, the sheets so white and the ocean so big and blue in the background, they look like sailboats, tossed away toward the horizon.

I can see that image on a quilt, no problem.

They're planning a day trip to the area sometime in the next few days, depending on the weather. My mom's really excited because she saw a TV show set in Trinity Bay a few years ago and has wanted to go there ever since.

I don't speak to them and they don't say a word to me. It's like they know I won't want to talk to them after what happened yesterday.

Something about the way they are hunched over the map

reminds me of our first move, to Murdochville. Months before, they had showed me a detailed map of the area, a resource and topographical map in one, they called it. It practically showed every bush and stone. It also made the area look so rich in minerals, I was sure we'd be driving straight into a pile of gold. Even though it wasn't exactly like that, the new house was still exciting. It had a great view of Needle Mountain and at night I could hear the wolves howling from its woods. The first night, even though I was twelve, I crawled into my parents' bed, snuggling smack between them. I could feel them smiling over my head.

The adventure had begun.

My mom catches me staring at the screen. "You know you're welcome to come, Cheryl," she calls across the room. "Today too. We're going up Signal Hill."

"Forget it," I say. "Not after you ruined my friendship with Jim. I don't ever want to go anywhere with you again."

"Cher, you're exaggerating," she says.

"No, I'm not. You saw how he couldn't wait to get away from us, after you accused everyone of dying. Nice job, Dad."

"Cheryl, your mom is right. You are exaggerating. Most people have been very understanding about what I'm doing."

"How would you like it if you found out someone was

studying you to see if you were going to wither up and die?"

"That's not what I'm doing, Cher, and you know it. We've had this conversation many times. You've known for years what the book is about. It's not the first time you heard about it."

"No, but it's the first time it's made my boyfriend hate me."

My parents just look at each other, completely silenced.

"You're so busy checking out how things are dying, you don't even notice when something is growing," I say. "Like my relationship with Jim. Or at least it was. That's probably finished now, thanks to you."

My mom comes over to me. "Oh, Cher. If Jim really cares about you, he won't let your father's book change that."

"Well, like you said, Dad, it's tradition. Jim has his whole family and history to be loyal to. Why should he put me ahead of any of that?"

"I don't see why he'd have to choose, honey," my mom says. "You're not on opposite sides."

"No, we weren't on opposite sides. I was getting along great with his family until you guys showed up and ruined everything."

My mom shrugs and looks at her hands. I wonder how

she'll manage hanging on to that chain today. I remember the swirling water far below, spitting up foam. What if I don't say anything and something bad happens? I know now that it really can, in the blink of an eye.

"Careful on the pathway, Mom. Some parts are hard."

"Thanks, honey," my mom says as she smiles.

***

"Cheryl," Nanny says, when I find her in her spot. "Jim's still in his room. Go on up, put a smile on his face."

"I'll try, Nanny. Where is everyone?" The knitted whale sweater is abandoned on the sofa chair, strands of yarn from all its pieces dangling down to the floor.

"Jim's mom has gone visiting with Joannie. Davy and Candy are out."

I've never been upstairs at Nanny's before. At the top, on a small landing, I find a tiny, cluttered bathroom. A pink frilly cover is wrapped over the toilet lid and a matching pink mat lies on the tiled floor. It's hard to imagine Jim doing his guy stuff in here, like leaning over the tiny sink to shave. He'd have to bend way down to see into the mirror on the medicine cabinet. I check my face in the mirror. I'm still not used to myself without black around my eyes. It doesn't look like me. I take a deep breath and practice looking casual, light-hearted, as though nothing weird happened yesterday. Maybe Jim really was physically sore and that's why he left the table. Maybe it had nothing to do with my father's book. I'll know pretty soon, by the way he treats me.

A second open door leads to what must be Nanny's room. It is cluttered with old-fashioned furniture, like a dresser that sits just inside the door, with a big square mirror and drawers so shallow it looks like they wouldn't hold a sock unless it was sideways. Lots of pictures, most black and white, are stuck to the rim of the mirror. Many are so old they're yellow. I assume some are of a younger Nanny and her husband, standing with their arms around each other, smiling against different watery backdrops. An ancient picture on hard paper shows a young man in a brownish army suit. He has a pencil-thin moustache running over his upper lip. He looks dead serious, his eyes squinting at the camera. Scrawled across the bottom of the picture are the words, "Grand-father July 1, 1916 Beaumont Hamel." Maybe Beaumont was Nanny's grandfather's name. That could mean Hamel is Jim's last name. I can't believe I still don't know it. I should have paid more attention that day in the hospital, but my mind was on other things.

I knock lightly on the only door that's closed, figuring it must be Jim's. "Hey, it's me," I call out.

"Cheryl?"

"What other girl are you expecting?" I say as I open up. Jim's lying on his bed, raised by a stack of pillows. There's a tray with some toast scraps and orange juice on his desk.

"How are you feeling?"

"Sore," Jim says, not looking at me, staring down at his hands. He doesn't say anything else and I just stand there, a few feet away, not knowing what to do. Yesterday, he couldn't wait to hold my hand. Today, I'm practically invisible.

I take a quick look around the room and see basically one thing: rocks. Every square inch of space on Jim's furniture is taken up by specimens. When I step closer to the shelf above Jim's bed, I notice that the rocks are set up like a museum, with pieces of cardboard under each one, identifying places and dates. Table Point Ecological Reserve, July 2001; Dorset Soapstone Quarry, March 2003; Pistolet Bay Provincial Park, 2004; Manuels River, Trilobites, 2002. Then I recognize the two fossils from Fortune Head, 2005, that Jim brought over all those nights ago. Beside them, displayed on a sheet of white marble, is a similar fossil. Its sign says,

Mistaken Point, 2006.

"Did you find all these yourself?" I ask.

"Most of 'em. Not all."

"Very impressive," I say. "I like that one." I point to one at random, moving closer.

"I'd be in deep crap if anyone found out about that one."

"Really? Why?"

"Because it's extremely rare. And you're not allowed to take fossils out of Mistaken Point," Jim says flatly, the usual edge to his voice when he talks about rocks missing.

"Well, they wouldn't exactly throw you in jail for taking a rock, would they?"

"It's not a rock, Cheryl, it's a fossil of a multicellular organism. And yeah, maybe they would." Jim finally looks up at me. His eyes are all dark, their yellow sparkle gone. This isn't exactly going the way I'd hoped. I think if I'd been standing this close to his bed a few days ago, he'd have pulled me onto it by now and we'd be doing a lot more than talking. "People come from all over the world to study there. You even have to take your shoes off out on the big rocks, so you won't scratch the fossils."

"Really? That's cool."

"Yeah, Mr. Wells said we had to be as light on our feet

as fairies, or ghosts. I guess that would suit your father's view, right?"

"Jim ... I, I'm really sorry about that. It's not what it sounds like. We did the same thing in every other place we lived. He just studies how big changes affect people's lives."

"And then he turns us into a chapter?"

"Yeah."

"But he doesn't know us."

"I know, but that's why he wants to live here, to get to know you. He interviews a lot of people and – "

"But he can't know what it's like just by interviewing. You got to live it," Jim says.

"I know. I think it's dumb too. What can I say?"

"And you don't even want to be here at all?"

"I didn't, before, no."

"So your father's here studying us, like a bunch of lab rats, and you don't want to get to know us 'cause you think we're a bunch of backwards – "

"That's not true. That's not what I think of you. Okay, maybe just a little – before I got here – I did. But not now. Honest. I think you're pretty cool."

"Oh well, I am so glad, Cheryl, that we are living up to your high standards." Jim sounds nasty, in a way I've never heard before. I wasn't expecting this. Now I don't know what to say, so I just keep glancing around. Two whole bookcases near the door are also filled with rocks.

"It's not just your father," Jim says finally, in a softer voice.

"What do you mean?"

"It's not just your dad that has me feeling crooked. I got this phone call this morning – "

"From?" I wonder if it was his dad, the only family member he hasn't spoken to since his accident. He doesn't answer. He just keeps concentrating on his fists that are clutching his blanket.

"Jim?"

Jim winces, as though the mere memory of the call has twigged his ribs. After a moment of silence, he says, "It was Mr. Wells, calling to say the trip to Horton was on. But of course, I'm too busted up to go."

"You mean that rock place?"

"Yeah, 'that rock place.' I know it probably doesn't sound like much to you, but it was a lot to me."

"No, I didn't mean ..." Now I don't know what to say. I didn't mean it was nothing. It just took me by surprise. It seems to me the last thing Jim needs is more rocks. Even the two bookcases beside the door are full of them, top to bottom.

"My father would say the same thing. He never did understand my interest in rocks," Jim continues. "And he never bothered coming home either, or even calling, you might of noticed. Having too much fun up in the oil sands, I guess, with his new girlfriend."

So that explains why no one has mentioned Jim's father, except Nanny, just that once, turning everyone stiff and silent.

"Sorry, I didn't know."

"Yeah, well, it's not the type of thing you make announcements about, right?"

I have absolutely no idea how to respond, so I just stand there, looking around, avoiding Jim's eyes.

"Well, maybe you can go next year," I say cheerfully. "If they go back."

"It's not all so easy for me, you know. My family doesn't have loads of money, you can see that. This trip was a one-off. Besides, they won't be going back next year. It might have led to something for me. Helped me get a scholarship maybe, make some contacts. Those are things I'm really going to need. Maybe you just don't get it."

Jim closes his eyes and clenches his mouth tightly. I get the feeling that if he could roll over easily, he'd turn away from me altogether.

"Jim?"

"I've got nothing more to say right now."

"I guess I should go then," I say. "I'll let you get some rest." I wait for Jim to open his eyes and ask me to stay, but he doesn't, so I turn to leave. Near the door, I notice a line of diplomas hanging on the wall. I don't have time to read them closely because I know Jim wants me to go, but I can see they are prizes for various science things: fairs and top marks in the class. Sprawled across the bottom of each is Jim's full name: James Parsons. I guess I got that wrong too – he isn't a Hamel. I close the door softly behind me, leaving him alone in his rock museum.

Downstairs, Nanny asks, "How was he?"

"Okay, I guess, but I think he wants to be alone for a while." I don't say anything about the phone call from Mr. Wells, in case Jim doesn't want anyone to know.

"And your mother?" Nanny asks next. "I seen her hands outside this morning, when I was watering the flowers. They looked some sore. There's an old Newfoundland cure for the rheumatism," she says. Then she pauses, as though waiting for me to show a sign of curiosity.

"What is it?"

"Carry a potato in your pocket," she says. A potato? Could she be joking? Or really losing it? But then I see that she's smiling, so I smile too. Besides, maybe it's not so crazy. Nothing else seems to help. Maybe something simple like a potato would do the trick.

"I'll let her know," I say.

***

A potato would come in handy just about now. My mom's hands are really bad. She's got them wrapped in hand towels that my dad put in the dryer for five minutes. Two more are in the dryer now, like he's setting up a rotation system – my dad's homemade remedy.

"It was so misty," he tells me. "It was like walking through water. We should've brought a snorkel."

I wait for my mom to say something about how Signal Hill was beautiful anyway. I mean, you can make mist out of grey fuzzy cotton on a quilt, with little glimpses of ocean peeking through. But she is unusually quiet.

"I'll make some tea," I say. It's either that or flee to my room, but for some reason, I don't want to be alone just now, not after Jim shut me out like that.

My mom nods a thank you, her damp reddish hair clinging to her forehead.

When the mug of hot tea is between her fingers, my mom smiles for the first time since she and my father came through the door half an hour ago.

"You were right, Cheryl. Some parts of that walk are pretty challenging, especially when it's wet," she says.

"Was the chain slippery?" I ask. If it was, I don't see how she could have gripped it. I have a vivid memory of Jim goofing around, doing his scarecrow from the Wizard of Oz imitation. That would've seriously freaked my mom out.

"We don't know, honey. We didn't make it that far. It was too hard and my hands were too sore. You need to grip every now and then, especially in the rain. I just couldn't do it."

That explains why my mom isn't telling me what she saw, the colours and shapes of the boulders and clumps of sea grass. My mom never misses these things, but it's like all her energy and focus is centered on the mug of tea, as if she's trying to add to the warmth that is soothing her swollen fingers. It's pretty clear that she won't be quilting anytime soon. It strikes me that I actually miss watching her quilt. In the past, our living rooms were always covered in colourful shapes, just waiting to be stitched together.

That's definitely not going to happen here.

"That's too bad, Mom."

"Don't worry, Ellen. We'll try it again, on a better day next time. Today was just too risky."

My mom looks down. She usually loves risk, but I guess that has changed too.

CHAPTER 11
to open water

I stay away from Jim's for the next few days, simply because I wouldn't know what to say to him. I keep seeing him turn away from me, like he wanted to shut me out. Maybe he needs some time alone, to get over feeling bad about Horton. Or, to get over the way I made him feel stupid about it.

My parents don't do any sightseeing either, because my mom's hands are too sore. She can't get another cortisone shot so soon, so she just takes a lot of painkillers and spends most of the day in bed.

Heavy rain beats down all morning on Thursday, a week to the day that Jim jumped into the ocean. It is constant and steady, barely altering its rhythm. The dark wood stain on my bedroom floor grows blacker from the continual drip trickling down from the window ledge. We keep every light in the house shining, even though my mom says that's an environmental faux pas, just to remind ourselves that it is actually daytime.

My dad has gone up to his new office again. He didn't dare ask me to come, but he also doesn't want my mom home alone, in case she needs something she can't get herself.

I bring her several cups of tea. Each time I approach her, I expect her to tell me that we're definitely leaving, but I guess she's still not decided, in spite of everything. I know my mom. She won't speak until she's sure. She never waffles and she's always steadfast. Through all our moves, she's never complained once, except to occasionally point out that she missed having a garden of her own. There wasn't much point planting bulbs in the fall if you were going to be leaving pretty soon after spring. In Osoyoos, where spring comes early, she planted large pots of tulips on our apartment balcony. But even those she had to leave behind when we headed for Saskatchewan. She wasn't upset though. She said the flowers would be her legacy to the new people. Who could object to having that great splash of red and yellow to look at?

At lunch, when I bring my mom a bowl of hot soup, I find her rifling through a box of her quilting supplies. Or trying to. I can tell the motion is hurting her hands. I'm thinking of asking if she wants some help when she shuts the box and gets back into bed, thanking me for the soup.

***

Davy leaves late that afternoon. I watch him from my bedroom window, swinging his bulging duffle bag onto the sidewalk. Joannie tries to lift it, then gives up and drags it toward Nanny's car. Davy says goodbye to Candy, play-punching her on the cheek, the same as when he said hello. She looks like she wants to follow him and fly away to a new life, if only her mother weren't holding her back.

Then Davy picks up Nanny, squeezing her tightly.

Jim is nowhere in sight. He must still be holed up in his room, like some kind of burrowing animal. If he were there, I might go down and test the waters, but there's not much point if he isn't. It's not like Davy and I ever bonded. And he seemed as thrilled about my father's book as Jim did. I'm better off up here.

"You'll miss your flight, son," his mom calls from the car. I guess she's saving her goodbyes for the airport, when she can have Davy to herself.

Davy turns and gives everyone a final wave with his big hand, sweeping it through the air like the windshield wiper of an eighteen-wheeler.

Nanny stands on the sidewalk waving as the car pulls

away. She stays like that long after the car has vanished, until Candy comes outside. "For god's sake, Nanny, you're waving at nothing. They turned the corner an hour ago." That seems to bring Nanny back to life, because she turns and goes in.

I lie on my bed and look around at my room. My eyes fix on my Japanese fans, at the silent painted women. My mom once told me they are *geishas*, whose role is to make men happy, however they can. All their lives they train to learn how to please men, to make them feel like the centre of the universe. That's really pathetic. I can't see myself ever wanting to be that way, all silent and submissive, swallowing my opinions. My mom's not that way, but she does know how to support my father and make him feel important. I could've done a better job of that with Jim. I guess I didn't realize just how much going to Horton meant to him. I thought it was just a little rock-hunting trip, but it was more than that. I just ended up making him feel like his rocks weren't important. I guess it was sort of like saying his life wasn't that important.

After supper, when the rain has finally stopped, Joannie comes over with Boss and asks me to walk with them. We've done it a couple of times since the day I went over to Jim's, the day I screwed everything up. Each time, she fills me in on Jim. Then she tries to talk me into coming over the next day.

"I kept figuring you were gonna show up today, Cheryl," Joannie says, as we head down Nunnery Hill.

"Yeah, well, I had to look after my mom again, so I couldn't," I respond, glad for the excuse. If Jim is encouraging his little sister to invite me, she doesn't let on.

Boss keeps tugging and pulling, leading us down to the bottom of the hill. It's like the ocean is drawing her in, until we are smack up against the wooden posts of the pier along the harbour. The water is pitch-black, rolling in against the boats, making them rock. The smell of fish wafts around us on a pretty strong breeze. We tie Boss up to one of the posts and sit on a block of wet wood between two fishing vessels, our feet dangling over the edge.

I take a quick look around the pier, like I do every time, to see if the goon squad is in sight. Luckily, it's all clear.

"So, how was Jim today?" I ask finally. "Did he come out of his room?"

"Nope. Davy had to go up to his room to say goodbye to him. Nobody knows what they talked about, but Davy was up there for almost an hour. Davy said the reason Jim is sulking has something to do with rocks, because he can't go fossil-hunting this summer. Davy said he blasts through rock all the time and if Jim wants, he can send him home a whole trunk full."

"Did Jim actually laugh?"

Joannie shrugs. She is kicking her feet high above the water, making her whole body swing.

"Careful, Joannie. You don't want to end up in the water."

"If Jim were here he could save me."

"Yeah, but he's not here. I am. And I couldn't pull you out, so calm down."

Joannie moves closer and leans her head against me. Out in the water, something splashes, too dark for us to see.

"Might be a whale," says Joannie after the sound has died.

"How can you tell?"

"By the sound. Same sound they make out at Mary's Hill."

"But a whale wouldn't be in the harbour, would it?"

"It might be trapped," says Joannie.

We listen for a while, waiting for another big splash, but nothing happens.

"Maybe it found its way out again," says Joannie. "They use sound, to find their way. Their noise bounces off the edges and tells them where they are. Jim told me that."

"Cool. I'll have to try that sometime if I'm ever lost."

Joannie laughs. The water splashes again, further out

toward the Narrows. "It's probably right about there by now," she says, pointing out toward the open water. The dark water and dusky sky blend together so perfectly it's like the world has turned upside down. Only the occasional star that manages to glitter through the clouds tells us where up is.

"You mean near the Narrows?" I ask.

"The what?"

"Narrows. Didn't you know that's what the opening to the harbour is called?"

Joannie shakes her head, her legs still swinging, hitting the wooden boards so hard I imagine her foot bones cracking. Then, suddenly she turns completely still and sighs heavily, taking in a deep breath.

"We're leaving tomorrow," she blurts out. "My mom just told us. Candy's throwing a fit and I don't wanna go either, but Mom says we been here a week and we can't overstay our welcome."

"Oh, wow, that's a surprise." Somehow, I hadn't even thought about Joannie leaving. It seems like she's always been here, she's so much a part of things. I remember how connected I felt at Nanny's when we had Jim's homecoming meal, eating the seal sausage. It made me feel part of something bigger than myself. Now, it's like everything is coming apart.

"What about Jim? Is he going too?"

"He promised he would, but now he says he can't. It's too close to school starting and everything."

I'm surprised by how relieved that makes me feel.

"Has he shown you his rocks yet?"

At that question, Joannie hangs her head. Clearly, he hasn't. Next thing I know, Joannie is crying.

"What's wrong, Joannie? Is it because you're leaving?" She shakes her head fiercely.

"He said his rocks were stupid, but I don't think they are."

"Neither does he, Joannie."

"Why would he say that then?"

"It was a phone call that upset him, not you."

"Mom was so mad after Dad called once, she ripped up one of her sweaters."

"She did?"

"Yeah. And she couldn't put it back together. Mom says if just one stitch is broken or dropped, the whole sweater is ruined."

I think of those mice again, the ones I unearthed back in Murdochville. I ran to my mother right away, without any hesitation. I wanted her to help me figure out what to do with them. They were like eight little wiggling pink balls, with slits for eyes.

If my mother were here now, I might turn to her the same way and ask her what I should do for Joannie.

"Come on, we better get back," I say. "Your mom will be worried."

We're walking toward the far end of the pier when I see one of the girls from the goon squad, the look-alike one. I brace myself. The last thing Joannie needs to hear right now is someone make fun of Jim, her all-time hero. Only he hasn't been too heroic with her lately. Otherwise, he'd have shown her his rocks, in spite of Horton.

I automatically look around for the rest of her gang, my arms tightening around Joannie, but this girl seems to be alone.

"Hey, you're Jim's friend," she says, coming over. I wait for her to say something nasty or tough, but she doesn't. For once, that sneering look is gone from her face.

"You know Jim?" Joannie says. I hold my breath.

"It's okay, Joannie. Never mind," I say, steering her away.

"He's my brother," Joannie blurts out.

"Hey, it was pretty cool – what he did. I mean, the rescue and all that."

I don't know why she's saying this. I'm afraid she's just setting up for some vicious punch line, like the one I got the other day. But when I look back at her she's smiling, like she's going out of her way to be nice to Joannie.

"Yeah, well, I better get her back," I say. "See ya."

She nods and heads off, probably to meet her clan. Which is too bad. It's like she was a completely different person alone, away from them. She kind of seemed like someone I might get along with, if I had the chance.

***

My parents join me outside the next day to say goodbye to Joannie and her family. It's a warm, bright summer's day, one of the nicest since we got here, which doesn't seem fair since everyone looks so miserable. My dad helps carry bags to the taxi and lift them into the trunk. He keeps saying how bad he feels that they called a cab. If he'd known, he would have driven them. I watch to see how Jim's mom will react. If she is sore at him, she doesn't let on. Maybe, in the end, she'd be the last person to argue that something in her life hasn't died, or at least changed. She never did get to see all her kids together before going home.

My mom and Jim's mom hug each other tightly. When they pull apart they look deeply into each other's eyes and nod, as if they are sharing a secret. I don't really get it, but I think it must have something to do with the fact that they're both mothers. It's like my mother can understand all the worrying Jim's mother has done lately, even though she's never almost lost a kid to the ocean.

Jim's mom gives me a warm goodbye too, drawing me close and tapping my back. "Just a little something," she says, pulling a plastic bag out of her handbag and handing it to me. "For being a good friend to Jim."

Inside, I find the whale sweater. I don't know what to say. It's the first gift I've gotten from anyone outside my family in years. I thank her and she surprises me by hugging me again. "Whales are beautiful things," she whispers in my ear.

I turn to Jim. He is here too, standing up pretty straight, leaning against the side of the house. He watches me put the sweater on, and I look for some kind of reaction on his face, some sign that he's feeling better. But there's nothing – his face is pretty blank, as blank as it was when I last saw him. I'm thinking of going over to him when he vanishes inside his mother's arms. She holds on to him for a long time, long after Candy is already sitting in the cab, the headphones to her MP3 plugged into her ears. She probably can't hear Jim say "don't worry" over and over again.

His mom's eyes are red when she pulls away and Jim barely looks up. Joannie, who has been surprisingly quiet so far, runs up to me and wraps her arms around my waist. She buries her head against my belly so hard I think she'll leave an imprint in my skin, even through the thick wool sweater.

"Promise you'll come visit me sometime, Cheryl," she says.

I've never promised anyone such a thing before. I've never had a mushy goodbye. What if I can't keep the promise, on account of us leaving or of Jim never speaking to me again? But when I look down at Joannie and see how eagerly she is waiting for the words, I know I can't let her down.

"I promise, Joannie, but I don't know when, okay?" Joannie squeezes my hand, sending a warm feeling through me. I wonder if the past few years would have been easier if I'd had a younger sister to look out for. I know my mom wanted to have more kids. Instead, she ended up with just me and I'm probably not the daughter she was hoping for. I feel a little stab thinking that her rheumatism might have something to do with me, and the way I am. As if all the affection she hasn't been able to share for the last couple of years has filled her up from the inside, swelling her joints.

Then Joannie lets go and runs over to throw her arms around Jim. I watch carefully to see if his face registers pain when she squeezes his ribs. It doesn't, but when she pulls away and heads for the taxi, Jim's unshaven face falls again, like his chin is being pulled to the ground.

Without looking up, he turns and walks into the house. Everyone, except for Nanny, is now in the taxi. My parents have gone inside. I feel like a total idiot all of a sudden, standing out there in the summer heat with a whale sweater on.

I thought Jim would speak to me at least.

Before I know it, I'm following him inside. He's at the bottom of the stairs, starting to climb, when I catch up to him.

"Jim?" He turns slowly.

"Yeah?"

"Why are you ignoring me?"

"I'm not."

"Well what do you call it?"

"Look, I've got a lot on my mind right now, you know?"

"Yeah, I know. Like your trip to Horton and stuff. I know, you told me, remember?"

"Yeah and I remember that you didn't seem to care that much."

"That's not true."

"Yes it is. Look, I know how it is. You may think you care, but you'll never really be able to understand, 'cause of how you live and everything."

"How I live?"

"Yeah, you know. Travelling around the whole country, moving from place to place so easily, and it's all like nothing for you. It probably seems dumb to you, that someone could be bummed out about missing a trip to a place called Horton. You know, like you said, *that rock place*."

"I didn't mean it like that."

"You didn't mean it, but it comes out to the same thing," Jim says. "I'm just a stupid rock geek, sulking over missing out on a little trip to Nova Scotia. What's the big deal, right? You just can't understand someone who lives like me, kind of scared that I might not be able to get where I want to go, to become what I want to become. And anyways, it just all fits in so perfectly with your dad's research, doesn't it?"

"What do you mean?"

"The way I can't even manage a trip to find rocks. Like what else can happen to hold me back? Your dad couldn't have picked a more perfect person to live beside."

"Yeah, and neither could you. I'm not exactly little Miss

Sunshine, or haven't you noticed?"

"It doesn't matter, Cheryl. You're just mad 'cause you're missing an underground shopping mall. I'm missing way more than that."

That blow whacks me in the chest. It's way more than that that I'm missing. I thought Jim understood. I thought we understood each other. We just stand there, his right foot frozen on the bottom step, his back half-turned away from me. The only thing that shatters the silence is the sound of Nanny shuffling down the hall. I turn and sweep past her, but she doesn't even see me. She is looking down at her feet, concentrating on the sound they're making, as if to distract herself from the fact that everyone is now gone.

***

None of us goes anywhere for the rest of the day. My dad spends hours on the computer, researching fishing villages affected by the cod moratorium. The list is pretty long so he's figuring out which towns he can visit and which ones he'll have to access in other ways, like via the Internet. My mom's wrapped in a blanket on the sofa behind him, calling out her opinions. I've just come down to get some more food to take upstairs, but I can hear them loud and clear.

"The government has given the university some grant money to boost access to computers in some of the outports," I hear my dad say. "Anthropology wasn't supposed to be that involved in the project, but my research might be changing that."

"That's terrific, honey," my mom says.

"Yeah, it is. It'll mean more people in remote areas will be online. That'll really benefit those communities."

This conversation feels staged to me, as though they rehearsed it and are now delivering some Academy Award-winning performance, carefully calculated to make my father's research look wonderful. Like he's doing it for Newfoundland and not for himself. I should tell him that Jim's family is already online, so they don't need his help. But then he might want to target them again, in case he hasn't gotten enough out of them.

"Most of the computers will be set up in town libraries, but in towns where they don't have libraries, they're putting them in wherever they can, even local stores," he continues. I wonder if the store Jim described, the one that sells underwear and sausages, will get one. And if they do, will my father be able to spy on that town, gathering information from local people.

I'm wearing the whale sweater Jim's mom made me. I'm still amazed by the way she could whip up a sweater exactly my size just by laying eyes on me a couple of times. She's like my mom that way, I guess. They both see things really deeply.

Every time I look down at the whale fins I hear Jim's mom say that I've been such a good friend to Jim, but I don't know if that's true. I've been going over and over what he said to me, trying to figure out if he was right. I hear him snap at me about how I've been all over the country, and how it all meant nothing to me. He made me sound like some kind of spoiled brat.

The words gnaw at me, like they've got teeth.

Then I remember the other thing Jim's mom said to me, about whales being beautiful. It's kind of like she was sending me a message. It's true that everywhere we went, Jim looked for whales. On Signal Hill he talked about seeing whales with his brothers from Mary's Hill back home. The way he kept staring out at the water as he talked, it was like he didn't want the memory of those times to end.

I trace the whale fins on my sweater, feeling the bumpy ridges of the thickly knit stitches. I think about the way if one stitch is cut the whole sweater is ruined.

If my life were a piece of knitting, it would still be in one piece. The moving around would just be big loops, but not a cut. Jim's life, on the other hand, has been cut. First, by his father, going off for work and then going off his family altogether, practically forgetting them except for his monthly payments. And now by missing his trip to Horton. Like he said, that could've been the first link in a chain to get him into a geology program. That means so much to him. I get that now, but I should have been able to see it more clearly before. I should've known how much fossils mean to him. Even an idiot could figure that out, just by standing in his room.

I close my eyes and try to imagine how Jim must feel when he actually finds a rare and special fossil. I can see him holding it in his hand and letting the find sink in, connecting with it and, through it, all of history. There'd be yellow sparkles of excitement in his hazel eyes and a mischievous grin on his face, playing the moment out for as long as he could.

He said I'd never get it and maybe he's right. Nothing I've ever done has given me that feeling.

It occurs to me that I've probably stepped over hundreds of amazing fossils. The deserts of Osoyoos are filled with geological treasures. And Murdochville too. After all, that whole area is known for its mines.

I just never looked close enough to see. I was too busy wanting to be elsewhere.

***

The whale is slicing through the water of the harbour, way down deep. The waves of its incredible voice weave through the thick, salty water. They are like flares that hit the ocean floor then bounce back up again, in a spiral of colour, to send the whale a message.

Even after I tear open my eyes, I see the flashes, almost like they are bouncing off my walls, giant sparks of purple and blue.

The whole room is humming and vibrating, as though a message is etched in the air, as clear as the lines on the fossils Jim brought over. I couldn't see the scratches, but I could feel them so clearly that finally I did see them. After a while, I could even imagine the little animals pressing down between the rocks, rustling leaves on their way.

Now, even though it's dark, I close my eyes to try to feel the message the same way.

It has to do with whales. Everything is pointing in their direction.

Maybe I have to help Jim see some whales. Maybe that would make up for Horton and show him that I really do care. Maybe that's what his mom was trying to tell me.

I tiptoe downstairs and log on to Google, Advanced Search, and punch in "whales Newfoundland." 895,000 sites pop up. When I narrow my search to "St. John's Newfoundland whales" only 540 appear. A couple of the tourist sites and a few of the personal testimonials keep referring to a place called St. Vincent's Beach. I go to MapQuest and see that it's located on the Avalon Peninsula, south of St. John's, probably about an hour or so away, judging by the mileage key. The sites all recommend that you get there either early in the morning or in the evening, just like the man told us at Middle Cove, if you want to see whales.

Which I do. In fact, at this precise moment I want to see whales more than I've ever wanted anything, maybe even more than I've wanted to go home. Going home doesn't even seem that important now. It's like some far away wish, a faint one that is no longer connected to me. Like it's still up there on that shaky plane, light as a whisper, high above the icebergs.

CHAPTER 12
on the edge of time

The sky is still grey, with only the tiniest specks of light poking through the clouds. I haven't been up before the sun since I had to catch that seven o'clock school bus in Saskatchewan.

Downstairs, I slap together some peanut butter sandwiches, then throw them and some apples, juice, and chips into a bag. I leave the note I prepared last night against the kettle — that way my parents are sure to see it.

As I get dressed, I start having doubts about my plan. Jim couldn't even look me in the eye yesterday — it was as if he really didn't want me anywhere near him. If he's in the same mood today, I'll have to persist. And I'll pretty much have to ignore the way it makes me feel, like there's big crack in my chest. Plus, I'm not even sure Jim will be able to drive. If he can't, I'll just have to do it. I know how, even though I don't have a license. I taught myself, out of boredom, in

Saskatchewan. I would just drive round and round our farm house on the deserted country roads. All the kids did it, some were driving tractors by the age of twelve, so my parents didn't mind.

I close the front door super quietly and step outside. The air is crisp and fresh. Early birds caw in the distance. I open Nanny's door as quietly as I can and step inside. The house is still, just as I expected. I tape Nanny's note onto the TV screen, then tiptoe up to Jim's room. His jaw falls open when he sees me.

"What the hell – "

"Good morning to you too," I say. "Can you get dressed quickly? I want to take you somewhere." I try to sound as cheerful as possible, like yesterday never happened.

"Take me somewhere? Where? I can barely walk."

"I'll help you, no problem. Besides, I came with you to Signal Hill and to Cape Spear. Now it's your turn to follow me." I stand there with my arms folded across my chest, letting him know I won't budge until he agrees. Eventually, Jim swings his legs over the edge of his bed. I can tell by his face that the motion still hurts. He isn't wearing a shirt, and a white bandage is wrapped around his rib cage. I can see the muscles of his chest straining below it.

"Here, I'll help you get this on." I grab a sweatshirt hanging on a hook behind his door, then pull it over his head and work his arms into the sleeves. Jim barely has to move. He's already in sweatpants so I just tell him to wear those. I bend down and pull some socks over his feet, then help him into a pair of running shoes. I think about how the old Jim would've cracked some joke about me dressing him.

"We'll need Nanny's car," I say. "Do you think she'll mind?"

"She might not mind, but I don't know if I can drive."

"Well, if you can't, I will." I help Jim down the stairs and pick up the picnic bag that I left in the porch. Boss comes running out of the kitchen, whimpering and jumping.

"Poor Boss is all confused," Jim says.

"Let's bring her," I say, grabbing the leash off the hook and attaching it to her collar. She's spinning with excitement.

I help Jim into the driver's seat, settle Boss in the back, then climb into the passenger seat. "Okay, we need to get onto highway 10 south," I say, looking at the piece of paper that I wrote the directions on.

"You mean toward Trepassey?"

"If you say so." I don't want to tell Jim exactly where we're going, it would ruin the surprise. Steering doesn't seem too hard, until he has to make a sharp turn. The leaning motion digs into his ribs, but he breathes through it.

"Are you okay?" I ask.

"I'll survive. I'm tough, remember?"

I hold my breath, hoping he won't crack a joke about my dad's book, but he doesn't.

We drive in silence for a long time. It's a bit lighter out now, with the sun starting to burn away the clouds, casting a muted light on the deserted landscape. I like the feeling of being alone out here, while everyone and everything is still sleeping. It's like we own the whole world, even if Jim still hasn't come round. We pass towns with strange names, like Bay Bulls, Burnt Cove and Aquaforte. Signs point out places called Black Head, Bald Head, and Shingle Head.

"People had a thing for body parts in the early days," Jim says.

"So I see," I answer, relief that Jim's finally a bit more talkative flooding through me.

"Better than noses. There's a Jerry's Nose on the island. And lots of arms, like Joe Batt's."

"Could be worse," I say. "I mean, they could've used other body parts, like butts and armpits, you know?"

Jim smiles but doesn't respond. A while later, I say,

"Hey, there's Mistaken Point," pointing to the road sign. "Isn't that's where you snatched your illegal fossils from?"

"Yeah."

"You mean if I hang my head out the window and yell I could have the RCMP after us?"

"Maybe." Jim's head turns to follow the sign as it disappears behind us, but he isn't laughing. He's probably thinking of all the fossil activity going on out there without him, similar to what his classmates will be doing at Horton Bluffs.

As we drive farther south, the landscape changes, becoming much more treeless and barren. Large round stones dot the gold-coloured ground, looking as though they have sprung up, randomly, from the earth. We drive for ages without passing any houses, until we near the town of Trepassy. I'm kind of relieved to see the ocean again, because it reminds me of why we are here.

"Maybe we'll see caribou," Jim says. "They like the bogs here. Sometimes you see whole herds of them. Block the road if they're crossing over."

"Wow. I don't even know what a caribou looks like."

"A cross between a deer and a moose," Jim says matter-of-factly. I wait for him to tease me about my urban ignorance, but he doesn't. "How much farther?" he asks.

"I don't know but I think it's soon." We've been on the road for over an hour already. St. Vincent's is obviously farther than I expected. What if Jim's in really bad pain and just doesn't want to tell me?

"I want you to stop when we come to a town called St. Stephens," I say, trying to sound excited. Jim just looks at me but doesn't say anything. Before long, he's pulling off to the side of the road.

"Okay, now we have to switch places. I'll drive the rest of the way." I hope he doesn't ask me if I have a license, because I don't want him to try to stop me from taking the wheel, if he cares. I run around to the other side of the car and help Jim out. I can tell that it really hurts him to push up against the seat and lift his weight. I help him walk around the car and into the passenger seat. Finally, I take out one of my crazy scarves, a purple and pink plaid one, with green caterpillars jumping around the stripes, and tie it around his eyes. "I don't want you to see where we're going."

Jim doesn't argue. He just sits still while I blindfold him.

I haven't actually driven on a highway before and I'm kind of nervous. The only good thing is that it's still pretty early and there isn't much traffic on the road. It's not exactly a superhighway anyway, like the 401 outside Toronto. For a split second, I picture myself emailing Janna and telling her about this little adventure when I get back. She'd probably think that I had seriously lost it. She might also think it sounded boring – driving around looking for whales, compared to what she and Stephan do.

"Watch out for moose," Jim says, seriously, without any sarcasm in his voice.

"Okay, thanks."

That didn't exactly put me at ease.

***

St. Vincent's Beach, according to the sign, is the low plateau of sand and rock stretching along the shore to our left. I turn into the parking lot, which is completely deserted, making me wonder whether those web sites were just lying, or pumping up the truth for the sake of tourism. If this is such a whale hot spot, wouldn't it be teeming with people?

I help Jim out of the car once more. His whole face contracts with the pushing-up motion. Boss jumps out of the car before I can grab the leash and runs off, leaping toward the water.

"Okay, put your arm over my shoulder and I'll help you walk." We follow Boss's path. Jim winces whenever he has to shift his weight on the loose stones. Once again, I wonder if I was nuts to do this. What if he cracks another rib while we're here?

"Not much farther to go," I say to encourage him. "Just – " I catch my breath. Out in the water a huge grey whale jumps up, in the shape of an arc. Its splash creates a huge boom over the water. Beyond it two more emerge like twin images of the first.

"What is it?" Jim asks, showing the first sign of excitement all morning. I pull him just a bit farther along, until we are standing at the top of a tall wall of dark wet rocks. The ocean is at our feet, on the other side of the mound. As far as I can tell, there is no shallow edge. The deep dark water comes right up to the rock wall.

I unknot the scarf from around Jim's head and pull. It's as though the whales were waiting for us to get in place before beginning their show. They are now jumping and spiraling, pirouetting even on the surface of the water, their huge mouths snapping at the seagulls that swoop down to tease them. The water roars as the whales split it open, then booms again when they dive back down, no more than twenty feet away. It's as though I could reach out and scratch their slick skin, they're that close.

I look at Jim, at the side of his face darkened by the bruise. A cloud seems to lift and his face breaks into a wide smile.

"This is totally amazing. Where are we?"

"St. Vincent's Beach," I say.

"I've heard of this place, but I've never seen it. How did you ..." Jim takes my hand. A whale jumps and the spray washes over us. Boss is running along the ridge, leaping as though she's trying to imitate the whales.

"I just Googled it," I say.

"You're too much," Jim says. Two whales jump and open their enormous mouths, as though they're talking to us. The spray of mist that surrounds us is a curtain that blocks out the rest of the world. It's just me and Jim and the whales. Before long, we are covered in water. And then we are standing close together, closer even than we were in that bunker.

Neither of us speaks for a long time. We just watch the whales slicing through the water, right at our feet.

"Aren't they awesome?" I call to Jim.

"Yeah, more than awesome," he says. There are so many

whales jumping now that we can hardly hear each other speak. The air is vibrating with their energy.

Jim puts his arms around me and pulls me against him. I squeeze back, my arms around his waist.

"Sorry. I forgot about your ribs," I say.

"So did I. I've forgotten about everything right now, even Horton. The sight of those whales breaching knocked it right out of my head."

"I am really sorry about your trip."

"I know. Look, about yesterday, I – "

"Forget it," I say.

We stand like that, watching the whales, breathing in the salty air, listening to the thunder of the water. I have no idea how much time has passed because everything is happening in some other time – whale time.

The sun is getting stronger in the sky, beyond the water, lighting up the whale's stage more and more every minute. It's like the whole world is just beginning, and Jim and I are standing right on the edge of time.

Then suddenly, from far off, the sound of car doors slamming cuts through the air. Our moment is about to be shattered.

"We're being invaded," I say, pointing at the parking lot.

"Damn tourists!" Jim says. "What pains in the ass."

"Is that what you think I am?"

"What? A pain in the ass?"

"No, a tourist."

"Well, aren't you? If you don't live here, you're a tourist, right? And you keep saying you don't want to live here."

I don't answer. I just nestle my head into the hollow of Jim's neck. When he nuzzles the top of my head with his chin, I feel my knees go weak. I tighten my grip.

I can hear the tourists now, coming closer. I bet they'll scare the whales off, with cameras or something. I don't want them cutting into this space. This perfect space.

I look up at Jim. He bends down and kisses me. His lips are soft and salty. Our tongues move together, like the whales. The kiss lasts forever, until the tourists start squealing and gasping at the whales. It's like we're being blasted apart again, just like in the bunker.

Jim rolls his eyes. "Let's get out of here," he says smiling.

I help Jim down from the hill and we walk, hand in hand, back up the beach to the car. I turn and call out to Boss every now and then to make sure she's following. She's completely soaked, but she looks incredibly happy.

Jim takes the driver's seat gingerly, but he doesn't start the car. He takes my hand instead. "You are full of surprises, Cheryl from the city."

"I wanted to do something to make up for Horton," I say. "I know it's not the same, but – "

"It was almost as good – pretty close, actually."

"Besides, you were right."

"About what?"

"Whales. They make everything perfect."

***

When we pull up to the curb, Nanny and my mother are out on the sidewalk talking. They've got a watering can between them and are taking turns using it for the flower boxes on the front windows. Nanny keeps looking down at my mother's hands. My mother seems to be talking for quite a long time, turning her hands over and back again. Nanny shakes her head as if she's feeling sorry about whatever my mother's saying.

"See you later," I say to Jim. I actually reach up and plant a kiss on his cheek, even though we're being watched. The sky doesn't fall.

"Yeah, I hope so."

I say hello to my mom and Nanny quickly, pretending I really have to go to the bathroom, to avoid being part of their conversation. Jim does the same, even though Nanny is starting to fuss over him and ask him questions.

I hear him say "I'll tell you later," as I step inside. I expect my mom to follow, but she doesn't. She continues picking at the flowers, snapping off the dead ones.

Inside, my father springs out of his kitchen chair when he sees me.

"You could have told us what you were doing, Cheryl. We never just vanish without telling you where we are," my father says. I haven't seen him this mad in a long time.

"But I left you a note," I say, pointing to it on the table.

"But it was so vague. 'Gone to see some whales.' What were we supposed to think?" he continues. "We wake up and you're gone. Then Nanny is at the door asking if we know where Jim is. And her car is gone."

I don't really know what to say. I could tell him about the whales at St. Vincent's and how they cheered Jim up, but it would destroy the magic, talking about the whales in ordinary words, to my father.

"I mean, the last time you two took off Jim landed in the

hospital. It's not exactly reassuring."

"He was saving someone's life, Dad, not diving off the rocks for fun."

"I know, Cheryl, but ... you just don't get it, do you?" He pulls out the chair beside me and sits down. "We brought you here and it's our job to make sure you're safe. How do you think it makes us feel to wake up and find you vanished? Your mother has been going out of her mind." I wonder if that's why she barely spoke to me out there. She was afraid of what she would say. Easier to take it out on the flowers, I guess.

Then my father does something that floors me. He takes my hand and holds it the same tender way he holds my mother's hand when she's hurting. My first instinct is to pull it back, but I don't. My father hasn't held my hand like this since I was a kid.

"I know the past few years haven't been easy for you. But we never did anything on purpose to hurt you. We actually thought it would be a great experience, seeing the country, living in so many places. You have to stop punishing us, Cher."

I feel tears well up behind my eyes and my throat's getting that constricted feeling that comes just before a good cry. But I can't cry in front of my father. It's not that my eyeliner will run, because I'm not wearing any. It's just something he hasn't seen me do in years. I'm like the very tip of an iceberg in front of my parents. They only see the ten percent above the water. The other ninety I save for when I'm in my room, listening to my music.

"You know, when I first got the idea to write this book, your mother and I talked about it for two years before deciding to set out. We knew it would be tough for you to go to so many schools. That's why we waited until you were finished with elementary school. But we also thought it would be fun and educational for you to see so many parts of the country. To see how people your age lived here and there. And even to make friends in different places. We thought the good would outweigh the bad."

My father then pulls back his hand, clasps his hands together and bows his head, almost as if he's praying. He seems so hurt.

I look up to see that my mother is now in the kitchen. She addresses my father. "Nanny told me what to do for my rheumatism. It's a bit crazy but she said it's an old Newfoundland belief. Want to hear it?"

"Carry a potato in your pocket," I answer.

My mother finally looks at me. "How did you know?" she asks.

"Well, I've been spending a lot of time with Newfoundlanders, right?" That's my way of telling them that I haven't hated everything about this move. I've even made a friend, more than a friend. Maybe I should describe that kiss out at St. Vincent's. That'll show them that I'm not being totally negative. All of a sudden it seems important that they not feel bad about bringing me here. "I mean, I have learned a lot about Newfoundland since we came here. Some stuff that might help you figure out how to do the research for your book, Dad."

"Well, I'd be glad to hear about it anytime," my father says, brightening. "I'm actually going to start interviewing people next week. One of my colleagues is helping me arrange it. He knows some of the fishermen who live in Petty Harbour, not too far from here."

"That's great," I say.

"And we might get some ideas at Trinity tomorrow. Did you want to come, Cheryl?"

"No, I think I'll stick around. I might do something with Jim," I answer, trying hard not to blush or appear too excited.

My mom opens the pantry door, roots around in a bag, then stuffs a big potato into her sweatshirt pocket.

CHAPTER 13
crossing over

My parents are leaving for Trinity really early this morning. I am vaguely aware of them moving around downstairs, but I stay in bed, pretending to sleep. I can't stop replaying yesterday in my mind, all of it, right down to the picnic we ate by the side of the road at Mistaken Point on the way home. Jim didn't want to get out of the car again, so we just opened the doors to let the breeze through. He said it made him feel good just knowing that all those fossils were out there, waiting to be discovered.

The front door clicks shut and I hear our car take off. They have a long drive ahead of them and won't be back until pretty late. That'll give me a whole day to myself and, hopefully, Jim.

Shortly after, I hear a bark that sounds a lot like Boss's down on the street. I part the curtains and peek down. Sure enough, Jim and Boss are on the sidewalk, looking up at my window. I guess Jim couldn't sleep either. I make a one minute sign with my finger and run down. By the time I get there, Jim is leaning against Nanny's car. Boss is tugging, dying to take off.

"Doesn't it hurt when she pulls?" I ask. All Jim needs is one good yank and his healing ribs will resnap.

"Well, yeah, but so what? I told you, nothing hurts us. We've been gashed by hooks, whipped by ropes and chains, lashed by giant waves. Left abandoned by merchants for entire winters with no supplies. We're indestructible. Nothing hurts us."

"Yeah, but still. Do you want me to take the leash?"

"God, Cheryl, I was hoping you'd ask. I can barely move."

"Is it because of yesterday? Was it a stupid idea? I bet I just made things worse."

"Don't worry. I'd have gone nuts lying there another day. I'll take it easy tomorrow. Besides ..." Jim takes my hand. "It was pretty perfect, wouldn't you say?"

"Perfect? Why? Because of the whales?"

"Those too. But I was thinking more about ..." Jim puts his hand on the back of my neck and strokes, in gentle circles. I've never been touched there before. It feels nice.

Boss tugs so hard the leash slides out of my hand and she

takes off to sniff in a patch of grass down the street. I turn to chase after her, but Jim pulls me toward him. "She'll be okay," he says.

I'm leaning right up against him now, my whole body touching his. I'm afraid I'm going to hurt him, but he doesn't look sore. He bends down to kiss me. It's not salty this time, but it's still nice.

"Hey, do you realize we can kiss like this before school, between classes, and after school," Jim says. Holy Heart. I haven't thought about it in a while. There's a fat envelope with the school's name in the corner sitting on our kitchen counter, but it's addressed to my mom. Even if it were addressed to me, I don't know if I would have opened it.

"I'm kind of scared though," I say.

"Of what? Getting kissed?"

"No, stupid! Of going to another new school. I just hate walking into a place where I don't know anyone, where I'm the new kid in class."

"But you won't not know anyone," Jim says. "You'll know me. I'll walk you straight to your classroom door and meet you for lunch. It'll all be different. It'll be different for me too."

Jim makes it sound kind of fun.

"What about those goons we met at the Village Mall?

Won't they give us a hard time?" I never told Jim about meeting the nicer one that night with Joannie. It might not be so bad, running into her.

"God! I couldn't care less about them. I know what I want and I stick to it, no matter what anyone else says or thinks. Nothing's going to stop me." Jim looks down at his chest. "Well, except Mother Nature, I suppose. Only it wasn't Mother Nature who made that family go so far out on the rocks. That was sheer human stupidity – same reason we lost the cod."

I wonder if my father's figured out how much conversations around here wind their way back to fish.

"Besides, you know, in my parents' day, back home, one walk around the bay with a girl and you were good as engaged. A peck on the cheek sealed the whole deal."

"Engaged! Are you out of your mind?"

"Relax, would you? I'm not saying anything about being engaged. I'm talking about making a commitment to someone, or to something, to being where you are instead of where you aren't. I've had to learn to do that too. It's not such a bad thing. You might want to try it some time."

Jim stares at the sky, where the sun is starting to poke through clouds. I know it's my turn to speak, but I don't know what to say. I suddenly feel as though I'm hanging on to that chain again, the one bolted into the rock on Signal Hill, hanging over the precipice. There are two ways to go. I can close my eyes and keep holding on, pulling myself to the other side, nice and safe. Or, I can let go, and fall into the wild ocean.

In a weird way, the second option would be like saying yes to Jim. Staying and going out with Jim would be taking a chance and jumping into something new, something that might toss and turn me and shake me up into a new person, with a new way of looking at the world.

"I've got an idea," Jim says. "Why don't you pop inside and grab Nanny's car keys off the hook. I want to take you somewhere."

"Are you sure? You remember what happened last time you took me on a road trip?"

"We won't be anywhere near water. Besides, we were okay yesterday."

"I know, but that one was my idea. Remember?"

***

"I'm surprised you never thought of doing this in your other places, Cheryl, with your other schools. The more familiar the building becomes, the less daunting it will be. It's what I'd call common sense," Jim says smiling.

"Well, in my other places, I wanted to pretend those schools didn't exist, right up to the last minute. It's what I'd call denial."

Jim pulls into the parking lot at Holy Heart. Facing us is a long whitish-grey building of four floors, almost completely covered in windows. It's certainly the biggest school I've seen since leaving Montreal. Jim points out the student entrance on one side and the theatre door at the other.

"Down there's the smoking pit," he says, pointing to a stairway that leads to a wooded area. We go down it then follow a laneway to the back of the building. Jim points out the windows for the gym and library. He even knows the history behind some of the cracked or boarded-up windows. Judging by the amount of beer bottle glass in the courtyard, I'm surprised more of the windows aren't smashed.

The walls are covered in graffiti, nothing huge like on the concrete overpasses of highways, but small tags, mostly people's names in puffy, cartooney letters. There's also the typical lines, like "school sucks," "wazzup", and "Grade A idiot," the same stuff I remember seeing on the high school near my old house. Jim walks right up to the wall and picks up a stone.

"What are you doing?"

He doesn't answer. He's too busy scratching "JP & CB" into the chipped paint. If he surrounds it with a heart, I'll kill him.

"We've gotta leave our mark, you know," he says. Then he turns the corner and calls me over. I find him looking into a barred window.

I have to go up on my toes to see, which is not easy to do in these boots.

"D'you see it?" Jim asks.

"What exactly am I supposed to see?"

"It's the hallway, where we'll walk in together. That staircase at the end is the one we'll take up to our classes."

The hall is completely still and quiet, lined with lockers. It looks so calm and harmless, like nothing bad could ever happen here. There's no trace of the activity that will take place once it's filled with people.

I never thought I'd say it, but my dad's kind of right. It's not a place itself or even what's in it that makes it what it is. It's the people and what they do with it. He says discovering what that is is at the heart of anthropology.

It occurs to me that my parents have made the most of wherever we lived. They tried so hard to fit in and become one with the place. My father even chewed on stalks of wheat when we lived in Saskatchewan, to try to look like a farmer. They wanted to be completely inside what was happening, as fast as possible.

I take Jim's hand and squeeze, hard.

***

Jim and I are watching a movie in the living room when my parents come back from Trinity Bay that night. Jim is lying on the sofa, resting his ribs. I'm on the armchair beside him. When my parents walk in we disentangle our hands. I catch the amused smile that passes between them the minute they see us.

They had a great time in Trinity, in spite of my mom's pain. She said the trip was worth the quarter bottle of extra-strength painkillers that it took to get her through the day.

"We even saw whales, Cheryl," she says, "playing around inside a little cove that we decided to explore. And seals too. Unbelievable."

I never told my parents about the whales we saw at St. Vincent's yesterday. In a weird way, I don't want them going there. I want it to be a place that only I saw, with Jim.

"That's great," I say. Jim and I look at each other. He doesn't mention our whales either.

"How are your ribs, Jim?" asks my dad. He has a sunburn across the ridge of his nose. I guess he didn't think to bring sunscreen.

"Better, thanks."

"Good, good. Well, you guys carry on. We'll just sort ourselves out." My parents disappear and we listen to them unloading bags and making tea in the kitchen. A while later, my father returns. He sits across from us and puts his feet, which are covered by thick wool socks, on the coffee table.

"It was bracing out there, very bracing," he says, sipping from his mug.

I roll my eyes, feeling like Candy. Why can't he just use a normal word, like cold?

"Did you find any dying people?" Jim asks. I think I'll die, but my father takes it well, smiling.

"Not one. It's quite something. People, on the whole, strike me as quite positive around here, Jim. Besides, if I may explain, my book is not a book about how people's way of life has ended and destroyed them. It's more about human resilience. About our ability to adapt to change. Even about the way science and technology shape and affect culture."

"Like the foreign trawlers scraping away our livelihood," said Jim.

"Well, yes, exactly. And it might be science that saves the culture too, by offering new options. We saw it on the Prairies, so many farms for sale. But others adapting, planting new crops. The native people I studied out in B.C. now have one of the most successful wine industries in the area up and running. And even in Quebec, where the iron ore and copper mines have shut down, they're now developing wind turbine technology. You know, archaeologists have uncovered remains of fishing vessels buried deep in the sands of deserts, where there's no water in sight. But the people are still living there, centuries later."

"You think that might happen here?"

"No one knows the future, Jim. Only the present and the past. I think you know a thing or two about that, right?"

I told my parents about Jim's trip to Horton, and about what fossils mean to him. I had to, to explain why I planned the trip to see the whales. My dad was impressed. He said not many young men knew so precisely what they wanted to do with their lives at Jim's age. "Or any age," he added.

"Yeah, a thing or two," Jim replies.

"What I'm doing is similar to what you do. You read

fossils to learn about the past. I read signs in the present to record that moment of change. It's that moment that interests me – when a culture crosses over."

"So I'm like a fossil under the microscope. You're reading my lines, looking for that moment," Jim says.

"If you want to look at it that way," my dad replies, laughing.

"I'm going upstairs. Goodnight everyone," my mom calls from the doorway. She's been really quiet since she came home, sitting alone in the kitchen. That's not like her.

"Wait for me, Ellen. I'm coming. See you soon, Jim," says my dad. "'Night, Cherie." I wish he'd stop calling me that, but I don't say anything in front of Jim.

My parents link fingers, loosely, before heading off to bed.

***

I'm saying goodbye to Jim outside his door. The sky above us is painted wispy streaks of red.

"Red sky at night, sailor's delight," says Jim. "Good day to be out on the water tomorrow."

"You know everything, don't you?"

"Nah, I just know what I know. There's lots you probably know that I don't know, 'cause of where you've been and what you've done."

Then I realize I don't even know what kind of whales we saw yesterday. In my mind, they were just whales, but Jim must know what kind they were.

"What kind of whales did we see at St. Vincent's?"

"Absolutely amazing ones, wouldn't you say?" Jim puts his arms around me, gently. I think both us of must be picturing the same thing – the whales leaping upward, making patterns in the air, snapping at the gulls then crashing down, only feet away.

Jim hasn't shaved in days and I like the stubble all over his chin. It suits him. "They were humpbacks," he says.

"What a horrible name. Sounds too much like hunchbacks. They should be called silverbacks at least. But what do I know about whales?"

"Not much, city girl. Not much," says Jim. "But if you stick around, you might learn a thing or two."

***

Marilyn Manson puts me to sleep, singing about peaceful

valleys and seas and pleasure and the fact that the whole wide world is out there, just waiting for me. It's like he's describing the exact way I felt out at St. Vincent's, the way I still feel when I close my eyes and bring it all back.

CHAPTER 14
footprints of time

*M*y parents haven't gone anywhere since Trinity, and my mom has stopped talking about places she wants to see. In fact, she's hardly said a word about anything. She's quieter than I ever remember her. My dad's been going to work every day, preparing for the semester that's starting in just a week. I keep waiting for my mom to start quilting, which is what she usually does around this time, but she doesn't.

I've been spending a lot of time at Jim's. He's getting more mobile every day, but he still can't do everything yet. He's been showing me his rock and fossil collection and I can't believe how much stuff there is to learn. Jim gets really into it when he's talking about them and I can just see him in ten years time, teaching university. My dad wants Jim to attend some of his lectures this semester at MUN, to get a head start. He says anthropology and geology are kind of related, through archaeology, and that Jim would learn a lot. He could also contribute a lot to the class because of his experience.

This is the week the group is off at Horton and I know Jim is thinking about it. Focusing on his rocks is helping him get through it. He's even asked me to help him rearrange his collection, to order it by date and type of fossil, and I volunteered to make better labels to put under them. I've borrowed our laptop which has a graphics program that lets me outline the labels with a string of footprints. After all, that's what fossils are: footprints of time.

I usually pop back home a couple of times throughout the day to check on my mother. She tells me I don't need to, but my dad wants me to – and I want to, too.

Today, I come home from Jim's to find her sitting in the middle of the floor, surrounded by her boxes of quilting supplies. Some are half-opened, their contents spilling over. Cotton batten flows out of one box like a snowdrift and swatches of bright-coloured fabric dot the hardwood floor. It's as though she was getting ready to dive into a project then forgot her idea.

She doesn't move at all when I come in, like she didn't even hear me.

"Mom?" I tap her on the shoulder and she whips around.

"Cheryl?"

"What are you doing?"

"I don't know ... I just wanted to see. I thought maybe if I looked at all this stuff, I'd discover that I could handle it. You know, the scissors, the needles, the rulers. All of it." She wipes her face with the sleeve of her housecoat and I see she's been crying.

"And?"

"It's no good. Even opening the boxes hurts me." My mom holds up her hands and I look at them closely. It's like I haven't noticed until now just how crooked they are. Her fingers aren't even straight anymore. They curve in the middle, like a twisty road sign and there are bubbles of skin around her joints.

"I'll have to give it up," she continues. "For now." She sits on the chair and sighs heavily. Neither of us speaks for several minutes.

"I never minded before," she says finally.

"Minded what?"

"Following your father around from place to place. Because I had this." She points to the boxes. "It gave me a sense of purpose, you know?"

I nod, as if I do, but inside I'm thinking how I never

realized that the moving was something my mom needed a strategy for. She seemed completely part of the whole venture, one hundred percent inside of it. I was the one on the outside.

"I'm going to have to go home, Cheryl," she says. "I don't want to, but I have to. You understand, don't you?"

I nod again, my heart racing.

"And you'll come with me, of course. It's what you've always wanted anyway, isn't it, Cheryl?" she continues.

"I guess so." But that was before Jim. She must know that things are different now.

"I know it's been hard on you, all the moving. I always thought it would get easier, that you'd learn to love the places we went to, like your dad and I have. I shouldn't have expected it to be the same for you."

"It's okay, Mom. It wasn't all bad. Especially here. I mean, you know, 'cause of Jim."

"Well then, that's good," she says. "It always helps when you make a friend."

I want to explode. Jim is so much more than a friend. Why can't my mother see that? Maybe she's been so focused on her hands and their pain she hasn't really noticed how close Jim and I are. It's like I have to spell everything out to my parents or they don't get it. I'm about to tell my mother that when she starts to cry again. I haven't seen her cry since her mother, my grandmother, died just before we left Montreal. It's kind of scary.

"Can I do anything for you, Mom? I can help you cut material or whatever."

"No, honey. There's no point in starting what I can't finish." The way she says it tells me she has definitely decided to leave. In her mind, she's already packed and back on the plane. With me beside her.

"I'll be okay, Cheryl. I'll just tidy up a little."

"Do you want me to help you?"

"No, no. I'd rather do it myself. I'll be okay."

I watch her stuff the material back into a box. She doesn't turn to look at me. She's too absorbed in what she's doing.

***

I don't go back to Jim's. I go upstairs, lie on my bed, and close my eyes, trying to imagine what my old room actually looks like. I can see bits and pieces of it, the purple beanbag chair and white iron bed, movie and dragon posters, and shelves full of old toys and the drawing stuff I used to love. But they kind of float around in my mind like separate pieces. I can't really assemble them into a whole.

Next, I try to picture my old neighbourhood, to bring it back – the square blocks with their brick and wooden houses, old and new together, the old ones with big porches, the new ones with big garages. I see the main street down near the train tracks where my friends and I went for pizza and ice cream. But it's all faded, like a picture that's covered in too much attic dust.

I think about the school behind my old house and picture myself walking into it. It's true I'd recognize some kids from elementary school, but just a handful and I don't really know them anymore. And Janna will be glued to Stephan. And, if I'm being honest, I don't really know her anymore, either.

Right now, Jim is more real than anything I've left behind.

I picture our initials, carved in stone on the back of Holy Heart. I had actually begun to look forward to going to school for the first time in years and now I don't know what's going to happen or what school I'll be going to. Jim practically had our lockers picked out already. How am I ever going to tell him that I might not be going there?

***

My dad's calling me down to dinner, which he made. That means canned soup and cold-cut sandwiches, his specialty.

We're all pretty quiet around the table. The only one who talks is my dad. It's like he's filling the silence with small talk and chatter about nothing important, like the fact that he met more of his colleagues today and saw the lecture hall where he'll be teaching his classes. He says he'll have to put his notes and slides on PowerPoint, that's what's expected now. Even my mom only grunts minimal responses. Then he starts talking about questionnaires that he's hoping we'll both help him with.

"Especially you, Cheryl. You can help me with questions geared to people your age. About what they're going through and everything."

I want to tell him that I wouldn't know how to answer questions about myself right now, how to put into words what I'm going through, never mind how to formulate the questions. But I just shrug a halfhearted okay.

We're just about finished when the front door opens and Jim walks into the kitchen. It reminds me of the first time he did that, the day he took me to Signal Hill, when he nearly gave my parents a heart attack.

"Hello, Jim," says my dad. "Have a seat. You're just in

time for dessert." He sounds so casual, I begin to suspect that my dad may have called Jim and told him to drop by. But I might just be paranoid, because of the trip to Middle Cove.

"Thanks," says Jim. He pulls out the chair beside mine and lowers himself into it slowly. I guess his ribs kind of squish together when he bends.

"How are the ribs?" my dad asks.

"Getting better, thanks," says Jim.

My fathers plunks a store-bought apple pie and a tub of vanilla ice cream onto the table, then grabs a stack of plates and forks.

"Everyone dig in and help yourself," he says. "Hope it's good. I was baking for hours."

"Aren't you marvelous!" says my mom, playing along.

I cut a piece of pie for myself, then decide to give it to my mom. The next piece goes to Jim. I guess I can't very well not give one to my dad, so I do. But everyone's on their own for ice cream.

"I got some news today," Jim says, scooping a ball of ice cream and flicking it on top of his pie.

All three of us turn to him. His dark eyes are all lit up, like when he talks about fossils. The news must be good.

"Just now. I got a phone call from the father of the girl I

rescued. You won't believe it."

"What?" I say.

"They're back home, in Oshawa, but the father wants to give me something. You know, like a reward. I said no at first, 'cause it didn't seem right. I mean, I didn't do it for that. But then he told me he works for Air Canada. He wants to give me a free return flight to anywhere in Canada, anytime."

"Jim, that's fantastic! You can use it to go to Horton next summer," I say.

"Or somewhere even better," Jim says. "Of course, Nanny says I should use it to fly out and see my dad and brothers. But I don't know if I want to. I've got to think about it, use it for something I really want. I'm not going to get another gift like this anytime soon."

"My advice is to use it to further your career, Jim," says my father. "There's more than one place to find fossils in this huge country. There are research teams working all over, even way up north."

My father would suggest something like that.

"Or, you might want to use it to come visit us," my mom says quietly. I just about choke on my pie. Jim turns towards me.

"Visit you?" he says.

"Yes. Cheryl and I are going back to Montreal. It's my fault. I don't want to go, but it's my hands, you see?" She holds up her fork to show off her bloated hands, but Jim doesn't look at them. He can't take his eyes off my face. I feel my skin burning.

"Montreal?" Jim says. "When?"

"As soon as we can," says my mom. "Before school starts."

"Anyone want more ice cream?" asks my dad, but nobody answers him. Jim is still staring at me, like he's waiting for me to explain or deny it. His bruise, which had faded to very light brown, just a shade darker than his skin, seems to be black again. Just this morning we were working on his rocks, talking about the new school year. Jim even asked if I wanted to go home with him at Christmas. He said his mom told him to tell me I'd be welcome. He said I better be prepared to see some real snow and ice. He must be so confused. Maybe as confused as I am.

This is even worse than that night at Nanny's, when my dad accused everyone of dying. Jim was angry that I never told him the true purpose of the book, but he'll never forgive me if he thinks I've been hiding this too.

I'm trying to keep my anger in check, but I feel it rising. My mother had no right to say anything. I would have told Jim in my own way.

"Mom! You always have to ruin everything," I say, throwing down my fork. "Why did you have to say that?"

"But Cheryl, honey. We talked about it this afternoon."

"No, you talked about it. You just assume I'm coming, like you always do. Did it ever occur to you to ask me what I want to do? Did it?"

"But, Cheryl, you've done nothing but say you want to go home ever since we got here. Ask your father. It's true."

I look to my dad and he nods.

"But that was before," I say.

"Before what?" my mom asks. And it occurs to me my mom doesn't know that Jim and I went out to Holy Heart and that he carved our initials in the brick. Or that I looked into the window and pictured myself actually walking down the hallway, holding Jim's hand. She doesn't know that I'm halfway through rearranging his fossil collection and making plans to go to the South Shore for Christmas. She doesn't even know that we saw those whales, leaping and writing their messages in the air.

She doesn't know anything.

"Before lots of things," I say, my eyes locked with Jim's.

"Cheryl?" says my mom.

Jim takes my hand, holding it right there on the table between the dirty bowls and plates.

I feel all eyes on me, waiting. It's kind of like walking into class the first day in a strange school, wishing there was somewhere to hide. Everyone watching to see how you'll perform.

"Before Jim," I say.

My parents look at each other, but say nothing. Jim squeezes my fingers.

My mom picks up her cup of tea, cradling it with both hands. Then, suddenly, as though the effort is too much, she drops it. The cup shatters into pieces as it hits her plate, cracking that in half too. My dad springs up to grab the dish cloth as the boiling water rolls over the edge of the table into my mother's lap.

***

I'm in the hole in my mattress, only it doesn't feel like a hole anymore. It feels like the exact right space to curl up in. Now, when I go to bed, I actually find myself shifting around, settling into its edges.

My parents are in their room across the hall. They talked

until half an hour ago, their voices muted through the walls. It wouldn't take rocket science to figure out what they were talking about.

It seems we can never just mesh smoothly in this family, all our different desires coming together, or pulling in the same direction. There's always a jagged edge somewhere, sticking out, off pattern.

That edge is usually me. At least that's what they were probably saying.

Jim didn't stick around for very long, and who can blame him? He finished his apple pie and ice cream, the world's most ordinary dessert, and headed home. He's probably in bed right now, thinking up ways to use his free ticket to get as far away from us as possible, cursing the day that Robbie and his family left.

Suddenly, I hear something hitting my window, making a sharp *ting*. I spring out of bed and look down to find Jim standing on the sidewalk below, a bunch of stones in his hand.

"Hey," he calls up.

"What the hell are you doing?" I whisper through the screen.

"You gonna let me in or what?" Jim points to the door. Good thing my parents lock it, in spite of wanting to fit in, or

Jim would've been chucking pennies at my bedroom door. I motion for him to give me a minute, throw on a sweatshirt, and tiptoe downstairs.

"What are you doing here?" I ask, opening up.

"I wanted to see you."

"But my parents. I can't wake them up. They've done enough for one night."

"We'll hang out down here. Don't worry, they won't hear a thing. You wouldn't believe how quiet you learn to be with four brothers and sisters when you want to sneak out and get a little exploring done without someone on your tail."

"Well, there's nothing to explore here, believe me." We sit beside each other on the sofa, Jim shifting around to settle his ribs in a good position.

"Oh yes there is. There's you. Like I never know what's happening next with you. One minute you're stowing away on a ship, the next you're showing me the best whales in Newfoundland. Two minutes later, you're on a plane to Montreal."

"I wanted to tell you, but I didn't know for sure. And I still don't. My parents are just used to me following them around, like some kind of dog."

"Don't be so hard on yourself. It's what most of us do

until we're old enough to stop."

"You didn't."

"Yeah, but my dad was so mad when I told him I was coming to St. John's. He wanted me at home, so he could stay away more easily, with my brothers. I was supposed to become the man of the house, you know?"

"And you didn't."

"No. My mom and dad fought about it – a lot."

"But it must've been kind of hard, coming here on your own, especially without your father on your side."

"Yeah, but I knew I'd survive. Besides, my mom supported me. She understood, in a way my dad just couldn't. Only saw things through his own eyes, you know? My mom wants me to do things, as long as it means staying in school. You should've seen the sweaters she donated to the big sale we had to raise funds for Horton. She didn't just give me some plain easy ones. No way. They had some complex patterns on them, like she put extra into them, thought a lot about them. Some had rocks on them, heaped in piles, all different colours. Sold for good money, money someone else is benefitting from by now."

I take Jim's hand.

"But the best thing is, my mom didn't put any pressure

on me, or try to make me feel bad if I decided to go. She let me decide for myself. You really should do the same."

"The thing is, I usually don't have to decide. This is a first."

"Well, deciding is a good thing, right?"

"Yeah, it's great. If I stay, my mom has to go home alone. If I go, I leave you. You actually had me looking forward to Holy Heart. You know, the whole walking through the hallways thing, hanging out in that charming courtyard. I've never done stuff like that."

"Don't forget kissing goodbye at the classroom door, you up on your tippy toes."

"Okay, now you're making fun of me. Next thing you know, we'll be trying out for some sucky high school musical."

"I'd make a great leading man, don't you think?" Jim turns his body and leans toward me and I snuggle closer. I can't get over how well we fit together. "If only these damn ribs would hurry up and knit."

"It's too bad Nanny doesn't know some weird cure for broken bones, like carrying a turnip or something."

Jim laughs. Then his face turns really serious and he leans even closer to me.

"The thing is, Cheryl, I just wanted you to know that I

want you to stay. I'm not trying to put pressure on you, but I wanted you to know." Jim traces my face with his finger softly and once again I feel him trying to read me, the way he would a fossil.

"And you wanted me to know now, at midnight?"

"No time like the present, as they say."

His hand combs my short hair behind my ears. We're both quiet, like we can't think what to say. Or like we don't need to say anything. Somewhere far off, a foghorn blows, warning boats that there are rocks ahead. For some reason, I think about my mom. Her lap got burned pretty bad tonight, even through her jeans.

"My mom's gonna be lost without my dad," I say.

"And without you?"

"Not so much."

"Are you sure?"

"Why?"

"I just … I remember the day she came to get me, to go to Middle Cove. She talked about you a lot. She gave me the impression she really cares. I mean, she really wanted you to have a good time. And then when she brought you a piece of the ocean in her hand. That was so cool."

"It was?"

"Sure. Not a lot of people would do something like that."

I hadn't thought of it that way before. I just thought she was being pushy, shoving the ocean in my face, trying to force me into the moment, any way she could. The way Jim describes it, it was sort of like an act of love.

***

I stay on the sofa after Jim has left, not wanting to move. The foghorn blasts again and this time it reminds me of the wolves on Needle Mountain. My parents used to take me to watch the hockey games at the local arena. All the kids in my grade seven class were there. In fact, the whole town was there, so the stands were packed. My parents cheered whenever the home team scored, so loudly it embarrassed me. I wanted to crawl under the cold aluminum bench every time they did it. At intermission, some kids took me out back. They had firecrackers which they stood up in the snow and lit. I stood against the arena wall and watched them explode in a burst of blue and orange against the back drop of Needle Mountain. They told me the wolves hated it when they did this. It made them howl, their long wails filling the empty space between the arena and the hills, ricocheting off the tin walls and tree trunks. Then they told me the wolves would come out of their dens at night and creep into town to take revenge. They were laughing, so I laughed too, to show I wasn't afraid. But that night I wanted to sleep in my parents' bed. When I told my mom it was because of the wolves she didn't laugh. She put her arms around me and pulled me close to her. She let me fall asleep like that, my head against her chest.

When I finally climb the stairs, my mom is on the landing.

"Everything okay, honey?"

"Yeah, I'm fine. Just getting some water."

"That's good," she says. "Look, I'm sorry for blurting that out in front of Jim, about going home. It was insensitive. I didn't realize, I guess."

"It's okay, Mom." And it seems odd that it really is. "I want to ask you something. Do you remember the wolves?"

"What wolves?"

"The ones that used to come into Murdochville at night?"

"The wolves never came into Murdochville. They were way up on Needle Mountain."

"But you let me sleep in your bed when I thought the wolves were coming to get me."

"Oh yeah, now I remember. Those kids were just teasing you. You took them to heart."

"But you let me sleep with you just the same."

"Of course, honey. You were scared."

I'm scared now, I want to tell her.

"Well, thanks, Mom."

"Thanks for what?"

"You know, for doing that. I was really stupid."

"Fear is never stupid, Cheryl. Never."

We can't see each other too well because the landing is dark, lit only by the moon, full as a fat potato in the small window.

"Well, goodnight, Mom."

"Goodnight, sweetie."

CHAPTER 15
the moment of change

It's impossible to read the street signs, the rain is lashing the car windows so hard. My father has the windshield wipers on high, but the water fills in the second it's been pushed aside. The howling wind is whipping the rain in all directions. At times it's horizontal, hitting the car from the sides. Other times, it seems to be shooting up from below. It's like we're under siege.

The plane can't possibly take off in this weather. The flight here was shaky enough, but today it'll be like flying through an earthquake.

My mother's hands are swollen, clutching her handbag on the front seat. This is exactly the climate she needs to get away from. If my father didn't have both hands plastered to the steering wheel, he'd be holding her left hand in his right, sharing his heat.

"We're almost there," my dad calls, yelling to be heard over the wind. Every now and then we hear a big crash, like the city's falling down around us. "Probably branches," he shouts. He's pulled himself right up close to the windshield, so he can see better, like an old man. "Let's try the radio."

My mother fiddles with the knobs and buttons, trying to get a station, but it's all static.

"We should have called the airport first," she says.

That would have been smart, I think, except it wasn't raining this badly an hour ago. It really just picked up as we were leaving. It seemed to come out of nowhere. Like Jim said, if you don't like the weather around here, wait ten minutes.

He said it again this morning, when he came over to say goodbye. It's like we were all trying to make small talk, to fill the time before we had to leave. Nanny dropped by too, hanging onto Jim's arm. Even with his injured ribs, he still walks better than she does. Her shaking has gotten worse. When Jim goes to see Dr. Patel this week, to check on his ribs, he's going to ask him if he can have a look at Nanny.

We're now part of a slow-moving line of cars crawling up Portugal Cove Road. All we can see of the other cars are the taillights. When one slows down, we all do, like we're a train. It amazes me that I remember all the street names: Portugal Cove, Elizabeth, Empire, Bonaventure. I guess they're imprinted on my brain, I worked so hard at memorizing them. Their initials spelled BEEP backwards. I thought that would be me, beeping everyone out of the way as I zoomed off excitedly to catch my plane home.

My father lets us out at the main door and goes off to park. He'll be soaked when he finds us, because no umbrella could survive this wind. I help my mother in with the luggage and we line up at the Air Canada counter. It's really busy. Lots of tourists are leaving and Newfoundlanders are going back to wherever they're now living. It seems that everywhere I look, parents are hugging grown children goodbye. Little grandchildren run around them, playing tag in between the adults' legs.

My father joins us a few minutes later, his hair and jacket soggy. We're all really quiet as we snake our way to the check-in. My parents never expected to be back here so soon. It's a good thing my father is already wet, because he looks like he's going to start bawling any minute. I see them back at Middle Cove, holding hands and running into the water to wet their feet. Knowing them, they probably squished right through the capelin. Jim said it made great fertilizer. If my mother lived here, I could see her bringing buckets of capelin home for a flower garden.

"Call the minute you get in, okay?" my father says for the third time, as we head toward the departure gate.

"Don't worry," my mother says.

"And do what I said. Don't be a hero. Think of your hands." My father wants my mom to hire some house cleaners to scrub the place down. He's afraid she'll try to do it all herself and hurt her hands even more.

"I will. Like I said."

"And no heavy lifting. You shouldn't need to. I'll help move whatever needs moving when I come in at Thanksgiving. Promise?"

My mother raises herself on her tippy toes and plants a long kiss on my father's lips. He folds his arms around her and within seconds they are clinging to each other. You'd think the flight was to Siberia, not Montreal.

"You guys," I say, tapping my mom on the shoulder. "You're holding up the line."

Jim wanted to come to the airport, but in the end he figured this should be a family thing. He said his goodbyes at the house. If he had come, I wonder if we'd be embracing too, right beside my parents. How weird would that be?

It's our turn. We're right up at the security gate. Somewhere along the line, my parents' two-way hug turned into a group hug and my dad's arms are around me and my mother. He pulls us together and we all squeeze and say goodbye at the same time.

In the middle of the huddle, my mother's hands reach out for mine, pressing as tightly as she can with her sore fingers as the guard calls out "Next."

***

I know my father will immediately be lost when he gets home. I can see him, wandering from room to room, his footsteps echoing through the house.

My mom's going to be the same, back in the old house. But she needed to go. The weather in Montreal isn't perfect and it can be way too humid, but it's not as damp as here. She needs to focus on getting her rheumatism better. She's already got an appointment with her old doctor. If she can get it under control, she might be able to work again. I know she's going to carry the image of the colourful row houses back with her. I can even see a quilted Cabot Tower rising out of the rock. If she wants any details on the pathway down the hill, she'll have to ask me, seeing as she never made the hike. It's vivid in my memory though. She might have the quilt done for when we're all together again at Thanksgiving.

My parents said Jim could come for Thanksgiving, too. They said they'll put him in the spare room, but we can sneak out so we can be together. Of course, my dad had to add that Jim could go visit the Geology departments at McGill and Concordia while he's there, maybe even Carleton and the University of Ottawa. Jim thought that was a great idea, which made my dad happy.

My dad will be sending along the boxes with my mom's quilting supplies by Express Post. This morning, when my parents were already in the car, I pretended I needed to go to the bathroom and went back inside. I tore open the box marked "Finished Quilts" and pulled out all the quilts my mom has made in the last few years. Then I quickly draped them over the backs of the sofas and chairs in the living room. I had one to spare, so I quickly ran upstairs and draped it over my parents' bed.

I stood in the living room doorway before leaving and took it all in. The quilt of Murdochville is a winter scene, with the desolate main street and its wooden houses leading up to Needle Mountain. The whole picture looks haunted, as though the mythical wolves are coming down from the hills to inhabit the empty buildings. Next to it are the fields around our farmhouse in Saskatchewan – the light blue flowers of the flax on one side, the sunny yellow of canola on the other. Surrounding everything is the creamy beige of the wheat under vast blue skies. The Okanagan Valley quilt depicts a crystal clear lake that reflects the hills of the lower Rockies. The canoes slicing through the water seem to be coasting on mountaintops.

It occurred to me that one of these quilts, maybe all of them, should be on the cover of my dad's book. It's yin and yang. The book is full of statistics and theories and technology, but behind the book was Mom, taking in the beauty of the land — the flowers and hills and skies.

I guess that's why I did it. I knew my dad would be lost when he got home, and I wanted him to feel that my mom was still here. There's no mistaking her presence in these quilts.

Anyways, I can see my dad back at the house, stroking his chin and thinking what a "puzzle" I am.

I wouldn't be able to argue.

Jim pretty much said the same thing, when I told him what I'd decided to do last night. Until I said it, I really didn't know what I was going to do myself. Jim was on one side, my mom on the other, both of them wanting me, but neither of them being pushy about it. Letting me decide for myself.

This is going to be a compromise, something that gives a little to everyone, but most to myself. A few weeks at home, to help my mom get settled. Then back to St. John's to do grade ten at Holy Heart. It's Jim's last year there and I want to be part of it. I also want to test his theory, to see if looking down that hallway will make walking it easier.

My mom understood when I told her.

As the plane lifts into the wet and windy sky, I strain to see through the grey. I want a clear and bright view of Newfoundland, but I'm not going to get it. It's all just grey. Even if it changes ten minutes from now, St. John's will be too far away to see.

I'll have to make do with what's in my head. I close my eyes and see the bits and pieces: Nunnery Hill, Cabot Tower, the Battery, the bunker at Cape Spear, Nanny and Joannie.

Oh yeah, and the whales.

Beside me, my mom is crying. She's trying to hide it, but the little tears escape the corner of her eyes faster than she can dab them with her tissue. The joints of her fingers look like bulbs of garlic. I know what my dad would do if he were here.

I reach over and hold my mom's hand. She seems surprised, but she doesn't resist. My father's explanation for his book comes back to me. The moment of change, he called it. That's what he tries to record. The point where the culture shifts, like the earth is sighing and rearranging its weight.

This could be that moment, for me.

Award-winning novels from **Lobster Press**:

Tin Angel
by Shannon Cowan / **978-1-897073-68-1**

Ronalda Page's idyllic life came to a halt when her father died and her mother was forced to sell the mountain lodge that had been in the family for generations. When the lodge burns to the ground with a man inside, Ronnie is the only suspect. Could she be guilty of murder?

"Rich with imagery and raw with emotion ... This is a must-read."
– *Quill & Quire,* starred review

"Strong themes of youth rights propel the story to an exciting and vivid conclusion, and readers will not be able to put down this marvelous, righteous tale that feels ripped from the headlines."
– *VOYA*

"... finely woven, heart-wrenching, coming-of-age narration."
– *Kirkus Reviews*

"Cowan gives her readers characters to connect with, characters to mourn and characters to despise, all of them unforgettable."
– *Vancouver Sun*

Shortlisted, Geoffrey Bilson Award for Historical Fiction for Young People
Selected, Quill & Quire "Best Books of the Year"

Posing as Ashley
by Kimberly Joy Peters / 978-1-897073-87-2

This spin-off of the award-winning novel *Painting Caitlyn* tells the story of Caitlyn's best friend, Ashley, who seems to have everything going for her. But deep down, Ashley's worries and self-doubt lurk. Once she enters the catty and hypercritical world of modeling, she is forced to make decisions that not only might disappoint those around her, but could also go against everything she believes in. Will Ashley walk the walk and chase what everyone else says she should want, or will she finally stand up for herself?

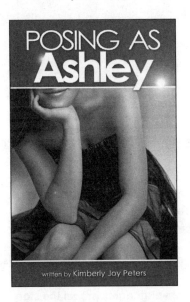

"With the same sincerity as *Painting Caitlyn*, Peters captures the fragility of the teenage soul ..."
– *School Library Journal*

"... destined to be a popular pick ... features an immediately likeable protagonist whose desperate need to always try to please everyone else in her life will resonate with many readers."
– *CM: Canadian Review of Materials*

www.lobsterpress.com

ABOUT THE AUTHOR:

Growing up in the diverse Montreal, Quebec, neighbourhood known as Park Extension, **Lori Weber** developed a fascination with cultural traditions and language. A careful observer by nature, she began writing at a young age, filling notebooks with stories that focused on the lives of her family, friends, and neighbours. Although Lori has spent most of her life in Montreal, she has also lived, studied, and taught in Nova Scotia and Newfoundland. She calls St. John's "everything and more than people say it is - charming, special, wet, and wonderful." Her memories of the area inspired the vivid setting of *If You Live Like Me*.

Lori's acclaimed novels for young adults include ***Klepto*** (Lorimer & Co.), which was selected by the American Library Association for the "Popular Paperbacks for Young Adults" list, and also the Formac "SideStreets" novels ***Strange Beauty***, ***Tattoo Heaven***, and ***Split***. She lives in Pointe-Claire, Quebec, and teaches in the English Department at John Abbott College.

Visit Lori online at www.lori-weber.com

Painting Caitlyn
by Kimberly Joy Peters / 978-1-897073-40-7

When Caitlyn starts dating Tyler, all of her problems seem to disappear. Older, gorgeous, and totally into Caitlyn, he makes her feel important, needed, and special. But as things get serious, she realizes her "perfect" boyfriend is as controlling as he is caring, and she is faced with a choice: she can either let this relationship define her, or find the courage to break away.

"... a realistic and powerful picture of how subtle and confusing abuse in its different forms can be." – *KLIATT*

"... a provocative story with an important message."
– *CM: Canadian Review of Materials*

Selected, International Reading Association "Young Adults' Choices" List

Selected, YALSA "Quick Picks for Reluctant Young Adult Readers"

Winner, Elementary Teachers' Federation of Ontario Writer's Award, Women's Program

Shortlisted, B.C. Teen Readers' Choice Stellar Book Award

Selected by the Maine Coalition to End Domestic Violence for the "Knowledge is Power: Building Healthy Relationships Through Reading" program